CATCH HOUSE

In memory of Gwen

JULIA -2023

Chapter One

The brass knocker was grotesque. I'd seen lions, foxes and even birds as door knockers, but never rats. I scowled at its ugliness, thinking it was actually quite fitting for such a filthy February. There had been unwelcoming weeks of dark days and dank evenings. No one in their right mind would've chosen to be out that night, it was bloody miserable. But there I was, lifting the tarnished tail of a metal rat, and striking hard. As I stared down at my work shoes splattered with wet sludge, the door to Catcher House swung open wide.

'Mrs Harker?' The estate agent was probably only a few years younger than me, in his mid-twenties, at a guess. He had a round, boyish face and a funny moustache hovered over his lip as he smiled.

I peered at him from under the rim of my hood. 'Yeah, hi. And you're Josh? Sorry to drag you out on such a foul evening.'

'Oh, no worries,' he said as we shook hands. 'Houses have to be sold whatever the weather. Quick, come in out of the rain.' He moved aside to let me in. 'There is one problem though. I can't get the lights to work. I've had a quick look around for the fuse box, but can't find it, but if you wait in the hallway, I'll have another look.'

'Oh, OK.' I wiped my feet on the doormat and stepped in, leaving the door half open so I could see by a chink of streetlight stretching across the tiles. Josh shone his torch into the cupboard under the stairs, while I stood there feeling awkward. I cleared my throat and took off my glasses, giving them a wipe with the bottom of my jumper. The house smelt stale, as if the doors or windows hadn't been open for a long time, but there was also an underlying floral scent that added a sweetness to the air. I scrunched up my nose and slipped my glasses back on to peer around the gloomy hall. The stair carpet was threadbare, and the window by the door was thick with grime. It was freezing. I put my hand on a nearby radiator; it was stone-cold. An involuntary shiver made me twitch, and I zipped up my coat.

'Aha,' A triumphant shout came from the cupboard, and at the same time, light flooded the hallway. I blinked and smiled as Josh backed out of the small doorway and turned off his torch. 'We have light!' he said. 'It must've tripped.'

'Oh, well done,' I said, shutting the door behind me. It didn't feel any warmer in doing so; if anything, the house seemed to entrap the cold, squeezing it tight between its walls.

Josh pulled some papers from his briefcase. 'The particulars,' he said. 'To be honest, this is the first time I've seen the house myself. I was hoping to get a quick scoot around before you arrived, but never mind.' He grinned.

'Ah, the truth's coming out now,' I laughed as I took the prospectus from him, 'Don't worry, we'll be fine.'

'My colleague came last week to take the photos and to measure up. As you probably saw online, it does need modernising.' He glanced up at the brown-stained ceiling and raised his eyebrows.

He was right, the place really needed a makeover; it would be TikTok heaven for some lifestyle influencer. But there was no way we could afford to live in Larkcombe, otherwise.

'Yeah, we're looking for a place to do up,' I said. 'My husband loves a project.'

'Perfect,' said Josh. 'Well, let's start in here.' He pushed open the door and switched on the light. We stepped in. 'This is the dining room. As you can see, the house is typically Victorian. Not open plan, mainly separate rooms.' he said.

I nodded, taking in the round mahogany table. It was a small room, and the furniture was way too big for the space. An old-fashioned black dresser towered over us, and eight chairs covered in red velvet were pushed in under the table, all upright and correct. With silver candlesticks lined up on a sideboard, it looked as if a religious ceremony was about to take place; or a séance or something. What a miserable room – the dark furniture was so oppressive; I couldn't imagine eating here. It was so depressing.

I walked over to the far end of the room and placed my hand on the wall. The plaster was flaking, and the faded wallpaper was peeling away. 'Is the kitchen on the other side of here? We could knock down this wall and have a kitchen diner.' I glanced optimistically at Josh, excited by the thought of me cooking at a range while the kids sat around a massive wooden table doing their homework.

'I'm not sure,' he said, flicking through his paperwork. 'Let's take a look.'

We made our way to the rooms at the back of the house. 'A small cloakroom,' said Josh indicating a tiny room on the right. He walked straight past it and into the kitchen.

Before following him, I peered into the downstairs loo and cringed at the limescale on the porcelain. Every few seconds a drip fell into the old cistern, the noise unnaturally loud in such a small room. The kitchen wasn't much better – the dividing wall looked as if it could be removed, but the room needed a lot of work. The units were from the 1970s, bright blue worktops, and a stainless-steel sink with a little curtained unit underneath. 'As you can see,' said Josh, 'you'd need to rip all this Formica out.' He opened a cupboard door and apart from some crusted wallpaper lining the bottom of the shelf, it was completely empty.

'Is anyone living here at the moment?' I asked.

'Yes, the owner's brother. He rents the house from her.'

'So, he can move out quite quickly then? If he's renting?'

'I don't see why not,' said Josh. 'There wouldn't be a chain, unless you have a property to sell?'

'No.' I said, cupping my hands against the back door window, trying to see into the garden. 'We're in rented too.' I rubbed a finger over the misted-up glass, but it was too dark to see outside.

'I can shine my torch around the back garden if you want to take a look?' said Josh, walking with an enthusiastic bounce to his step.

I smiled. 'No, no, don't worry. I've seen the pictures online. I'll bring my husband back during the day, if I like it.'

'OK. Let's go and view the living room.' As we walked along the hallway, there was a faint smell of stale cigarettes. I hadn't noticed it before. It was as if disturbing the dust floor had agitated something. Suddenly, the light flickered, and we both glanced up. 'I hope it's not going to trip again,' said Josh. He frowned and then pushed open the living room door.

In a brown leather chair, sitting stock still, was a man. His watery eyes staring straight at us.

Chapter Two

'Jesus Christ!' Josh jumped and gripped my arm as the house prospectus fluttered to the floor. I stared at the man. The only sound was a clock ticking, each second seeming to last a minute.

The silence became unbearable, I had to say something. 'Sorry, but didn't you know we were coming? Didn't you hear us? I'm so sorry.'

The stupid idiot had just scared the life out of me, why was I apologising? And more to the point, why in hell had he been sitting in the dark? I took a few steps away from him, my heart racing. He still didn't speak. He glared at us, as perspiration glistened on his pallid face. He was dressed in a pair of faded beige cords and an out-of-date patterned jumper that had stretched with age. He had food stains on his clothes, as if he'd forgotten to take them off and wash them.

'I'm terribly sorry, sir. Your sister told me to let myself in,' said Josh as he scooped up the papers from the wooden floor. 'She said you'd be out. I did knock first, just in case, and there was no reply, so I … I'm terribly sorry.' He ran his fingers through his hair and took a few steps forward.

'Get out. I'm not moving. Catcher House isn't for sale.' The man who must have been in his late fifties, balled his hand into a fist and thumped the coffee table next to him. I flinched. Despite his small build, the force was so strong it sent a mug toppling onto the parquet floor, smashing into three pieces. Brown liquid dripped down the table legs, pooling by the man's slippered feet. 'I said, get. Out.' His voice rasped quietly and that disturbed me more than if he'd shouted. An angry heat burned in me.

Josh guided me out of the room, his cheeks bright red from either embarrassment or annoyance – or possibly both.

'I can only apologise sir, for any confusion. I'll phone your sister as soon as I get back to the office. We'll let ourselves out.'

I swallowed and turned towards the man, my nails digging into the palms of my hands. 'I don't get what your problem is,' I said. I hated confrontation and my voice faltered, but his reaction had really got to me.

He glared, full of hate.

By the time we reached the stone steps and hurried down to the pavement, I was shaking. 'I'm so sorry,' said Josh.

'Don't apologise.' I brushed damp hair from my face, irritated. 'It's not your fault, there's obviously something wrong with the man.'

Josh pushed up his umbrella, and we stood under it; solidarity and a shared sense of injustice allowed us to feel comfortable being so close to each other. 'OK, look, I'm not sure if you're going to be interested in the house now, but shall I ring you tomorrow morning? After I've talked to Mrs Debonair about her brother?'

I gave a small smile and shrugged. 'Yes, and I'll speak to my husband. I liked what I saw so far, but if we do decide to come back for a second look, you'll have to make sure that man isn't going to be there.'

'Absolutely,' said Josh, 'Well, it was great to meet you Mrs Harker, and I'm very sorry.'

I waved my hand, as if batting off his apologies. 'Look, please don't worry, call me tomorrow.' Turning, I ran to my car, keen to get out of the rain. The familiar *thunk* of the central locking was reassuring, and I slipped into my seat exhaling loudly. Not wanting to hang around, I started up the car and pulled on the seatbelt, the wipers automatically springing to life. Peering at the house, my stomach dropped. The man was standing by the window. His figure was shadowy, and his face a silhouette, but the tips of his unkempt hair were highlighted by the lightbulb behind him. It seemed wilder, sticking out at all angles like a clown's. A cold dread chilled my skin and despite the dark, I sensed he was watching me. With a shudder, I hit the indicator with the side of my hand and spun the wheel into full lock. Trying to control my panic so I didn't press my foot too hard on the accelerator, I joined the traffic to take me home.

Back in the comfort of our flat, I poured myself a glass of red wine. Tom stirred a saucepan of spaghetti sauce, and the smell of garlic and basil wafted around the kitchen. Isla, sat at the table colouring in a picture of a flower fairy, her tongue poking out the side of her mouth as she concentrated.

'It was so odd. He scared the life out of me.' I sat next to Isla on the bench and took a gulp of wine, the velvety texture warmed my throat.

Tom laughed. 'It's hilarious!' he said. 'I wish I'd been there. I bet he's just some grouchy old bugger who wants his own way.'

I frowned. He always made light of things; I wanted him to take me seriously. 'It's not funny, Tom. It was weird. We'd been in the house for at least five minutes and turned on the lights and we'd been talking and opening doors and things. He definitely knew we were there.'

'Maybe he was deaf?' said Isla looking up and biting the end of her felt-tip.

'No, he wasn't sweetheart. He could hear us when we spoke to him. And don't forget the lights – he certainly wasn't deaf *and* blind. He was sitting in the dark. His chair facing the door. He was waiting for us.'

'Seriously, Julia, you're so melodramatic. I'm sure that wasn't the case. He's probably just a bit weird.' Tom looked at his reflection on the shiny metal of the extractor fan. He rubbed his chin, checking the length of his stubble. 'Anyway, do you want to go back and see it again?'

I looked away from him, taking out a box of matches from the table drawer and lighting a candle. 'Yes, I do. It's in our price range and the area is perfect. We'd be silly not to.'

Isla was busy putting the wrong-coloured lids on to her pens. Red on black, yellow on blue, green on brown. Reaching out, I took the pens and changed the lids around to the correct colours.

Is it near the shops?' said Isla.

'Yes, only a few minutes' walk. Near that gorgeous coffee shop with the cosy sofas you like.'

'Yay! I want you to buy it, Mummy. We can go for coffee every day and get milkshake.'

I put my arm around her and squeezed; she giggled and leant against me. I rested my chin on her head; I was tired, and my brain was scrambled after a busy day. Yet despite my failed attempt at house viewing, the thought of us living in Larkcombe with its independent shops and cool cafes was so appealing. It was a proper 'grown-up' house, and I could do some proper adulting at last. Instead of pretending to be the perfect wife and mother, maybe the dreaded imposter syndrome that always plagued me on the school playground would finally disappear.

After tipping the drained spaghetti into bowls and ladling the sauce on top, Tom stuck his head around the kitchen door. 'Alex, tea's ready!' He picked up two of the bowls and carried them over to the table. 'Speak to that agent tomorrow then, make an appointment for the weekend.'

'I will,' I nodded taking mine and Isla's bowls from him. Isla sprinkled Parmesan onto her sauce.

'Go steady with that,' said Tom. 'It's for all 4 of us ... Alex! Tea's ready.'

Alex came through with his hands in his pockets. 'I was just finishing off the game,' he said. 'Oh, spaghetti, yum! Isla stop pigging all the Parmesan.' He sat down and shovelled the spaghetti into his mouth, not bothering to wrap it around his fork. 'Did you like the house, Mum?'

'Don't speak with your mouth full of food, Alex. And yes, we'll go back and see it. And it's on the bus route for when you go up to Brookmeads next year, only ten minutes ride, so it's perfect.'

'There was a weird man there,' said Isla. 'I'm not having his bedroom. You can have that room, Alex.'

'The man won't be there if we move in, Stupid,' said Alex. 'You're so dumb.'

Isla glared at her brother and stuck out her tongue.

'Pack it in, you two.' My head began to ache and arguing children was the last thing I needed. 'Eat your food, please both of you.'

While the kids kicked each other under the table, and Tom talked about his latest plumbing job, I absently ate my supper, not concentrating on the taste or what Tom said. I'd started to think about that man again.

Chapter Three

10 O'clock on Saturday morning, Tom, Isla and I stood outside Catcher House. We'd just dropped Alex off at football practice so he couldn't come with us, but Isla was excited – she held my hand and gazed up at the house trying to work out which bedroom might be hers. 'I hope it's that one,' she said pointing to the room on the left.

'Why do you like that one, sweetheart?' I said, smiling.

'Cos it's got pink curtains,' she said.

'Very good choice,' said Tom. 'But what happens if I want that room? I like pink.' He winked at her, and she squealed and launched herself at him, her little fists beating his middle. 'Stop, stop! I give in. You can have it.' Tom grabbed her hands, and they were both still laughing and messing around when Josh walked up to us, smiling.

'Hello Mrs Harker, and Mr Harker? Nice to meet you. And who have we here?' he smiled at Isla, who tucked herself behind my legs.

'Say hello, Isla,' I said. 'She's pretending to be shy.'

Isla peered out. 'Hello.'

Josh winked at her. 'Nice to meet you, Isla. I'm so glad you could all make it. Mrs Debonair is inside. I spoke to her last night, and she was really embarrassed about what happened. She said her brother doesn't want to move, but she's adamant that the house is on the market, and he'll have to lump it. Her words, not mine. Anyway, to cut a long story short, her brother won't be here.'

'Good,' I said, relieved. Last time I was here it had been so unsettling, but now, the sun was shining and everything seemed better; the patterned tiles on the doorstep, the neighbours' beautifully managed courtyards – so much better.

'Shall we go up?' Josh gestured towards the steps.

Tom nodded. 'I like it already.'

Mrs Debonair must have been watching out for us because she swung open the door before we could knock. She was an attractive, slim woman with ashen hair tied back in a low ponytail. At a guess, I would have said she was in her early sixties, stylishly dressed in flared jeans and a black polo neck jumper. Although she smiled politely and apologised for her brother's behaviour, her eyelids were heavy. Such deep, haunting blue eyes – I had to look away.

'I'll let you wander around by yourselves,' she said. 'Nothing worse than having someone looking over your shoulder. I'll wait in the lounge. You'll be pleased to hear that my brother, Roger, has gone out for a walk so we shouldn't be disturbed.'

'Thank you,' I said, glancing at the hallway table littered with unopened mail, all for Mr Roger North. My chest tightened, but I was determined that man wouldn't take away my enjoyment of showing Tom and Isla around the house.

We wandered into the kitchen, and this time I could see the garden. Josh unlocked the door, and we stepped out onto a patio, overgrown with weeds. It needed a lot of work, but it was a good size. It was surrounded by an old brick wall and sloped down about 20 metres to a bottle-green gate.

A small mossy greenhouse was attached to the wall, made from the same bricks. A few glass panels were missing, and it was clearly being used as a shed. Along with a rusty spade and a heavy pickaxe, all sorts of garden tools lay on the flagstones. A few grow bags were on the ground, so it had obviously been used for the right reasons at some point.

Isla ran up to an old, gnarled apple tree. 'Look Mummy, we can make apple pies.' She picked up a wrinkled apple from the ground, and a small slug clung to the shrivelled skin.

'Not with those apples, I hope.' said Tom. 'Put it down, love. It's mouldy and rotten. Shall we go in and see the rest of the house?'

Isla stared at the apple with a look of disgust on her face, then threw it down. I watched as it hit the ground, the pulp mashing into the soil under a spindly rose bush. Isla wiped her hand on her coat, then slipped it into mine. I squeezed her little fingers and tried not to think of the rotten flesh she'd recently been holding.

Once we were back in, Josh led the way to the living room; I shivered, it was still bloody freezing. Flicking through a newspaper, Mrs Debonair sat in the same chair as Roger had been in, although this time, it was turned around to face the television. She raised her head and fixed us with those penetrating blue eyes. 'Don't mind me,' she said. 'Come in. This is my favourite room in the house. It's lovely when there's a fire lit.'

I nodded, the room certainly had potential, but I'd hardly describe it as lovely. The grey paint on the skirting boards was chipped, and the unclean yellow wallpaper looked like the type you get in pubs.

Mrs Debonair stood and walked towards the window. 'And there's a perfect view, right down the road from here.'

I took in a long breath and walked over to join her. Roger North wouldn't have seen me in the dark, especially with the rain against the window, but when I'd got into the car, the interior light would've come on – he would have seen me then. I shuddered. What was it with that man? Something about him made me so uneasy, I wished I could stop thinking about him. Isla looked up the chimney, her little blonde pigtails swinging as she bent her head. 'Mummy, we can put our stockings here at Christmas. Santa won't have to come up in a lift like in our flat.'

Everyone smiled and Mrs Debonair said; 'I remember as a child my mother knitted us some stockings to hang around the fireplace here. We used to hang them from these.' She showed Isla two black metal hooks attached to the wooden mantel, which now had a fire poker and a horseshoe hanging from them.

'You lived here as a child?' I said, in surprise. 'How long have your family owned the house then?'

'My parents bought it after they were married,' she said. 'Let me see. That must have been in 1959 or thereabouts.'

'That's interesting,' said Tom. 'So, Mrs Debonair, it'll be quite a big thing, selling the house then? Full of memories I suppose.' He walked over and ran his fingers against the green patterned tiles that decorated the fire surround. 'So beautiful.'

'Please call me Josephine,' she said, smiling at Tom. 'And I've not lived here for years now. I have a place in Down End. Unfortunately, I need to sell this house for one reason or another, so memories will have to belong in my head, and not here,' she sighed and smoothed her jumper. 'To be honest, I'd rather not have some memories at all.'

We shuffled uncomfortably, standing quiet for a few moments to see if she would continue. The only sound was the rhythmic ticking of the old wooden clock on the mantelpiece. I had to break the silence. 'Why is it called Catcher House?'

Josephine raised her eyebrows. 'Not the nicest of reasons, but it's bad luck to change a house name, so we kept it. In Victorian times it was owned by the rat catcher.'

'Oh,' I said, feeling half thrilled, half repulsed at the idea. 'Well, at least that means there were no rats here then.'

'On the contrary,' said Josephine, 'rat catchers often bred rats to plant around the city to create more business for themselves, but that's a different story. Don't let that put you off buying the house.'

We laughed politely, and when she turned to look back out of the window, Tom nudged me with his elbow and shifted towards the door. He was keen to get on with the viewing, so I thanked Mrs Debonair, then followed him upstairs. There were three bedrooms and a family bathroom. All rooms had small fireplaces. Only the master room at the front was being used, the other two were empty except for a few cardboard boxes and some odd pieces of furniture. The room Isla had admired from the street looked particularly sorry for itself – the pink curtains which had seemed pretty from down below, were tinged with mould patches and had curtain hooks missing. The faded orange carpet was worn around the edges; it looked as if something had chewed it.

Isla peered through the doorway and screwed up her nose. 'I don't like this one anymore, Mummy. I want that back room.'

I laughed. 'We don't know if we're definitely buying the house yet, sweetheart, but if we do, we'll decorate your room any colour you want. And put a new curtain and carpet in, so no need to worry.' I placed a hand on Isla's shoulder and patted her gently.

The bathroom was not much better. I'd been hoping for a Victorian style porcelain bath, but instead, an olive coloured 1970s plastic three piece had replaced anything of any value or taste. The taps were coated with limescale, and I didn't even dare look inside the toilet bowl. Isla screwed up her nose.

'It needs a bit of work,' said Josh with a sideways look at Tom.

Tom nodded and we went back out to the landing. He glanced up at the ceiling. 'Do you know what the attic space is like? I know some houses have converted them into bedrooms. Do you know if we could do that here? It would be handy having a spare room.'

Josh flicked through the particulars. 'I'm not sure,' he said at last. 'Would you like me to ask Mrs Debonair if you can have a look?'

'Might as well, now we're here,' said Tom. 'Yes please.'

I stared upwards. A layer of dust and cobwebs hung around the gaps between the hatch and the ceiling – it obviously hadn't been open for a long time. I didn't want to go up there. Tom could look if he wanted; not me though. I hated attics.

Chapter Four

In the car, Tom couldn't stop talking about the house. Josh had told us there were two other couples going that afternoon, as well as a property developer. 'I reckon we need to put an offer in straight away. Before those other people even get to see the house,' said Tom. 'Otherwise. we'll end up in a bidding war.'

'Is that even a thing in England?' I said, remembering a conversation I'd had with my dad about the Scottish way of buying houses where they had sealed bids.

'You've not heard of gazumping?' said Tom, his eyes darting left and right as he pulled the car into the main high street. 'But to be honest, I don't really know. And I don't think we should wait to find out. Look, it's on at £425,000. I think we should offer the asking price, on the proviso they take it off the market today.'

'Hang on, hang on!' A panicky feeling rose in my stomach. 'Look, let's take Isla to that park near the downs and we can have a coffee to talk about it.'

'OK, but I don't want to hang around. It'll be snapped up really quickly.'

I turned to look out of the window. It was a big decision. Moving house, moving from the area we'd been in for the last ten years. The kids would have to change schools. But it was closer to the senior school where we planned to send Alex. I leant my head on the car window. Isla was a shy girl. Would she make friends easily? But the house was just what we wanted. It would be silly not to go for it.

The road next to the play area was busy. Tom only just managed to get a parking space because someone reversed out. I let Isla out of the back, and she skipped towards the wooden castle, her trainers slipping in the mud and her coat hanging off her shoulders. 'Do up your coat,' I called after her. 'It's freezing cold.'

Isla pretended not to hear me and carried on towards the castle.

'She's fine,' said Tom. 'Let her enjoy herself. I'll get the parking ticket and the coffees you get that bench over there.'

He pointed, and I followed the path around, watching Isla climb up the wall of the castle. She hung from a metal bar with both hands and swung back and forth a few times, before kicking up her legs and hooking them over the wooden wall. She let go of the bar, dangled upside down with the fluffy bobble on her hat swaying side to side. 'Look at me, Mummy!' she shouted.

With a grin, I stuck up my thumbs.

'She's like a little monkey.' said a woman who stood next to a pile of fat shopping bags, bulging with clothes.

'She's always been like that,' I said, walking over to join her. 'Everywhere we go, she climbs. It's exhausting.'

The woman's little boy hauled himself up the wall and sat next to Isla at the top of the castle. Isla gave a small smile and looked at the ground, but the boy started chatting to her regardless.

'Unfortunately, she's not so confident around people – but I suppose everyone is different,' I said.

'Absolutely,' said the woman, who hugged herself to keep warm. 'Wilf will chat to anyone but get him to walk up some steps without falling over is a different matter. My mum says he's got two left feet.'

I laughed. 'Do you live around here? We're thinking of buying a house in Skelton Road. Which means Isla will probably go to The Beeches Primary.'

'Oh really? Yeah, we live about five minutes from here. Wilf goes there too – he's in year 2. How old's Isla?'

'She's just 7, so she'd be in the same year.' I watched as Isla laughed with Wilf and the two chased each other around the platform on top of the castle. 'Well, It's great she's made a friend already. That makes me feel better about moving. I'm a bit worried about her changing schools.'

'Well, if you do move, make sure you come and say hello in the playground. My name's Lizzie.' Tucking pink tinted hair behind her ear, which had about six piercings in, she gave a smile, her bright orange lipstick lighting up her pale face.

'Aw, thanks. It's so good to meet you, I'm Julia.' I returned the smile and then noticed Tom walking towards us with two coffees in his hands. I waved. 'That's my husband coming over – he's going to try and convince me to buy the house.' I pretended to grimace.

'You should,' said Lizzie, nudging me with her elbow. 'You'll fit in really well.'

Tom sauntered up and handed me a cardboard cup of spiced pumpkin latte.

'Tom, this is Lizzie, she lives near here, and Wilf would be in the same school where Isla will go.'

'Hiya,' Tom said, then raised an eyebrow. 'Well, you seem to have done a great job in persuading my wife to move here, Lizzie.'

Lizzie laughed and tilted her head to the side. 'I did my best. Look, it was so fab meeting you both, but I'll let you get on. And I'll say it just once more, you *so* must move here. It's such a cool community for families.' With a quick turn of her head, she flicked her hair over her shoulders, picked up her bags and we said goodbye.

I leant back on the bench, cupping my hands around the coffee cup, thinking what a fabulous place the park was to bring the kids. Behind the play area was a fenced off pond, and I watched Lizzie wandering over to another family who were feeding the ducks. A little further away was a Victorian style bandstand painted in gold and red with a lead roof and an ornate, bronze handrail. 'Well?' said Tom. 'Shall we go for it?'

I turned towards him. 'For once in my life, I'm going to be spontaneous and say yes.' My words tumbled out in excitement. 'It's got so much potential, and the area is perfect.'

Tom's eyes shone. He took my hand and squeezed it tightly. 'It'll be amazing,' he said. 'Get us away from those gross new builds near us. I'll give the estate agent a call now.' He pulled out Josh's business card and punched the number into his phone.

As he spoke, I put my thumbnail to my mouth, and chewed – had I made the right decision? The image of that man flashed into my head – Roger. What had he said? *Get out. I'm not moving.* Was that a bad omen? I shook my head. I was being silly. Over on the roundabout, Isla sat like a little princess while Wilf pushed her around. No, I'd definitely made the right decision. Besides, the ball was rolling now, and I couldn't upset Tom by changing my mind. I put down my cup and shivered. The wind picked up and the dark clouds scudded ominously across the sky. Buttoning up my coat, I listened to Tom negotiating. He smiled and winked at me. My shoulders relaxed. I told myself that everything would be fine.

Chapter Five

The sale went through quite easily as far as the solicitors were concerned. The only problem was Roger North. No matter how many times Mrs Debonair tried to speak to him, he seemed to get great pleasure from tormenting us. Tom had even gone around a few times to speak to Mrs Debonair about it.

Although I never knew for sure, I didn't think Roger had a job, because he always seemed to be at home. When the surveyor went around to the house, he wouldn't let him in. On the third visit he finally managed to gain entry, and that was only because our solicitor sent Mrs Debonair a letter. Even then, the surveyor reported back that Roger had been super rude to him and tried to block him from going up into the attic. Luckily the surveyor wasn't the type to take no for an answer. And of course, there was nothing wrong up there, it was apparently in very good condition, so Roger was being bloody awkward.

It was an early March evening when the call came through. We were sat at the kitchen table, eating pie and mash. Tom, who'd been expecting the call, snatched up the phone.

'How come he gets to have his phone at the table, and I can't?' said Alex, his face contorting into an angry frown.

'Ssh,' I said, putting a finger to my lips. 'It's the estate agent.'

'That's such good news,' said Tom, waving a victorious fist in the air. 'Thanks Josh, for everything.' He placed the phone back on the table and looked at me, his face turning red with excitement. 'The deposit's transferred. Completion is a week today. It's ours.'

Isla banged her cutlery on the wooden table, 'Yay, yay, yay!' she shouted.

'So cool!' said Alex, and grinned at his dad, who stood and put his arms around my shoulders and kissed the top of my head.

I put my hand on Tom's and squeezed, an exhilarated thrill rushing through me. Catcher House was ours. 'Let's crack open that bottle of prosecco in the fridge,' I said, 'celebrate in style.'

'Can we have a coke, Dad?' said Alex.

'I expect so,' he said, pulling out both bottles from the fridge. 'To think kids, in a week's time, we'll be in.'

Alex gulped his water, then emptied the contents of the large coke bottle into his and Isla's beakers; the plastic crunched as he squeezed it between his hands. Tom uncorked the prosecco with a pop and poured it into the glasses. 'Well, here's to us,' he said, raising his drink.

'To us,' I said, and I leant over and kissed him on the cheek, enjoying the feel of his stubble against my lips.

*

On the day of the move, my stress levels went through the roof. Throughout the week, I'd romanticised it in my head – making tea for cheerful removal men, walking into each room, and saying goodbye to our flat, remembering all the best bits of living there. But the reality was not quite the same. The removal men were miserable bastards – only interested in getting the job done; and as for the memories – all I could think of was how bad the blackcurrant squash stain looked in the living room once all the furniture had been removed. The landlord would definitely take that off our deposit.

The kids had gone to school. Alex was going to carry on there until the end of the summer because it was his last year, but Isla would go to her new school the next week.

Tom packed the last few items from the hallway cupboard, but there wasn't anything else I could do. I stood in the communal garden and watched the removal men fitting the furniture into the lorry like pieces of a jigsaw puzzle. The early spring sun brought a little heat to the air, and I rolled up the sleeves of my sweatshirt. As I let my body relax in the warmth, I wondered how 10 years of life could fit into one lorry.

Eventually, everything was boxed up. I sighed in relief when the phone call came from the estate agents saying we could now get into our new house, and Mrs Debonair would meet us outside with the keys. As we drove up Skelton Road, my stomach twisted with excitement and nerves. The lorry had managed to park right outside Catcher House – Mrs Debonair had thought of putting yellow cones in the road to stop anyone else from parking there. 'Brilliant,' said Tom. 'I was worrying about where the lorry would park. It's always so busy. Hop out and move that cone for me, love.'

Tom pulled the car over and I jumped out. As I picked up the cone, Mrs Debonair came down the steps, her hair tied up stylishly in a red print scarf. She waved the keys in the air. 'All yours,' she shouted above the noise of the lorry ramp as it lowered to the ground. She was much happier this time, the worry lines that had previously marked her forehead didn't seem quite so deep.

'Thank you, Josephine.' I smiled and took the keys. 'Did your brother's move go OK? Was he alright about leaving in the end?' I cringed at my attempt to sound caring.

Mrs Debonair sighed and waved her hand dismissively. 'Oh, yes, yes. Don't worry about him. He's all safe and sound in that hostel on the corner of the high street for now until he can find a place.' She licked her lips and paused before speaking again. 'He *said* he hasn't been able to find anything quite as nice as Catcher House, so he's going to wait until something suitable comes up for rent. I'm afraid he's a bit of a … well, you know.'

I nodded, and my heart sunk. The thought of Roger North living so close made my skin crawl. Why didn't Mrs Debonair invite her brother to stay with her temporarily? But I figured I wouldn't want him staying with me, either, if he was my brother. 'Well, I hope he finds something soon, I'd hate to think that he's unsettled because we bought the house.'

Mrs Debonair let out an over-loud laugh. 'He had to move out, whether you or someone else bought it. He's absolutely fine about it now. He's just bitter because the house was mine to sell, not his. Our father refused to leave Roger anything of value, he said he lacked responsibility. Lucky for me, eh?'

'Oh,' I said, not quite sure what to say. It didn't seem fair that Roger didn't get anything.

Mrs Debonair must have realised what I was thinking. 'Don't feel sorry for him,' she said with a smile on her face. 'Of course, I've given him some money to go towards his next place. Now where's your husband? I need to show you both how the boiler works.' She turned and walked into the house, and I waited for Tom to finish speaking to the removal men. He ran up the steps with a big smile on his face.

'All OK?'

'Yeah, all good,' I said, and then lowered my voice. 'Except Roger North is going to be living down the road in a hostel. I hope he's not going to be a pain.'

'Jesus, Julia, don't spoil the day by worrying about that bloody man,' he said. 'He won't bother us, so stop fussing. Now, where's Mrs Debonair? I need to ask her a few things.'

*

That night, Tom and I sunk onto the sofa with boxes and furniture all around us. The kids had finally gone to bed, exhausted from exploring the house and high on excitement. Resting my head on a plumped-up cushion that really belonged in the bedroom, I was happy to be in our new house but a little overwhelmed by all the boxes that needed unpacking. But it had gone ten o'clock and I was knackered – I couldn't bear to look at another cardboard crate that night. The television hadn't been connected, so we made do with scrolling on our phones, sitting in comfortable silence. Outside, the rain hit the sash window, and I wished I'd hung the curtains up – it made me uneasy thinking that anyone could be watching us. I put my phone down on the wooden floor and walked over to the light switch. 'I'm turning this off,' I said. 'I don't want people staring in at us through the window. '

Tom frowned. 'Don't be stupid, Jules, we can't sit here in the dark.'

I flicked the switch, throwing the living room into semi-darkness. 'I don't like it. It'll be alright, we've got a bit of light from the hallway.'

'Well, it's stupid,' said Tom. 'I'm going to bed. I'll see you up there.' He got up and walked past me without kissing my cheek like he normally did. My stomach sunk a little, but I figured he was just tired; maybe I *was* being stupid? I took a few steps towards the window to look outside. The weather had turned, and it now poured down. With the rain battering the glass, it wasn't easy to see anything. I wiped away the condensation, cupped my hands and peered out. Our front garden was in the dark, except for the silhouetted steps leading down to the pavement, and a blur of orange from a streetlight. Of course, there was no one standing in the pouring rain staring in. I was just unsettled being in a new house. I'd put up our old curtains tomorrow, even though they probably wouldn't fit the window. I'd feel more comfortable then. I lowered my hands and a car drove by; its headlights making the raindrops look like tiny diamonds on the glass.

Turning away, I picked up my phone – time for me to go to bed too. As I walked up the stairs, I peered over the bannisters and my heart leapt to see we'd put a chair in exactly the same spot where Roger had been sitting. I stopped and stared. How had I not noticed that before? Tomorrow, I'd move it to a different position, no way was it staying there.

Chapter Six

As the days went on, we soon had the house sorted. There were a few boxes in every room that needed unpacking, but there was loads of time to do that over the next few weeks. The kids were happy. Alex had found out that Callum, a friend from his football team, lived a few doors down, and he went to the park most days to kick a ball around. Isla was pleased with her new bedroom – I'd hung up some pink and purple voile material across the walls to make her room cosier and to give it a 'princess' feel, just until we could get around to decorating. The horrible pink curtain that had hung from our bedroom window found its way to the tip, along with a number of other manky things that had been left in the house.

After their stuff was moved out, Mrs Debonair had paid for a cleaner, but they'd totally ignored some things in the bathroom cabinet – sticky bottles of medicine, opened tubes of haemorrhoid cream, and even some hypodermic needles. It turned my stomach as I swept them with my rubber glove into a bin liner. Maybe Roger was a diabetic? I didn't know, but it was typical of that man to leave something like that for other people to find. My animosity for him had grown tenfold over the weeks we'd been waiting for the sale to go through. He'd deliberately made things hard for us, and I wouldn't forget that. If I ever saw him in the street, I'd give him a good ignoring.

Tom and I had taken a few days off when we'd first moved in, which was great– and it didn't take me long to feel more settled. I began to enjoy planning all the renovations we needed to do, and Tom was in Heaven – working on his own housing project was a dream come true for him. Unpacking and sorting things in the house had been exhausting though, so I was more than ready to get back to work.

On the Monday morning, Tom had left early for an emergency call-out on the other side of the city, and Alex had gone to call for Callum. The house was quiet without the two boys, and when I tried to get toothpaste off the front of Isla's new school jumper, a strange scraping sound came from the next room. Isla's bedroom. 'What's that noise?' I frowned and draped the flannel over the sink. Isla wasn't interested, she pulled away from me and looked into the mirror, trying to clip her fringe back with a hair slide. She was desperate to make a good impression on her new school mates.

What the hell was it? I dashed along the landing to Isla's room. With my hand on the doorframe, I stood still and listened. Nothing. The voile material had come loose from the upper corners of the walls and had flopped down onto the wardrobe, so maybe that had made a noise? But honestly? I didn't believe that was true. There wasn't anything else, though. I shook my head; it was weird.

Twisting my wrist, I glanced at the time – we were going to be late. 'We need to go Isla, quick, get your shoes on.' That was the last thing I needed, arriving late on Isla's first day at her new school.

We were in the hallway, just about to go out, when a thud came from upstairs. This time it sounded like loose masonry or something – stones or tiles slipping. Tiles? My heart sank. I opened the front door and looked at the roof. Nothing seemed out of place. It must be around the back of the house. The wind was picking up, something must have come dislodged. There was no time to look, we were late, and besides, there was nothing I could do if a tile had come off the roof. Damn. 'I think it's something around the back of the house, Isla. I'll phone Daddy and see if he can come back at lunchtime to have a look. We better get going.' I ran back up the steps and grabbed my coat and thrust Isla's new book bag into her hands.

'Maybe it's the chimney, Mummy,' said Isla, as she skipped along next to me. 'I heard a bird tweeting from my fireplace this morning. Maybe the bird's pecking at the bricks.'

'Maybe, darling, it could be that,' I said, trying not to sound too depressed - birds in the chimneys? We'd need to sort that too. Had we taken on more than we'd bargained for with this house? I wasn't used to old properties; my parents always had new houses. What if there was a lot of things wrong with it?

As I drove down the road, I tried to force down the negative thoughts; it's nothing that couldn't be fixed. It would be fine once Tom looked at it – he'd probably be able to repair it himself.

Isla was a complete star going into her new class. I took her to the school office, and two little girls came to meet her, saying their teacher, Miss Acrington, had sent them to fetch her. They were going to be her 'buddies'. She held their hands and walked away, giving me a little smile over her shoulder. 'Bye Mummy.'

'Bye darling, have a super day.' The door shut with a bang, and my heart gave a small flutter. She was growing up so fast, growing in confidence all the time. I was proud of her.

*

The gravel in the office car park crunched as I reversed into a space. Moments later, a cherry-red Mazda drew up alongside. It was my best friend, Thalia. Her faux-fur Russian hat fitted stylishly over her cropped platinum blonde hair, and she waved at me, smiling.

We both stepped out of our cars and chatted for a minute before she wrapped her arms around herself and shivered. 'It's bloody freezing out here. Come on, quick!' She strode across the car park and into the office, with me following close behind. It was warm inside, and there was a smell of bitter coffee. While throwing my jacket over the chair, I texted Tom about the strange noise. He replied straight away, saying he'd sort it out; and I let my shoulders relax.

Soon, I'd forgotten about the house and got into the swing of a normal working day – taking bookings, sorting out plumbers' schedules and typing up quotes. I loved my job – especially because it was where Tom and I met. He'd been at GS Plumbing Services for ages before he left to work for our competitor. He was still friends with many of our lads. Thalia and I both worked in the same office – she dealt with accounts, and I was mainly administrative. Although we did have a couple of female plumbers, we were the only two in the offices, and over the last seven years, we'd become firm friends.

'I'm going to the shop to get some sushi, want anything?' Thalia stood and stretched her arms above her head, revealing her flat, brown midriff as her blouse became untucked from her skirt.

'Yes, that'll be great,' I said. 'Just the usual.'

'Has Tom messaged back about the roof yet?' she said as she pulled on her coat.

I picked up my phone; he'd texted a few minutes before. I eagerly opened the message.

NOT SURE WHAT YOU HEARD BUT THERE'S NOTHING LOOSE ON THE ROOF. I CHECKED THE ATTIC. NOTHING THERE. MUST BE THE WIND UNDER THE TILES. x

'Oh,' I said, not sure whether to be pleased or worried. 'He said there's nothing wrong. That's so odd, Thalia. I really did hear something. Twice.'

She waved her hand in the air. 'Oh, don't worry. If it's anything serious, you'll soon know about it. Get the kettle on, and I'll see you in ten minutes.'

In the kitchen, I filled up the kettle, thinking. Wind under the tiles wouldn't make a scraping noise. Uneasiness crawled into me like a parasite, and I didn't like it. I don't know why such a small thing could put me on edge, but something didn't feel right. I hoped Tom would be around if it happened again. I pulled my cardigan around me as I waited for the kettle to boil, although the heating was on, my fingers felt like ice.

My hands trembled as I got the mugs out of the cupboard, and I knew it wasn't just from the cold. I really hoped the stress of the move and doing up an old house wasn't going to make me ill again. When Isla was born I'd suffered from post-natal depression and paranoia, and I didn't want that constant hell again. Gazing at my reflection in the stainless-steel kettle and seeing what Tom called my 'silly worried face', I told myself to get it together.

Chapter Seven

During the rest of the week, no one heard the sound again. Tom joked with the kids that I'd been hearing things. 'She wasn't, Daddy,' said Isla over supper one night. 'I heard it too.'

'Maybe we've got a ghost,' said Alex.

'Alex, don't say that; you'll scare Isla.' I glared at him, and he looked down at his plate, pushing his broccoli to the side. Isla grinned. She looked perfectly happy with the idea of a ghost. She'd been reading a book recently about friendly ghouls who haunted a school, and she was quite taken with the idea. To be totally honest, it was me who was scared because I knew where this was going, and Alex didn't surprise me when he spoke again.

'I heard footsteps last night, and I'm not even joking,' he said. I fixed him with a stare; was he serious? There was no sparkle in his eyes, his face, deadpan. He was being totally genuine.

Tom smirked. Of course it was all a bit of fun to him. He put his hands in the air and waggled his fingers. 'Ooh, tell us more, l love a spooky story.'

'Was it a friendly ghost, Alex?' said Isla. Her eyes widened and she put down her knife.

'I don't know if it's a ghost or some of those old pipes banging or what, but the last two nights I've heard footsteps, that's all.' Alex's expression was still serious, and he held my gaze. Unsettled, I glanced over at Tom. He winked.

'Is it you, Tom?' I said, shooting him a dirty look. 'It is, isn't it? Daddy's always needing a pee in the night, that's what you'd have heard,' I said, not wanting the kids to be frightened.

A shudder went through me. I didn't believe any of my own words. Because I'd heard the footsteps too, and Tom had been in bed beside me – fast asleep.

It wasn't until Saturday, when Alex had gone to football, and Tom had taken Isla swimming, that I had the house to myself. Both Tom and I agreed we'd decorate Alex's room first because the damp was really bad. But before stripping the wallpaper, I made the most of the peace and sat for a while at our tiny kitchen table. Despite the pleasures of freshly ground coffee and a cinnamon bun, my chest was heavy as I gazed around at the amount of work that needed to be done. I couldn't wait for the wall to come down so we could have more space, and light. I wanted new kitchen units pretty soon too; the ones we had were practically falling apart, even the shelves above the worksurface were sagging after years of holding heavy pans and stuff. On the middle shelf, sat the biscuit tin, and annoyingly, the lid was off. Tom was so irritating; didn't he know they'd go stale? It wasn't the kids; they couldn't stand the fig rolls that he dunked in his tea.

I reached up and peered into the tin – it was empty apart from the wrapper – the greedy pig! Surely, he hadn't eaten a whole pack since yesterday. What a joke. Shaking my head, I sat back down to finish my bun, using my fingertip to wipe up the sugary glaze.

But drinking coffee and eating buns wasn't getting Alex's bedroom done, so I forced myself upstairs to get on with it. As I dragged the furniture into the middle of the room and threw dustcovers over it all, the morning sun shone through the window, casting an unfamiliar yet welcome warmth over everything. I'd told Alex at breakfast time it would be best if he slept on the sofa until his bedroom was ready, which he was hardly ecstatic about, but I reminded him if he wanted his room decorated, he wasn't in a position to complain.

Although I wasn't a great fan of DIY, I quite enjoyed myself with my headphones on, listening to playlists. The wallpaper was old and brittle, and after sponging it down with warm water and sugar soap, it peeled off the wall easily. It was so satisfying removing large strips all in one go. Before long, a pile of damp paper lay everywhere, sticking to the floor and woodwork. I decided it was time for a break and went downstairs to make myself another coffee.

While waiting for the kettle to boil, I phoned Mum to tell her about the wallpaper coming off so easily. 'Are you still ok to come for lunch tomorrow?' I said.

'Of course, but I don't want you to go to any trouble, Julia, you have enough to do as it is.'

'It really isn't any trouble at all, I need a break. Having a roast with you and Dad will be great. But if you want to help, you can bring a pudding.' I tucked the phone between my shoulder and ear and poured boiling water into the cafetiere.

'Oh, OK,' said Mum, sounding pleased. 'I'll do a crumble, or shall I do Tom's favourite? One of those cheesecakes?'

'Tom always gets one of your cheesecakes,' I said with mock indignation. 'I fancy a crumble.'

Mum laughed and agreed she'd make a cherry crumble and would bring some custard as well. It would be so nice to have them around and take our minds off the house. Dad would like to see Tom's plans for the kitchen renovation too.

After finishing my coffee, I grabbed a bin liner to clear away the mess in Alex's room. Some paper had even stuck to the window, and as I peeled it off, I saw Tom parking the car outside our house. I waved, and my heart squeezed as Isla's little face with red shiny cheeks pressed against the car window. She waved back at me, and I smiled to see she was wearing her little pink mittens, even though it wasn't that cold. Before going down to see how they'd got on at the swimming pool, I inspected the floor, checking I'd picked up all the wallpaper.

Tom was in the kitchen, putting on the kettle, but Isla had disappeared into the living room; the TV more interesting than talking to me. 'Have a nice swim?' I said, picking up their bags and pulling out the wet towels and costumes.

'Great,' said Tom. 'She's swimming a length without any problem now.' He put his hand out to reach for the biscuit tin, and frowned to see there was nothing inside.

'Biscuits don't automatically appear you know.' I raised my eyebrows and smiled.

'What? I'm sure I only had a couple out of that new pack, where have they all gone?'

'You must have had them, it's not us, we hate them. Maybe you're secretly eating them in your sleep?' I joked.

'Ha, ha, very funny. I must have had more than I thought. Oh well, I'll have a KitKat instead.' he placed the tin back on the shelf and opened the cupboard. 'I saw that woman today, you know the one who we met at the park? Her name's Lizzie, remember?'

'Oh, yeah,' I said, as I crammed the swimming things into the washing machine. 'I do remember. I've been in such a rush at the school gates I haven't had a chance to speak to anyone yet. Next week I'll make more of an effort. What did she say?'

Tom sat down at the table and broke his KitKat in two, before taking a bite. 'She said she saw you rushing in on Wednesday but didn't get a chance to catch up with you. She mentioned a book club you might like to go to. She said to speak to her next week about it. A group of other mums or something, involving cake and wine. Sounds right up your street.' He nodded his head at me and smiled.

'Great, thanks,' I said, pleased. It would be good to meet a few other mums. 'Anyway, come and look at the paper I've removed from Alex's room.'

Tom followed me upstairs, and into the bedroom. 'Oh wow, you've done a great job. Well done, love.'

'It was so easy and quick.'

He looked around, and then his eyes caught sight of something under the window. 'There's some writing down there,' he said. We walked over and I crouched down. I hadn't noticed it earlier; too focused on my own private challenge of getting the wallpaper strips off in whole pieces.

Pulling my sleeve over my hand, I rubbed the wall and peered closely. It was tiny writing. 'Oh! It's not very nice.'

Tom crouched down next to me and read the words out loud. '*Fuck off Faither.*' He whipped his head around to check Isla wasn't there. 'Bloody hell, I wonder if Roger wrote that?'

'I bet it was him,' I said. 'Just as obnoxious as a kid. Funny word, Faither isn't it? Must be an old word for Father.' I ran my fingers over the words. 'Better get one of your markers and colour over it for now, we don't want the kids to read it.'

'Yeah, don't want to give them any ideas either, or they'll be scrawling on the walls too.' He walked out of the room and came back a few minutes later with a black pen. He bent down and drew three thick lines through the words. 'Is there any more?'

Glancing at the walls, there didn't seem to be. 'No, I think that's it,' I said. 'I bet his dad was mad when he found out. How old do you reckon he was when he wrote it?'

'He must have been a teenager, but who knows?'

'Funny place to write it, right down by the skirting board – odd.' I frowned, as I imagined Roger as a boy, being so angry to scrawl nasty things on the walls.

'He is odd, though, isn't he?' said Tom as we both stood up. 'And kids do weird things sometimes. Well, it's gone now, and we'll paint over it so no need to think about it anymore.'

I nodded and put my hand on the small of his back. 'Come on, let's get some lunch.' As I walked out of Alex's room, I had a horrible feeling in the pit of my stomach. It wasn't unusual for teenagers to swear at their parents, but for some reason, it disturbed me.

Bloody Roger – he wasn't here in person, but his presence certainly was.

Chapter Eight

That evening, Tom and the kids were going to stay with his mum over in Bath. There was a play on at the local theatre, which his mum had been involved with. She was a seamstress and made the costumes for the performance. Typically, it clashed with my choir's annual dinner – we always had it in March because Christmas and New Year were too busy, and it also tied in with Irie's birthday. Irie was our choir director. She'd formed the all-women's group ten years ago – she was a force of nature, and we all adored her.

It was a shame I was going to miss the play; I loved theatre. If I hadn't fallen pregnant with Alex, I'd have gone to study drama at university, but I got married instead. Such is life.

But I wasn't going to complain, it was a night out. As I put on make-up and listened to some music, Alex came in and threw himself onto the bed. 'Do I *have* to go? It's for kids.'

'Your point being?'

'It's for kids, it'll be so boring.'

'It says suitable for 8- to 12-year-olds, and when I last looked, you were 11, so …' I poked him with my hairbrush as he groaned. 'Don't be so ungrateful. Your gran's bought tickets and she's excited about taking you. You'll enjoy it when you're there. Besides, it will mean you won't have to sleep in the living room tonight, either. And Dad said he's going to take you for breakfast in the morning.'

Alex sat up, looking a bit more interested. 'OK,' he said. 'But can you tell Dad we're allowed to buy an ice-cream and coke in the interval?'

'I bet your gran's already thought of that, you know what she's like. Now, go and get changed, you've got 10 minutes.'

'Changed? Seriously? Can't I go like this?' He looked down at his tracksuit bottoms and T-shirt, both stained with mud.

'Nope – get your jeans on and a clean shirt, now go.' I chased him out of the room laughing.

*

It had been a long while since I'd been on a night out. My stomach bubbled with excitement as the scent of perfume and citrus fruit drew me into the warmth of the cocktail bar. Thalia was just behind me, and above the noise of the music and the hum of conversations, she spoke close to my ear. 'Irie said she's booked three booths at the back.'

The place was heaving, and we had to sidestep and squeeze through the groups of people until we found our friends. Irie spotted us, and she waved both arms in the air – gold bangles dangled off her wrist, glinting in the soft light from the chandelier. With hugs, kisses and excited laughter, we sat down at the table, where glasses were thrust in front of us, and margaritas poured. The salt and lemon around the glass tasted sharp and sour, and delicious, and I sipped my drink, straining my ears to hear the conversation around me.

We stayed for about an hour, before heading out of the bar and into the cool night. I fell into conversation with some girls I hadn't spoken to for a while, and we walked along to the courtyard where our Italian was. We crowded around the door – there were at least 20 of us, so we formed a kind of queue, and that's when I heard my name being called.

'Hey, Julia.'

Someone tapped me on the shoulder, and I turned to see Lizzie, the woman from the park.

'Oh hi, Lizzie isn't it? You alright?'

She looked fabulous in a long flowing, purple dress. A silk printed scarf was wrapped around her head, and she wore a pair of flowery DMs. Her lipstick matched the dress; she totally carried off the look.

'I'm fine thanks. On a night out!' She waved her hand in the direction of two women who sat under a patio heater at the next restaurant. 'What about you?'

'It's my choir's night out. Been for some cocktails, now need some food to soak up all the alcohol.'

'Know the feeling. Did your gorgeous husband mention that we'd seen each other? Did he tell you about the book club?'

'Yeah, he did…'

'You must come, there's not many of us, we need new members. First Thursday of every month and we take it in turns to go to each other's houses.'

Thalia nudged me. I knew what she thought. Lizzie was too left field for her – Thalia, although beautiful, was not one for alternative dress. In fact, she despised the hippy look, and it didn't help that Lizzie wore patchouli perfume which was beginning to sting my nostrils.

We swapped phone numbers, and I promised I'd go to the book club. She hugged me goodbye as if she was an old friend, then drifted back to her table. By then, the rest of our group had gone into the restaurant, and Thalia held the door open for me. 'Bit OTT, isn't she?' she said, as we walked into the restaurant.

'A little maybe, but she seems nice.'

'And what's all this about '*gorgeous husband*'? I'd watch her if I was you.' Her voice was loaded with suspicion.

Irritated by Thalia's comment, I put my hands on my hips. 'She's only being friendly, don't assume everyone is like you, Thalia – not everyone's after someone's husband.'

Thalia stopped walking and looked at me with hurt in her eyes. 'Do you really think that of me? I'd never make a move on a friend's partner. I can't believe you'd think that of me.' She turned away and strode towards the table.

I cringed. I hadn't meant to upset her. But sometimes she was too judgemental, and she always seemed to find bad points about my other friends. But I knew she'd never do anything to hurt me, and she was right – she'd never flirted with Tom. Ever. And she was the world's biggest flirt. As I reached the table, I put my arm around her shoulders and whispered, 'Sorry, Thalia, I was out of order. Forgive me?'

She turned and looked at me for few seconds. I must have looked so wretched because she smiled and kissed me on the cheek. 'All forgotten. Now, sit down, will you? We need to order some wine.'

Chapter Nine

It had gone twelve by the time I got home. It was the first time I'd been in the house on my own at night, a strange sense of expectation hung in the air. But even if the others had been there, it wouldn't have been any less quiet– they'd be in bed, fast asleep. I shut the front door, and leant against it for a few moments, swaying a little. My head spun; I was drunk. I kicked off my heels and walked into the kitchen to get a glass of water. The pipes behind the tiles clunked; a deep thudding that only stopped when I turned the tap off. It was a horrible noise. Keen to get to bed, I downed the water in one, the cold liquid made my teeth ache.

Holding the banister to steady myself, I went upstairs. The landing bulb didn't have lightshade, and it cast an ugly brightness across the carpet and into Alex's room. Eager to see my attempts at DIY, I stepped in and admired the bare walls. My head swam with alcohol as I steadied myself against the bed post, and I enjoyed a few moments of contemplation. What shade of blue would suit his room? (he'd already told me that it was to be the same colour as the Tottenham strip – but there was no way the whole room would be navy blue).

It was then I saw it. Right under the window, above the writing Tom had scrawled out earlier.

More writing.

My stomach lurched. Almost losing my balance, I walked over. In block capitals, written in red ink, were the words FUCK OFF.

I dropped to my knees. My guts twisted and the blood rushed to my head as I ran my fingers over the words. 'What the hell?' I swallowed hard, glancing around the room, expecting to see someone standing there. I shook my head in disbelief. Who had done this? Was it Alex? But he hadn't seen the first bit of writing, so surely he'd not have written a similar message in the same place? No. Not Alex. He'd not do something like that anyway. Isla neither. Was it Tom, trying to have a joke with me?

I fumbled for my phone in my jeans pocket and took a photo of the writing. It looked so sinister, like a still from a horror film. Not caring about the typos, I sent it to Tom. He'd probably be asleep, but he'd see it as soon as he woke up.

Leaning against the door frame, I willed Tom to answer. But there was nothing. My head began to thump. The unclean woodwork was sticky against my cheek, and after too many drinks, the dirty smell made me retch. I needed to get to bed.

Despite the graffiti plaguing my thoughts, I did manage to fall asleep. It was a fitful, dream-filled sleep with terrible images and strange faces. When I woke up, I was clammy – my pyjamas clinging to my skin. I turned to look at the clock. It was 4:55. Thank God. Time to sleep more. My pyjama top was wet from sweat, so I sat up and pulled it off, then wriggled out of the bottoms, throwing them to the floor. After a sip of water, I rolled over to Tom's side of the bed where the sheets were cool.

Not being able to drop off, I thought about the night out – about Lizzie and Thalia. About the writing on the wall. It had been a strange evening. The orange streetlight glowed through the crack in the curtains, and I switched on the radio, lulled to a gentle doze by the shipping forecast – *Forth, Tyne Dogger, Fisher – Easterly or South-Easterly 5 or 6 in North and East. Rain then showers. Moderate or good.*

Then *Thump.*

Thump. Thump.

My eyes snapped open. Again – *thump. Thump.*

I shot up to sitting, straining my ears and holding tight to the duvet. It had come from above me; I was sure. I tried to breathe quietly, opening my mouth. But there was nothing. No more noise. After a while, I allowed my shoulders to relax and lay back down. It was probably the tiles – Tom would have to go up on the roof and have a proper look. Or we'd have to get a roofer in. I squeezed my eyes shut, and this time, I didn't fall to sleep. I lay there, holding onto the frill of the pillowcase until I was aware of the sky lightening through the crack in the curtains, and the soft sound of the birds singing.

Chapter Ten

'Look, I've told you, it wasn't me. I swear to God.'

Tom leant against the kitchen table, holding his hands up in defence. In the living room the kids were watching TV, and the noise of a cartoon blared out; some animated character laughing, as if mocking me.

'Who the hell was it then, Tom? Not the kids – Alex thought I'd gone mad when I asked him. I could tell by his face it wasn't him.' I was preparing vegetables ready for Sunday lunch, the peel got thicker and thicker as I worked a knife angrily around the potato.

'Of course it wasn't Alex.' Tom looked out of the window, deep in thought. 'Maybe it was always there?' he said in calmer voice. 'Maybe we just didn't notice because we focused on the black writing below? Maybe it showed up when you shone the light on it?'

I shook my head. 'No. It's too clear and too obvious for us to have missed it.' I took the joint of lamb out of the fridge and began to unwrap it. A hangover was making me more sensitive than I'd normally be – my eyes were tired from lack of sleep and my head still hurt. But I was scared, and I needed Tom to take me seriously.

He sat down with a sigh. 'Well, if it's not the kids, and not me. Did *you* do it as a kind of joke?'

As I washed my hands under the warm tap, I didn't even bother to reply. 'I think we need to ring the police,' I said at last, drying my hands on a towel and throwing it onto the worktop. 'Someone must have got into the house. Unless it's something else…'

'Love, this is ridiculous. It's not going to be anyone who got into the house. Who does that? And what do you mean … something else? Surely you don't mean a poltergeist?' He shook his head and raised his eyebrows.

'Well, I don't know. And don't be scornful, it's not me; it's not my fault.'

Tom scraped back his chair and put his hands behind his head. 'Look, you can call the police if you want, but I honestly don't think they'll take you seriously.'

I stared at the table and nodded. 'I'm going to. And the other thing that happened was that banging noise again. Can you get up onto the roof and have a proper look? Or go into the attic? It really was the last thing I needed after the writing – this house is doing my head in. I'm beginning to think it's haunted.'

Tom's lips pressed together so firmly it looked as if he'd swallowed them. 'You need to get a grip Julia. Or you'll be going back to the doctors again. I really can't hack any more of your senseless worries.' He stormed out of the kitchen, and my eyes stung as they welled with tears. I blinked and picked up my phone – dialling 101.

*

Tom was in the shed, rummaging through his toolbox when I went to find him. 'I got through to the local police,' I said. 'They're going to send someone around this evening.'

'Good. Look, I'm sorry I snapped at you, but it's all so weird. I worry about you too, you know? I don't want you to get ill again.' He came over to me and kissed me on the cheek. 'I'll go up in the attic now and have a look, OK?'

Pleased he was taking me seriously at last, I sniffed and nodded my head. 'Don't forget Mum and Dad are coming for lunch today.'

'Yeah, that's fine, it won't take me long, will it? What time are they getting here?'

'About twelve o'clock.'

'No problem.' He picked up his head torch from the shelf, and strolled purposefully into the house, with me following after.

The kids had turned the TV off. I peered into the room to see what they were doing. Alex was on his phone, Isla knelt by the coffee table, colouring in. 'Nan and Grandad are coming in a while, kids, OK?' They both nodded without looking up, so I pulled the door to, and ran upstairs to join Tom.

The hatch door was like an entrance to hell. Never had an attic seemed so unwelcoming as this one. Evil seemed to emanate from the other side. It was crazy, but a sudden sense of dread tore in the pit of my stomach, and as I chewed the inside of my mouth, a taste of blood coated my tongue.

Tom opened the hatch with the metal rod and slid the ladder down. I stood back as it thudded on the carpet. Glancing up, he switched on his head torch and started to climb. He reached the top and scrambled in, and I followed, gripping the rungs tightly. I didn't go right up; instead, I rested my forearms against the attic floorboards and peered in, screwing up my nose at the musty smell. It wasn't completely dark, there was some light from a dormer window, and Tom's torch cast a strong beam across the attic.

Behind the chimney stack, birds clawed and chirped, the sound eerily peculiar. Something crunched under my fingertips. Cringing, I snatched my hands up from the floor and in disgust I flicked off the remnants of dead flies.

And as my hands moved, Tom shifted violently too. With a yell, he shot up and knocked the back of his head on a beam. 'Shit!' he said.

'What? What is it? Are you OK?'

A rustling. Quick footsteps. The torchlight flashing erratically as Tom moved across the attic. Then an exclamation. A shout from the darkness. It wasn't Tom's voice. It was someone else's. I screamed.

'What the fuck are you doing in our attic?' yelled Tom.

He hurried back towards the hatch and crouched down next to me. 'Someone's there. Someone's there!' he said, breathing heavy and fast; his face pinched as he squinted into the darkness. With my eyes wide, I tried to climb up next to him, but he grabbed my wrist.

'Stay back, Jules. It's some nutter.'

I *knew* I'd been right. Someone *was* there. In the dim light, I strained my eyes to see. Right at the end of the attic was a man, hunched over a pile of blankets.

'Right, I'm calling the police,' shouted Tom as he put his hand on my head, and pushed me down, scrabbling behind me, desperate to get out.

My feet slipped; with a gasp I clung onto the rungs of the ladder. Adrenaline rushed through me so fast it took my breath away. I couldn't believe it. Couldn't believe what I saw.

Because I knew the man in the attic.

It was Roger North.

ROGER 1975

Chapter Eleven

Roger sat on the edge of his bed, looking out of the window. He often sat there, watching people walk by, the clouds in the sky, and the jackdaws in the oak tree across the road. It was the one consistent thing in his life that brought him a sense of comfort. The jackdaws were always there, and so was the sky and as for the people – there was always someone out there. Often in twos or threes, friends, families, work colleagues dressed in suits and carrying briefcases. He wondered if he would ever have a briefcase when he was grown up?

'Roger, teatime.' His mum's gentle voice was so soft he might not have heard her if his door hadn't been open. He slid off his bed and drew his curtains, before heading downstairs and into the kitchen. The room was silent, except for the hum of the overhead fluorescent light, and the tapping of Mum's serving spoon as she dished up the boiled potatoes. The windows were misted over with condensation from the saucepans. Faither was at the far end of the table, and his sister sat in the chair opposite his.

'Please sit, Roger,' said Faither.

So, Roger sat. His mother placed their meals in front of them, but no one picked up their cutlery. Instead, they bowed their heads and put their hands together as Faither spoke.

'May we be blessed by God as we share this food, and as we work and live together for the good of all. May the seal of God's love rest upon this food and upon this day now drawing to a close. May we and our gifts of food be under the tent of God's peace. Amen.'

'Amen,' they all repeated.

Roger glanced at Faither from the corner of his eye, waiting for him to pick up his knife and fork first, then he waited for his mother. Not until both had begun eating, did he begin. At first, he was so hungry, he could only concentrate on filling his stomach. He shovelled the potato into his mouth, barely chewing. After a few moments, he was aware of Faither's glare, and his outstretched arm, ready to tap Roger's wrists with his fork. Roger immediately slowed his eating down – he knew what that gesture meant. It meant if he didn't stop bolting his food, Faither would stand over him and …. He didn't want to think about it. It was so horrible when it happened last time. But like everything, as soon as you try not to think of something, it becomes the only thing you can think about. Thinking about Faither's large, red hands scooping up potato and forcing it into Roger's mouth until he choked. Not being able to breathe because the potato went up his nose and blocked his throat.

Roger winced as he remembered. No, he wouldn't rush, instead, chewing each mouthful for at least twenty seconds. He looked up at Josie. She wasn't enjoying her meal. She didn't like cheese and egg flan. Josie pushed tiny pieces of pastry and egg onto the back of her fork and placed it into her mouth, as slow as a tortoise munching a lettuce leaf. She swallowed and grimaced, glancing at him before sipping from her glass of water.

After everything had been eaten, Roger laid his knife and fork next to each other on his plate, and waited for Faither to tell him he could get up from the table. 'You may collect the plates, Roger.'

Roger did as he was told and started to wash up. Josie was excused from the table, and she reached for the tea towel draped over the oven door handle. She picked up a plate to dry.

'Did you have a good day at school, dear?' Mum placed her elbows on the table and cupped her chin in her hands, smiling at her husband.

Faither pulled a handkerchief from his pocket and patted his mouth. 'It was a difficult day,' he said. 'The children were somewhat fractious, on account of the nurses coming to do the BCG injections. It didn't make for easy teaching.'

'I'm sorry to hear that. I expect you managed them well enough, though.'

Faither smiled. 'Of course.'

Roger knew what that meant, and he tried not to think of the poor boys who would have had a blackboard rubber thrown at them for talking in class. He knew Faither's reputation, which was one reason why he wasn't popular at school. Being in the first year at secondary was hard enough – being Mr North's son was worse.

'And Roger, did you have a nice day at school? What did you learn today?' said his mother.

'Yes, thank you, Mum. We had biology today. We dissected a cow's eyeball.' His mother nodded and pursed her lips.

'I hope you're behaving now, boy,' said Faither sternly. 'I don't want any more complaints from your teachers about emotional outbursts. I hope you're learning some self-control. I don't need to speak to you again about that temper of yours, do I Roger?' He rustled in his pocket. A few moments later, he struck a match before deeply inhaling one of his cigarettes. Roger dared not turn around, but he could sense Faither's eyes burning into the back of his head.

'No, Faither,' said Roger, watching the black marks come off the saucepan as he scrubbed hard, back and forth, harder and harder until the metal shone.

'And how about you, Josie? Did you have a nice day at school?' said Mum.

Every night. The same questions. If Roger taped the conversations they had, he was sure it would be exactly the same every evening. He couldn't blame his mother though; she was only trying to break the silence.

'O-Levels this year, my girl. I hope you're working hard.'

'Yes, a good day, thanks.' said Josie, in a monotone voice. 'And yes, Faither. I am working hard.'

As Roger stared into the washing up bowl with his head bent, he knew Josie was trying to catch his eye; trying to roll her eyes to form some sort of camaraderie with him, but he didn't have the nerve. It wasn't worth the risk. As she passed him to put a glass on the shelf, she deliberately bumped his shoulder.

'Roger, as soon as you have finished the dishes, please clean the shoes. I'll lay them out on the newspaper by the front door.'

'Yes, Faither.'

Once all of Roger's chores were finished, he was sent upstairs to do his homework. He didn't have much. Only a bit of maths and a bit of geography. He sat at his desk, and picked up his Swiss-army knife, pulling out the blades and inspecting each one carefully. There was a thin, sharp blade that was perfect to scrape the dirt from his nails, and he spent five minutes digging out the grime and flicking it on the floor. He was relieved Faither hadn't noticed how grubby they were when they were having tea.

With a sigh, he folded all the blades down and put the knife into his desk drawer; he needed to get on with his long division. He concentrated hard and didn't notice Faither walk into his room. Not until he stood right next to him, his shadow casting a greyness over Roger's exercise book.

Roger looked up, his stomach pitching.

'Do you know what you have done?' Faither's neck protruded out of his shirt collar as he towered over. His pale blue eyes bulging. 'You have got shoe polish on the rug. Why do you think I put newspaper down? Do you think I do it for fun?'

'No, I'm sorry. I didn't realise. I'll clean it up immediately.' Roger pushed back his chair and stood, he began to walk towards the door, but Faither gripped his forearm, digging his fingernails into his skin. So tight. He leered close to Roger's face, so he could smell cigarettes on his breath.

'You *will* clean it up my boy.' He dragged him out of the room, down the stairs and thrust him onto the rug by the front door, where there was a small fingertip sized stain of black polish. Roger felt sick as Faither shoved his son's face down, his nose rubbing on the rug, the friction making his skin burn. 'Lick it,' he said. 'Lick that polish, and then get a cloth and some washing up liquid and do it properly.' He gave one last shove, and then strode back into the lounge, leaving Roger on his hands and knees, panting hard.

Chapter Twelve

The only good thing about going to church was the juice and biscuits afterwards. Well, not the only good thing. Seeing Christina Moretti from the third year was also good. Roger got a heavy aching when he saw her. She was always there every Sunday, with her parents and her three brothers. He'd never spoken to her, but she often talked to Josie afterwards, and he would stand and listen to them.

It was one of those summer days where the sun was really hot, and the birds sang manically – everything was overpowering and intense. Roger wasn't a fan of hot weather. He didn't like how he sweated now he was older, and he didn't like the way it made his skin go red. Faither also went red in the sun – they were both pale-skinned. The complete opposite to Christina Moretti and her family, but they were from Italy.

Mum said he couldn't wear his shorts but had to wear his smart trousers and a check shirt. It was too hot for that, of course, but he wouldn't argue. They always walked to church because it was only ten minutes away. Roger lagged behind his parents with his head down. Josie was in front. A group of boys wearing shorts and T-shirts walked past them. One of them bounced a ball and Roger stepped off the path and onto the road to make way. They ignored him. 'Rude bastards,' he said under his breath. He turned to look over his shoulder, tightening his hand into a fist. He recognised them – they were in a different tutor group, but he often saw them on the playground during breaks. He never played football though. He thought it was a stupid game.

Despite Faither barking at them to hurry up, they still arrived late. It was Josie's fault – she'd put mascara on, and when Faither had seen her, he'd gone crazy and sent her back upstairs to wash it off. His face was like thunder as they entered the church - he pushed them towards the chairs right at the back and Roger made sure he was at the end of the row so he could have more space. He was pleased that now he was older, he didn't have to go the Sunday school. He hated it there; the teachers were so strict – at least going into the main church meant he could watch Christina. Leaning a little to the left, he could see her sitting at the front. Her long black hair, as smooth as glass, hanging loose over her shoulders.

Normally, he only pretended to listen to the sermon; he knew Faither kept an eye on him to check he was concentrating. But that day, something sharpened his senses, and he found he *was* actually listening. The preacher was a man who Roger knew quite well. Mr Harris worked in the local library, and he sometimes came around to their house during the evenings to have a cup of tea with Mum and Faither.

Mr Harris stood on the top step with his hands stretched wide, he was a big man, with long, curly grey hair and looked quite imposing. 'If you open your hearts to Jesus, the rest will follow. I gave him my love and opened my body to the holy spirit, and from then on, life has been good, oh, so good!'

Someone from the middle of the church shouted out, 'Amen!'

Then a general murmur began. Roger closed his eyes. He never liked this bit. Yes, he wanted to find the peace and joy that Mr Harris seemed to have found, but he hated the thought of the holy spirit entering him. His chest tightened, aware that Faither was now speaking in tongues, gibbering that nonsensical language which was supposedly the Holy Ghost. It gave him the creeps; he wished they went to a different church without all the drama. He cringed as his mother who was normally so quiet, called out, 'Hallelujah!'

Although they'd never discussed it, Roger knew Josie didn't believe either, he peered at his sister, who sat on the other side of Faither. She had her head tilted back, with her eyes closed – her way of blocking out the voices around her, but at the same time, looking as if the spirit had touched her so she wouldn't get into trouble with Faither. The electric organ started up, and people raised their hands in the air. Some danced. Some gripped the chairs in front of them, needing to steady themselves and hold on tight as the gift of the spirit entered their bodies.

Roger stood – his way of coping was to sway with his eyes closed – listen to the music, pretend to be entranced, count the beats, try and work out the musical notes – anything to distract him from the worship. *A sharp, C sharp* … He opened one eye, slowly. Christina Moretti stood and clapped. Roger wondered if she really believed or if she pretended like he and Josie did. She *looked* as if she was enjoying herself.

Soon, Mr Harris raised his arms and gradually the voices quietened, people sat back down, and it felt like the calm after the storm. Roger sat too. He thought of the boys in the street, the ones with the football. What would it be like, to go to the park on Sunday, instead of church? Playing with the kids from his class? Buying an ice-cream from the kiosk and sitting on the grass with the girls in their short skirts as they watched the boys kicking the ball around. Because that's where he'd be – with the girls. Because the boys didn't like him. He knew that. And Roger didn't like football. So, he'd be with the girls, and he'd be able to look at their tanned legs and …

'Roger, come on boy, get out of your seat.' Faither tapped him on the shoulder, and Roger realised everyone in his row was standing. It was time to go.

*

The church had a small courtyard at the back, and during the summer, everyone congregated there to drink tea and eat the homemade biscuits. Josie and Christina sat on the red brick wall which surrounded the herb garden, and Roger stood as close as possible so he could hear their conversation. At first, he thought they were talking about a boy in school, then he realised it was a pop star.

'David's the most talented, Josie, seriously. I'm going to get his All the Fun of the Fair album for my birthday, I can't wait.'

'Yeah, but Roger Taylor's more handsome. I'm going to see if I'm allowed to go and see them in concert. Apparently, they're playing in London in the autumn. I might be able to persuade Mum if it's for my birthday.'

'I'm not allowed,' said Christina. 'My dad said concerts aren't the place for girls my age.'

'Seriously?' Josie's face fell. 'In which case, my dad will definitely say the same.'

The girls put their heads together and started to whisper. Roger shuffled over, to listen, but they were too quiet. Christina looked up and caught his eye.

His face burned – he knew he was going red, and he dropped his eyes to the paving stones.

'Roger, stop eavesdropping,' said Josie. 'Go and talk to Christina's brothers.' Then she turned to Christina. 'I can't believe he's called Roger too, how unfortunate is that?'

Christina smiled and let out a little giggle, then they huddled together again, so Roger couldn't hear. He rolled a pebble under his shoe and kicked it, so it bounced and hit the sole of Christina's sandal. Glancing up, she scowled at him. His eyes stung and he turned away and walked back into the church. Angry with himself for kicking the stone, angry they caught him listening, and angry she'd scowled at him. It had really spoilt his day. He gritted his teeth – although he hated himself for what had happened, he figured it was good that she wasn't allowed to go to the David Essex concert. She didn't deserve it.

Chapter Thirteen

Roger liked to collect things. He found it soothed him to arrange his possessions into an order. If his day at school ever went wrong, it calmed him down. At that moment, his favourite things to collect were discarded brown bottles that smelt medicinal and were sticky around the lid; empty blister packs of aspirin which crackled as he pushed his fingers into the plastic indents; cardboard boxes which had contained indigestion tablets – the possibilities for his medical collection were endless. He kept everything in an old shoe box under his jumper pile, but soon, as his collection got bigger, he'd need to find another hiding place.

Faither would be angry if he knew about his collection. Last time, he collected animal bones – frail bird skulls and mouse skeletons he found in fields and fish bones from down by the river. He even found a deer hoof one day; the hair was still attached in places. When Mum said it smelt in his room and eventually tracked down the bones on a tray under his bed, she'd told Faither, and he'd gone mad. Roger shuddered as he remembered being smacked around the head and told to bury them in the garden. It had been a very cold January, and the ground had been rock-hard. He'd been handed a spoon to dig the ground with, and he wasn't allowed back into the house until everything was buried. He remembered how cold his fingers were, and sometimes when he tried to force the spoon into the hard earth, it skittered off; the force juddering up his arm, causing the metal to crunch against his knuckles. It stung so much.

After that day, he always made sure to wrap any animal remains in clingfilm to contain the liquids and the smells. It didn't last forever, but it was fine for a while, to give him time to examine his finds without Faither noticing.

The other collection Faither hadn't liked were the cards from sweet-cigarette boxes. The cards were tucked behind the pink-tipped, chalky-white candy sticks, and every time he'd opened a box, he smelt the sugary smell of vanilla and pear drops. Faither banned him from eating sweets, but Roger didn't tell Faither about the newsagents putting his paperboy wage up by 30p a week. He kept the extra money for himself to buy the candy sticks.

When Faither found the candy-scented cards tucked in Roger's sock drawer, he made him tear each one up, one by one into tiny pieces. Roger's eyes filled with tears as he watched the pieces of card burning on the coal fire in the living room. Josie had sat on the settee watching, glancing at Roger now and again to see his reaction. She'd often been at the wrong end of Faither's temper too. He'd taken her tape recorder away for a month when she'd played her 'horrible pop music' too loud. Poor Josie. Why did Faither have to be so strict and so horrible? Often, Faither would put the pocket money in the kitchen piggy bank instead of giving it to him – it was where all their loose change went, and this money was used for buying piano music and books. But they were the books Faither chose, not his choice or Josie's. Roger tried his best to keep his head down, but nothing seemed to be good enough for Faither. Even his mother was scared of him, and she always took her husband's side. But Roger didn't begrudge her; he knew she didn't have a choice. The occasional bruising on her upper arm was evidence enough.

Roger picked up one of his medicine bottles. It had contained cough tincture, and the lid was hard to twist off because the mixture had crystallised around the edge. Once he got it open, he held the bottle to his nose. It smelt of cherry, and although it was now empty, he licked the rim, enjoying the sticky, sweet taste on his tongue. Next, he picked up a smaller bottle. This had contained aspirin or something and it didn't really smell of anything, but there was a piece of cotton wool inside that was soft and squeaky when he rolled it between his fingers.

While studying his possessions, he thought about Christina Moretti and what happened at school that day. She had been perfect. Her silken hair, her long eyelashes, and her thin body – all her features made him think of a fawn. But since she'd laughed at him at church, he had grown angry with her. He was so disappointed. His resentment had grown since Sunday. By the time he'd seen her at school on Wednesday, hanging outside one of the portacabins with her friends, an intense hatred towards her had burned inside him. He'd crouched down behind the steps leading from the back of the portacabin and watched her. His disgust for her building up and up, until he could stand it no longer.

With his hands in his pockets, he'd sauntered over towards the group of girls. His stomach lurched as she caught his eye, and then she turned away. That was it, if she hadn't done that, if she'd smiled at him or said hello, Roger would probably have changed his mind and carried on walking past. Even if she'd raised an eyebrow. But to completely ignore him, and turn her back …

A fire burned in his gut, and without thinking, he'd veered to the right, and walked straight into her, his shoulder cracking against hers. Although he was a few years younger than her, and quite slight for his age, he banged into her so hard, she lost her footing and fell, a gasp coming from her lips. A thud sounded as she hit the ground.

'Hey!'

'What the hell?'

'You bastard!'

Her friends' shouts echoed around the courtyard, as he ran away across the school field. His heart pounded in time to his feet hitting the hard, dry earth. He ducked under the barbed wire fence and into the surrounding woods. The branches of the trees scratched at his skin as he ran, but he was relieved to be out of the midday sun; the cool shade of the overhead leaves sheltering him from the heat. Behind him, he heard the lunch-time supervisor yelling and then the sound of a whistle pierced the air.

At first, he ran, but soon the woodland had become too dense, and he had to slow down and walk. He wasn't sure where he was going, all he knew was, he had to get away from the school. Eventually, he came to a clearing, where a rope hung from a thick branch and two discarded plastic orange school chairs lay on the ground, stained green from being outside for so long.

He looked up, and realised if he climbed the rope, he could reach the higher branches of the tree and hide there until the end of school. He knew staff would come looking for him. Roger wasn't very agile, and he panted loudly as he hauled himself up. The rope was thin, and it was hard to stop himself from slipping, his hands burning from the friction.

Eventually, he reached the branch, and he swung himself over so he could sit astride. The bark dug into his thighs as he shifted his weight along, finally twisting himself around and leaning against the tree trunk. He closed his eyes, inhaling deeply, trying to calm his mind and his racing heart. The birds had stopped singing when he climbed the tree, but after a few minutes, they began again. He listened. putting words to their song, like lyrics to a tune. With his head resting on the tree, and his fingertips stroking the bark, he began to relax and feel more himself.

Twenty minutes later, Roger heard twigs snapping and low voices. 'Do you think he's still in the woods? He might have gone along the back path, by the river.' Roger recognised the voice. It was Mr Hall, his form tutor.

'I think he's in the wood somewhere. He wouldn't have gone far.' And that was Miss Sheringham, the woman who ran the Serenity Centre. He liked her. She was always kind to him. Whenever he couldn't cope in class, or his emotions got too much, he often went to see her. Roger peered over the branch, holding his breath, then he whipped his head back – they were only a few feet away from the tree. 'I think he's around here,' she said. 'This is obviously where the kids make a camp of some kind. Look at those chairs.'

'Roger!' shouted Mr Hall. 'Come on lad, you won't be in trouble. We want to make sure you're safe, that's all.'

Roger sat as still as possible. No way was he coming down. He knew what would happen. They'd get Faither from the staff room and ... but before he could think any further, there was another shout. Miss Sheringham had looked up into the tree and spotted him.

'Roger, there you are! Look up there, Mr Hall. Do you see him?' She pointed and walked closer to the tree; her head tilted back.

'I'm not coming down,' shouted Roger. He gripped the branch so tight the damp moss and bark caught under his fingernails.

'Roger, look, it's dangerous. You're really high up. Now, come on down, and we can talk about this. You've made this a lot worse by running away,' said Miss Sheringham.

'I'm not coming down. You'll tell my dad.'

The two members of staff went quiet and looked at each other. Then Miss Sheringham said in a gentle voice, 'You told me about your father last week, didn't you? You said he'd been nice to you. He'd bought you a packet of crisps and took you to the park. I'm sure he won't be cross if I explain it all to him, will he? If I tell him how you've been upset.'

Roger bit his lip as he remembered the fib he'd told Miss Sheringham. How could he get himself out of this situation? Even if he stayed up here, and they went away, they'd still tell Faither. He had an idea.

'If I come down, will you promise not to tell my dad?'

Again, the two teachers looked at each other. This time, Mr Hall spoke. 'OK, Roger. I promise. If you come down, I won't tell your father. On the condition that you talk this through with us. Alright?'

Roger nodded, and then put his hands one in front of the other and slid himself along the branch, towards the rope.

'Good lad,' said Mr Hall. 'You know it's for the best.'

Chapter Fourteen

Mr Hall and Miss Sheringham kept to their word. Roger was taken into the Serenity Centre and given a beaker of water and a Penguin chocolate bar from Miss Sheringham's lunch box.

They left him to sit on his own to 'think things over'. After twenty minutes or so, Miss Sheringham came back. Roger didn't look at her. He sat on a blue bean bag next to a bookcase, reading the titles. *Children's Guide to Making Friends. Don't Be Selfish. It's Good to be Different* – he turned away. Did kids actually read these books?

Roger glanced up at Miss Sheringham. She was a small woman, with brown hair tied up in a bun. Her smile was wide, and she had one of those faces that made him feel happy just looking at her. She sat on a chair opposite him.

'Lots of books,' he said.

'There are, you can borrow one if you like. Seen anything you think you'll be interested in?'

Roger shrugged. 'Not really,'

'That's OK,' she said. 'We can just talk. Now, tell me what's all this about Roger? Christina tells me you knocked her over before running off. She's worried about you. Why did you knock her over?'

Roger shrugged again. He wouldn't tell her that he was crazy about Christina. He wouldn't say he got angry because Christina didn't love him back. Miss Sheringham wouldn't understand that. 'I didn't mean to knock into her. It was an accident.' He looked down and fiddled with the zip on the beanbag. The tiny polystyrene balls were easy to pick out, and he squeezed them between his fingers.

'Then why didn't you apologise, instead of running into the woods? You must realise that made you look guilty?' Miss Sheringham clasped her hands together and leant forwards.

'Yeah, I know. I panicked.' He folded his arms and stretched out his legs, rolling a felt-tip lid back and forth under his shoe.

'Why don't you want us to tell your dad? Is everything OK at home, Roger?'

Roger froze. The felt-tip lid crushed under his foot. 'Everything is fine,' he said at last.

Miss Sheringham glanced at his foot and nodded slowly. 'Well, if you need to talk to me about anything, you know where I am. In the meantime, please can you apologise to Christina, and we'll say no more about the matter, alright?'

'Yes.'

'We won't tell your father in this instance, but if your temper gets out of hand like last time when you hit George McKenzie, we will definitely have to speak to him. OK?'

'Yes, I promise my temper won't get out of control again, Miss.'

'Good, well you can go back to class now. What lesson do you have?'

'French.'

'Ah, oui, oui. Au revoir then, Roger, and remember, my door is always open.'

Without saying anything, Roger stood, noticing the door was closed, and he had to open it to leave. *So no, Miss Sheringham, your door isn't always open. Doors just aren't.*

*

But all that nastiness had been earlier on, and now he was back home in his bedroom, Roger no longer felt bad. He'd said sorry to Christina outside the school gates, and she'd been very gracious in accepting his apology. Even though the whole situation had been horrible at the time, it was OK now. He let his shoulders drop as he examined his medical collection – just holding the brown plastic bottles and smelling the medicine comforted him, like in the same way you might get comfort from a soft blanket and a cuddle from your mother when you felt ill. He lay down on his bed, an empty blister pack in his hands, he imagined Christina's voice. *'Roger, I'm so sorry we had a falling out. I do love you. Really, I do.'*

He imagined her slim body lying behind him, spooning him, with her arm thrown over his waist. Closing his eyes, the corners of his mouth turned upwards as he thought how her soft hand might touch his. He crunched the blister pack in pleasure at the thought of her holding him.

'You mean the world to me, Christina,' he whispered.

'And you mean the world to me, Roger,' she replied. Or so it seemed to him.

'Do you mean that?' he sat up and stared at the vision in front of him, his stomach lurching at her words.

'Of course, silly.' she said.

Roger laughed and his heart lifted. He packed up his medical collection, opened his wardrobe door, and slid it under his jumper pile. Just in time. Heavy footsteps sounded on the stairs.

'I wish Faither would go to hell,' Roger said under his breath. He climbed onto the bed and stood up, scratching his fingernails along the ceiling. He changed his voice to an evil mocking tone. 'Deep into the bowels of the abyss, along with the devil.' He was pleased to see Christina laughing.

'Who are you speaking to?' Faither barged into the room without knocking.

'No one, Faither.' Roger dropped to the bed and sat back on his heels.

'Don't lie boy. I heard you.' He closed his eyes when he spoke. Roger hated it when he did that. It was almost as if he couldn't bear to look at him. 'You said something about the devil. Who are you talking to? You do know, that when we speak to God, sometimes the Demon intervenes? He has ears and can hear you. We need to pray for you in church this weekend – I'll speak to Mr Harris about this. Do you hear? Now, come downstairs, I have a job for you. Keep you busy.'

'Yes, Faither.'

Faither sighed and crossed the landing towards Josie's room. Roger turned and gazed at his pillow. 'I've got to go, Christina. I'll see you later.'

Her sweet voice swam in his head as he got off the bed. 'Bye, bye, Roger. I love you.' As he stepped out of his room, and silently closed the door, he vowed to himself that there was no way Faither could find out Christina was in his room. It was a miracle, that's what it was.

*

When Roger got downstairs, Mum was at the stove stirring some bubbling stew. He peered into the pot – strings of chicken floated on top of the greasy liquid amongst the little oval barley grains, but at least it smelt good. Mum raised the spoon and let him have a taste. He opened his mouth, and the burning liquid scorched his tongue. 'Ow, that's hot' he said, wafting his hand in front of his mouth; a jab of anger spiking inside him.

'Sorry, love, I should have warned you.' She quickly put a hand on his arm. 'Are you alright?'

'Yeah, but it hurt.' He sat down, holding his tongue with his thumb and forefinger. Some papers were laid out on the table. 'What are these papers for?'

'Faither wants you to do a little job for him. They're from the church. You need to help him copy the names and addresses from there and put them in his address book.'

Roger nodded and sat at the table, pulling the papers towards him. The creak on the stairs told him Josie and Faither were coming down, and as they walked into the kitchen, he noticed Josie's head was bowed, her shoulders slumping. Roger picked up a pen and started to copy the names into Faither's leather book.

'Josie has something for you. Hand it over to your mother, Josie.' Faither sat down opposite Roger, smirking.

Josie held a piece of black material in her hands. It was lacy and Roger realised it was a bra. In a rush, Mum snatched it from her, a look of worry in her eyes.

'Sorry, Mum. A friend gave it to me. It's too small for her now, and she thought I might like it.'

'We don't have that kind of clothing in the house,' said Mum, her voice breathless and high pitched. 'You have 2 white brassieres that are perfectly adequate.'

'Throw it in the bin, Josephine. NOW!' Spit shot from Faither's mouth as he pointed at the bin in the far corner of the kitchen. 'You're not to speak to this girl who gave it to you, do you understand? No contact whatsoever.'

Josie's cheeks were wet. She'd dropped the bra into the bin, and the metal lid crashed with finality. A red blush spread from the hollow of her neck up to her forehead. Stumbling out of the room and thumping up the stairs, her sobs echoed around the hallway.

The kitchen became silent. Roger put his head down and continued with the job he had been given, his stomach churning.

Chapter Fifteen

A few days later, Mr Harris came around, half past seven on the dot. Like always. He was never late. Mum had put a plate of digestive biscuits in the living room and sorted out the tea things in the kitchen. Roger could hear Faither welcoming Mr Harris, as if he was some long-lost friend. He laughed and sounded so friendly and cheery, that Roger wondered if he had a personality change whenever Mr Harris visited.

As he'd been instructed, Roger came downstairs when he heard Mr Harris arrive, and Faither smiled and said, 'Good lad. Why don't you go and help yourself to a biscuit in the living room, and I'll get poor Mr Harris a glass of water. It's so hot out there, isn't it?'

'It certainly is,' said Mr Harris as he pulled a handkerchief from his pocket and wiped his forehead. 'Hello, Roger, how are you?'

'Very well, thank you,' he said, before hurrying into the lounge to make the most of the biscuits – a treat that only occurred when they had guests. He sat on the floor, cross legged in front of the coffee table, wondering if Faither would call Josie down too, but it didn't seem as if he needed her. Instead, his mother came in, carrying a tray. The teapot, the cups, and a glass of squash tinkling against each other.

Mr Harris sat down, stretching out his legs and crossing his ankles. The settee sagged with age. Underneath, Roger could see the shape Mr Harris's bottom as the cushion bulged through the gaps of the supporting straps.

Faither brought in the glass of water for his guest. You'd think he carried a golden chalice, the way he presented it to him. He loved to make people think he was the man about the house, the perfect host. Roger clenched his fists and looked away.

'Here we are. I let the tap run so it's nice and cool,' he said.

'Thank you,' said Mr Harris, taking the glass. 'And how are you, Moira? Doing well, I hope?'

'I'm doing very well, thank you, John. And how are you?'

'I can't grumble,' he said. 'The library and the church are keeping me busy – no rest for the wicked, is there?'

Everyone laughed, except Roger. It wasn't really funny. He took a bite from his second digestive biscuit, the malty, sweet flavour crumbling in his mouth.

'I hear from your father that you're having trouble with things at the moment, Roger, is that right?' Mr Harris's small grey eyes darted from Faither, to Mum, and then to him. The biscuit crumbs caught in the back of Roger's throat, and he coughed.

'Hand over mouth, please, Roger,' said Faither, as he sat down in his leather armchair.

'Tell Mr Harris what's been happening,' said Mum gently, leaning over to pass him his glass of lemon squash. Roger took a mouthful and swallowed.

'Nothing. Nothing's happening.'

'That's not true, now, is it Roger?' said Faither, cocking his head and raising an eyebrow.

'Don't worry,' said Mr Harris, lifting his hand as if he was stopping a car in the road. 'I'm sure Roger's just a little embarrassed. There's nothing to worry about, we can all talk openly here. As servants of God, we are willing to forgive whatever's been happening.'

Roger glanced up but didn't know what to say. He could hardly mention that Faither was never willing to forgive.

'He's been fighting at school and doesn't seem to know how to control his temper,' said Faither at last. 'A boy, George McKenzie, had a black eye after Roger hit him. I can't begin to tell you how humiliating it is for us as a family.'

Mr Harris nodded as if he understood. He drained his glass of water and placed it on the table.

'And there's something else which is very disturbing, John,' continued Faither. 'I believe he's been speaking to … how can I put it? All I can say is … I believe he's been communicating with demons. Every night this week. I hear him talking, but when I go into his room, he's by himself, smiling and laughing.'

Mr Harris nodded sagely. 'I hear you my friend, but let me get the facts clear. In what form do you believe the demon takes?'

Roger rolled his eyes. There was no demon, except maybe, Faither. He smirked at this thought. Faither the Devilish Demon. He imagined him with a long red tail growing out of his backside.

'He seems to think it's amusing, Mr Harris.' Faither's eyes burned into Roger, blue as a gas flame, daring him to argue.

Roger sat up straight, his eyes widened. He cursed himself for letting down his defences – he'd probably get a beating for that later. He tried to make amends. 'Sorry, no, Faither, I don't think it's funny. I smiled because I'm enjoying my biscuit.' He made a show of licking his lips.

'Mm,' said Faither, narrowing his eyes. 'As I was saying, I think Roger is in danger of becoming possessed; if he isn't already.'

Roger's mum sat up straight and her bottom lip dropped. 'William! Don't say such awful things. He's a bit different, that's all. Aren't you Roger? I don't think this is really necessary. All we need is someone to give Roger some spiritual guidance, some direction.'

'Quiet, Moira.' Faither put up his hand. 'I am speaking to John. Please just pour the tea.' He interlinked his fingers and rested them on his stomach. 'I believe a demon has entered his soul. He doesn't have any friends. I hear him laughing and cursing to himself behind the door – it's quite unnerving, I must say. I would like you to speak to the Pastor on my behalf, it's better coming from you, as an Elder.'

Mr Harris took his tea from Roger's mum. 'Thank you, Moira, very kind.' He picked up a teaspoon and stirred his drink around and around. 'I think we might need a little more proof, William. You can't suddenly decide the boy is at risk from possession because he's got in a few fights at school, and you hear him talking to an unknown entity. If we're being realistic, he's probably just speaking to himself. Roger, what are your thoughts on this?'

Irritation flashed in Faither's eyes. Roger picked at the skin around his nails until a pin prick of blood appeared. He cringed. He loathed blood, it made him feel sick. 'I don't know,' he finally said. This was excruciating; he hated it. There was no demon, what was Faither on about? Christina visited him every now and again, that's all, and she is in no way a demon.

She's an angel.

'I'm not sure about this,' said Mum, and she sat back down, her cup wobbling on its saucer. The veins on the back of her hand were like blue roots protruding across her pale white skin.

'Shut up, Moira,' said Faither. Mr Harris opened his mouth and closed it again. Mum dropped her eyes and stared at the floor. Realising he made a bad impression, Faither painted on a smile. 'But thank you, my dear. It's very sweet of you to be concerned, but there really is nothing for you to worry about. John and I will organise everything.'

'I will speak to the Pastor, and he can decide in which direction we should go. Is that acceptable to you all? Moira? Roger?'

'Yes, thank you John, very acceptable,' said Faither. Now, on another note, I wondered if I could get your advice on some suitable reading material for the children. The school doesn't seem to have anything appropriate in their library and Josephine's teacher was very dismissive when I broached the subject.'

*

That evening, after he'd cleaned the shoes, Roger went upstairs to escape from his parents. He sank onto the bed and waited for Christina to arrive. Normally, she came when he closed his eyes and imagined her next to him. If he did that, she'd often appear. It was funny, but whenever he saw her at church or at school, they both pretended they weren't friends. It was their little secret.

He opened his eyes and there she was, facing him. She kissed him gently on the nose, and Roger's stomach jumped. 'I love you,' she said.

'I love you too,' he replied. 'In fact, I worship the ground you walk on,' He smiled, tipping his head back against the pillow, feeling joy surge through him. But without warning, the bedroom door flew open, and Faither stormed in. Roger sat bolt upright – reaching out to Christina, to protect her.

'Who is it you're worshipping?' shouted Faither. His shirt sleeves were rolled up, and his face was clammy from the heat of the day. He marched across the room and grabbed hold of Roger's arm. He hauled him off the bed and dragged him to the floor, Roger winced as a ligament popped in his shoulder.

'I spoke to God, honest Faither. It was God I spoke to.' Roger squeezed his eyes tight, breathing fast, as the pain shot down his arm.

'I don't believe you. Tell the truth, boy.' He spat out his words as if they were poison. He pulled back his fist. Was he going to punch him?

Roger curled into a ball and put his hands over his head, trying to think of the worst thing he could say to hurt Faither. 'Alright,' he shouted, 'it's the devil I'm speaking to. I hate you and I hate God. So, what you gonna do to me now?'

Faither lowered his arm and stepped away. Roger pushed himself up, leaning on his elbow, his eyes tired and aching. What had he done? Why did he say that?

Faither pinched the bridge of his nose. Without saying another word, he averted his eyes and backed out of the room. The door slammed behind him.

Roger swallowed the lump rising in his throat as Faither turned the key in the lock. He leant against the wall, burying his face in his drawn-up knees; the material of his corduroys soaking up his tears. He dug his fingernails into the skin of his forearm; scratching, then pushing hard into the flesh, until he began to bleed. In disgust, he wiped the blood with his thumb and smeared it on the carpet.

JULIA -2023

Chapter Sixteen

Like a zombie, I sunk into my office chair, exhausted. It was the Monday after we'd found Roger North in our attic, and it still disturbed me. The thought of food made me feel sick, and I'd skipped breakfast. My hair was a greasy nightmare – styling and fiddling about with it hadn't been an option, so I'd fastened it back with a plastic grip. I'd managed to put on a bit of make-up, but still, dark rings hung like horseshoes under my eyes. Of course, Thalia noticed straight away.

'Jesus, Julia, you look like death warmed up.' She sat down at her desk and stared at me. 'Are you alright?'

Steam from my coffee warmed my face, as I cradled the cup for comfort. 'I feel shit,' I said with a weak smile.

'I'm not surprised,' she said. 'You've had a horrendous time. Tell you what, why don't we go for a spa day next weekend? My treat.'

'Maybe,' I said. 'I'll think about it. Alex has football, and I'll have to ask Tom if he can look after Isla.'

'Why do you have to ask him? You should tell him. You're not the main carer, you both are. Or ask his mother – she's only in Bath, isn't she? You need a break; you look ill, and this is a health matter. You're going to collapse in a heap by Sunday. So, get on the bloody phone now, and tell him.' She knotted her eyebrows together, dark lines forming as she frowned.

I laughed at her rising temper. Thalia didn't quite get the nuances of parenthood, but she had a point. I did need a break.

'I'll speak to him tonight, I promise,' I said.

'OK, well, make sure you do. I'm going online now to book the spa. Then we'll go for cocktails and out for dinner. Agreed?' She picked up her phone and started scrolling.

'OK, thank you! Sounds perfect.' I smiled at her. She was so protective over me, and although at times it could be too much, I really appreciated it.

As Thalia began booking our spa day, I leant back in my chair and thought about my weekend from hell.

Tom and I had stood under the attic hatch, staring at each other, completely gobsmacked. His hands shook as he'd pulled his mobile from his back pocket and called the police. I went into our bedroom and sank onto the bed. It couldn't be real. Swallowing hard, I phoned Mum and told her what had happened. We agreed it was best to cancel lunch and I would phone later to let her know what the police said. After the call, I went downstairs in a daze, not sure what to say to the kids – I wished I didn't have to say anything at all, I didn't want to frighten them. But of course, they'd see the police arrive, so I decided to make it simple.

With fake cheerfulness, I sat on the sofa, grinning like the Cheshire Cat. 'You know the man who used to live here?' Neither of them looked particularly interested. 'Well, he's come back without asking us, and we found him in the attic collecting some of his old stuff. Nothing to worry about, but we thought we'd call the police, so he doesn't do it again. OK?'

I didn't mention the blankets, or the fact that he'd probably been living up there. My smile hid the horrible thoughts humming in my head.

'What the hell?' said Alex, laying his game controller on the table and standing. 'What a weirdo.'

My head was throbbing, so I ignored his comment, I had enough on my plate without dealing with the kids as well. The living room looked like a tip, and as if the police would judge me on an untidy home, I put the cushions back on the sofa and shuffled Isla's colouring sheets into a pile.

'Can you both stay in here please? Until the police leave.'

'I want to see the policeman,' said Isla, her eyes widening.

Tom had come downstairs and leant against the door frame. He shrugged. 'Well, how about you say hello, then you both come back in here afterwards,' I said.

'OK,' said Alex. 'Will they arrest him?'

'I expect so,' said Tom.

'What did he come back for? And why didn't he just knock on the door and ask? What did you say to him, Dad?' Alex forehead was creased with anxiety; he suddenly looked very young.

'Woah! Too many questions. Look, you've nothing to worry about. It's all under control, OK?'

'Daddy will protect us, Alex. He's strong.' Isla seemed more excited than scared, and she ran towards the window, so she could look out for the police. 'Will they have the siren going?'

'Probably not, love. It's not really an emergency.' Together we watched for the car to draw up outside the house. I rested my head against the wooden panel by the window. It smelt of wood smoke and a strange floral scent that I couldn't quite place. I figured it must be some polish that Josephine's cleaners had used.

The police arrived within half an hour. Two constables – a tall, wiry man called PC Jamac, who's muscular arms I couldn't help noticing, and PC Hinchcliffe, a woman who blinked too much. PC Jamac climbed into the attic with his torch, and I stared up at the hole, dark and gaping like a cavern. Eventually, he peered down at us. 'Looks like he's done a runner. The window catch is broken, that's where he's been coming in and out.'

He climbed back down, the rungs on the ladder creaking.

My head buzzed; I couldn't think straight. Had he been into our bedrooms? Had he been into Isla's bedroom?

Nausea hit me full on, and I leant against the wall. PC Hinchcliffe must have noticed, and she took my arm and led me downstairs. 'Let's get a cup of tea,' she said. 'With lots of sugar.'

We sat at the table, and she put the kettle on, while PC Jamac took out a notebook.

'Start from the beginning. Did you know this Roger North?'

We told him everything, even mentioning the biscuits that had disappeared from the tin, and the writing on the walls. 'Do you reckon it was him who did that too? He must have been coming down into the house when we were out.' I swallowed hard. 'You don't think he touched the kids, do you?'

Tom looked at me in horror – I don't think that had occurred to him.

'I doubt he came into your house through the attic door. I looked at the catch and I don't think it can be opened from up there. I suspect he's still got a key to the house.' said PC Jamac. 'At a guess, he's been getting in through the dormer window and sleeping in the attic, but he's gone back out the window and used a key to get into the house to steal your food and try and frighten you. I suggest you get that window repaired and change your locks. But we'll put out a warrant for his arrest. Don't worry, we'll catch him.'

'How's he getting up to the window?' I said. 'Surely, it's not that easy to climb onto a roof? And why? Just why would someone do that?'

PC Jamac shook his head. 'I don't know. Let's go and take a look outside.' He rubbed his hands together, as he got up from his seat and Tom led the way through the back door.

The four of us stared up at the house.

'There's a tile broken up there on the left, look.' PC Hinchcliffe pointed to the roof, just above the bathroom.

'I see how he's done it,' said Tom. 'He's climbed up the apple tree, onto the roof of the old outside toilet, then he's pulled himself up from there. Maybe using that wisteria and the window ledges to climb onto.' We all watched as he pointed out the route he thought Roger North would have taken.

'It's a tight squeeze,' I said, looking up at the dormer window. 'If he was any bigger, I shouldn't think he'd have fitted through it.' The attic window swung open and slammed in the wind, banging against the wooden frame. I shuddered as a chill went through me.

'As I said, you need to fix that window as soon as you can,' said PC Jamac. 'The glass is going to smash if you're not careful.' He looked over his shoulder. 'And put a lock on your garden gate, he obviously got in that way.'

Eventually, we went back into the house. The kids were still in the sitting room, and PC Jamac popped his head around the door to say goodbye to them. 'See ya, kids. No need to be scared – you're going to be safe now.'

PC Hinchcliffe looked at me sympathetically, her eyes blinking rapidly. She put a hand on my arm as I opened the front door. 'Don't worry,' she said. 'Once that window's fixed and the locks are changed, you'll be safe. I've had a look around and the rest of your security seems adequate. Try not to let it get to you – we'll do our best to catch him. By the sounds of it, he needs a bit of help mentally – if you know what I mean.' She put her finger up to her forehead, as if implying he had a screw loose. It didn't help. Joking about his mental health only made me dislike her, despite her previous kindness. I turned away without saying goodbye.

That afternoon, Tom phoned a locksmith, then took a trip to the local DIY store and bought everything he needed to repair the window catch and some bolts for the doors. I had to get out the house. I took Isla to the park and was relieved to see Lizzie with Wilf. She sat on a bench, looking at her phone, while Wilf climbed up the castle. Isla ran over to join him, her red coat flying in the wind.

'Hiya, Lizzie.' I sat next to her on the bench. Looking pleased, she put her phone in her bag.

'Hey, how're doing? Good weekend so far? I've been abandoned today. My husband, Simon's gone into Uni to plan some student social event – I'm sure he goes to more student socials now than when he was an actual student.'

'Alright for some,' I said with a smile. 'We had an awful weekend, so far I'm afraid.' I told her everything that had happened and her jaw dropped. 'You see, I'm terrified, in case he watched the children while they slept. He could have done anything. Taken photos, touched them…' I put my hand over my mouth, as if to stop the awful words coming out.

'Oh no, Julia. I'm so sorry!' Lizzie put her arm around me and gave a tight squeeze. 'You really mustn't worry. The police will catch him, and as for touching the kids – I'm sure they'd have woken up. You mustn't torture yourself with such terrible thoughts.'

'I know, I know,' I said. 'I do tend to do that – I had a really bad bout of anxiety after Isla was born. I reckon it was postnatal depression really. Anyway, I do have a very vivid imagination, and it runs away sometimes. It drove Tom mad.' I looked up at Lizzie, surprised how I'd opened up to her. But it had felt right. She was so friendly and warm. But I didn't tell her everything. I didn't tell her I'd actually had a breakdown. That was not something I wanted to talk about.

'I'm here for you, anytime you need a friend to speak to,' she said. 'Call me day or night, OK? Remember I'm only around the corner. If Tom's ever away, and you need company, just let me know. But you mustn't worry – the police will get him, and everything will be all over before you know it.'

Her kind words made things seem so much better. And I had to stop worrying about the kids – she was right – they would have woken up if he'd touched them. My shoulders dropped, and I relaxed a little. Everything would be fine, I told myself. But little did I know things were going to get a lot, lot worse.

Chapter Seventeen

All that afternoon, I'd thrown myself into finishing Alex's bedroom. Furiously painting the walls blue and the skirting boards white. I had to keep busy to take my mind off what had happened.

That night, as Tom and I sat down to watch something mindless on TV, we got a phone call from PC Jamac. 'Mrs Harker? Good news. We've arrested Roger North, so you have nothing to worry about now. He's going to be interviewed, and we'll see if we can get to the bottom of this for you.'

'Oh, thank God!' I smiled and put my thumb up to Tom. 'Has he admitted to it all?'

'Well, I'm afraid I can't go into details. All I can say is, I'm sure you'll be safe now. We'll keep you updated of course.'

'Thank you for letting me know,' I said.

'No problem, you sleep well now. And if there's anything else I can do, give me call. Goodnight.'

'Night; and thank you.' Grinning at Tom, I lay my phone back on the sofa. 'He's been arrested. Not sure what will happen to him, but at least he won't be in our attic anymore.'

'Good.' Tom stood up. 'Thank God for that. I'm going for a shower. I'll pop into the kids' rooms and let them know. Don't want them having nightmares.'

'OK, good idea. Are the doors bolted?'

'Yeah, course,' he said. 'Now, are you going to stop harping on about that bloody man, Jules? We need a fresh start. If we're going to make a go of it in this house, you've got to stop worrying, alright?'

'Fine,' I said, turning away as he left the room. I plumped up the cushions and lay down on the sofa. Flicking the channels, I soon settled for an American sitcom –

something with no crime or darkness. But I wasn't really watching it – my heart was heavy and the room, so depressing. The décor was bad enough, but there was also a horrible atmosphere; an oppressiveness making it difficult to breath, as if the pressure in the room wasn't right. But I suppose that could have been my stress levels, or maybe something else, a gas leak? The internal alert system in my brain began to pulsate, as all the worst-case scenarios played out; I'd better buy a carbon monoxide tester, just to be on the safe side.

*

The next Saturday, Thalia had kept to her word, and I met her outside Bath Spa. A small queue wound around the building, and we tagged on the end. In front of us was a loud group of women on a hen-do, the bride-to-be wearing a fake tiara and a sash. They shared a bottle of prosecco, and the head bridesmaid offered us a swig; her status printed on the front of her pink T-shirt. We declined with a smile. 'I haven't been here for ages, thanks so much,' I said. 'Such a good idea.'

'You needed it,' replied Thalia.

'I do need it, I tell you. I've been so stressed about all this business. And with the house renovations, it's been a nightmare. But do you know, I feel better now Roger North's been arrested.'

'I bet. That guy has some serious problems. You knew he was a nutter right from the beginning, didn't you?'

I cringed at Thalia's description – I knew what she meant, but I didn't like that term. But I let it pass – Roger North had been a nasty piece of work, and Thalia was my best friend.

We moved further along in the queue, nearing the front desk, and I couldn't wait to get into the warm. It was one of those dank March days, where the damp hung in the air and bit into your bones.

'How's Tom coping with it all?' said Thalia.

'He's OK. He was livid at first, but now he's trying to forget the whole thing – he doesn't like me talking about it. He keeps saying I'll drive myself mad if I keep thinking about it – he's worried I'll have another episode. You know.'

'I don't think you will,' said Thalia. 'You know what to do if you start feeling anxious and out of control again. Don't let him sweep things under the carpet, that's the worst you can do – if you need to speak about your worries, you must let it out. OK?'

Smiling, I linked my arm through hers. 'Thanks, Thalia, you're the best! Now, come on, let's forget about it and have a good time.' We stepped up to the desk, and the receptionist checked our tickets. Within minutes we were in the changing rooms, the smell of minerals and essential oils had already begun to work their magic. I took off my glasses and put them away; for the next couple of hours, I was happy to see the world in a blissful blur.

The white dressing gowns smelt fresh and crisp, we wrapped them around ourselves and headed straight for the saunas and steam rooms. We chose the Roman steam room first, with its stone seating, and fluted columns. The heat from the steam and the aroma of rosemary and mint was instantly relaxing. We didn't speak for a while, comfortable to sit together in silence.

After trying all the rooms – the infrared room, the celestial relaxation room, and the ice chamber, we dived into the showers to warm up, before going to the rooftop for a swim in the outdoor pool. As we stepped from the lift and onto the terrace, I gasped; it was so cold. Laughing and shrieking, we hung our towels and robes on hooks, before hurrying down the steps. We swam around in the warm water, then sat on a ledge, gazing out across the Bath skyline with the steam drifting around our shoulders like a mist.

'So, give me an update on your latest conquests,' I said. Thalia had many dates, but she wasn't interested in forming long-term relationships. She preferred the thrill and kick of meeting new people. New sex.

'Funny you should say that,' she said, her brown eyes twinkling. 'I had a date last night with a man called Bentley. IT consultant.'

'Bentley?' I smirked.

'Yes, Bentley. But he said to call him Ben.' She pursed her lips and narrowed her eyes, before smiling. 'It was a bit awkward at first, I thought I'd have to escape and climb through the toilet window or something like that, but then I told him I sang in a choir, and he suddenly came to life. Turns out he writes songs in his spare time. We got on fine after that.'

I raised my eyebrows. 'And…'

'Julia! You know me better than that. I'm a lady of class. Never on a first date. But we've been texting, and things have been getting heated. So, who knows next time?' With a smile, I paddled my feet gently in the water and leant my head back, thanking my lucky stars I had a friend in Thalia. The worries of the last few weeks washed away in minutes.

I gazed up at the clock on the wall. Our two-hour session was nearly up – my heart sank, but then I remembered we still had cocktails and dinner to go; I splashed Thalia with a handful of water before climbing up the steps to get my gown on.

Chapter Eighteen

Luckily, things began to calm down. Roger North was on bail under the condition that he couldn't contact us or come down Skelton Road. He was also ordered to see a therapist. His case was due to come up in the middle of April, only three weeks away. The police had visited our house, taken the evidence needed, and although North claimed he had every right to be in the house, he wasn't denying he'd been there. The police seemed to think it would be a clear-cut case.

Isla had settled well into her new primary, and Alex enjoyed the independence of getting the bus to his old school, until it was time for him to go up to secondary in September. The house renovations were going well, we'd finished Alex's room, and we'd started on our bedroom. Tom had spoken to builders, and we had a date in the summer for the dividing wall between the dining room and kitchen to be taken down.

*

I was excited when the night of book club came around. It was my first time, and it was going to be at Lizzie's house. I'd read quickly to catch up with their chosen book of the month; someone had chosen a hefty piece of literary fiction, and I'd struggled my way through, finishing off the night before, with a quick skim read of the last few chapters.

Alex was downstairs watching a programme with Tom about the sports industry and performance drugs, and I'd read Isla a few chapters of her favourite author and tucked her up in bed. I'd actually really enjoyed it, and wished I could suggest that as a book club read – but I wasn't sure how people would react to a children's novel. I knew some people would turn up their noses, despite how good the writing was.

Cherry red lipstick was in order, and I brushed my hair, before sticking my head around the living room door. 'See you later, then.'

'Bye, mum,' said Alex.

'What time are you back?' said Tom, not looking away from the TV.

'Not sure. About ten I should think. I'll text you if I'm any later.'

OK, have a nice time.'

Lizzie lived a few roads away, and it only took a few minutes for me to walk there. I rang the doorbell and stood back to admire her house. It was similar to ours, except it was an end terrace and had more space at the front – more of a garden really. Through the glass, I saw a fuzzy frame of someone coming towards the door.

'Julia, Come in!' She threw her arms around me, giving me a hug – her perfume was overpowering, and I held my breath for a few seconds. She looked stunning and as glamorous as ever, in a primrose-coloured boiler suit and a silk red scarf tied around her neck. I told myself that it was her job to look good – she was a stylist and a personal shopper. There was no need for me to feel a frump in my jeans and black top.

I stepped into the hallway and followed her through to a large kitchen diner where a group of people sat around an expensive-looking rectangular table. I recognised a few of the faces; mainly mothers from Isla's class. I nodded and said hello as Lizzie did introductions.

'This is Julia, she's new to the area. You know Ali, don't you? And Angela?' Both women smiled and said hello. 'This is Deirdre – she owns that gorgeous vintage clothes shop on Baron Road, you know the one? I buy so much there and send all my clients in that direction.'

Deirdre laughed. 'She's a serial shopper, which is good for me,' she said.

I laughed too, then looked at the next person at the table, waiting for an introduction. She seemed younger than me, perhaps in her mid-twenties. 'And this is Olivia – she lives down the road,' continued Lizzie. 'Her mum's coming in a few minutes. We'll start as soon as she arrives. A glass of wine, Julia?'

Sitting down opposite the woman called Deidre, I happily accepted Lizzie's offer of wine, I needed a drink. It was overwhelming coming into a group of women who already knew each other. But they were friendly and chatty, and it didn't take me long to feel my shoulders relax and to uncross my arms. The doorbell rang. 'Good, that'll be your mum, Olivia. We can start soon.' Lizzie hurried across the room, and I heard her opening the door. 'Hi, Josephine.'

At that point, I didn't put two and two together. One minute I was sipping my drink and listening to Ali talk about her daughter's case of ringworm, and the next minute Josephine Debonair stood in the kitchen, her coat hanging from her arms. Roger North's sister. I froze. At first, I couldn't say anything, and I wondered if I should pretend not to recognise her. But that would have been stupid. Why on earth didn't Lizzie tell me? She must have known the woman was North's sister. Surely?

She beamed at everyone, saying, 'hello, hello,' and as she sat on the only remaining chair at the head of the table, her eyes met mine. The scrutiny of her stare drilled into me like bullets from an automatic rifle. 'Oh.' The room went silent. 'Julia.'

I nodded. 'Hello Mrs Debonair.' Not sure how much everyone knew, I glanced around to see everyone's reaction, but no one seemed to notice the awkwardness. My mind raced, what should I say? The stem of my wine glass was near to snapping, I was gripping it so tightly.

Leaning forward, I tried to get Olivia's attention, hoping she'd break the ice and save the situation. She must have known about her uncle, and maybe she knew I lived in her mother's old house – Would Lizzie have told her? But she looked down, pulling her tightfitting cardigan around her large chest and fastened the straining buttons as if cold.

'A glass of wine, Josephine?' said Lizzie. The decision was taken out of my hands – the moment of saying anything had gone. I bent down and fished out the book from my bag.

'So, who wants to start the ball rolling?' said Lizzie. 'Angela, you chose this one, do you want to tell us why?'

With a fixed smile, I thumbed through the pages of the book. My stomach was in knots. Embarrassment brought a fire to my cheeks, and I shuffled uncomfortably as I sat through half an hour of book discussion. Occasionally I commented on a few things, but mainly I let them do all the talking. What would I say to Josephine? There was no doubt about it, something had to be said.

My chance came when Lizzie announced we'd have a break for some nibbles which she had baking in the oven. People started talking about other matters, the book quickly forgotten. Deirdre got up to go to the bathroom and Ali and Angela stood to help Lizzie plate up the food and top up the wine. Olivia smiled at me across the table. 'Did Lizzie tell you Mum was coming?' she said.

'No.' I gave a small smile in Josephine's direction. 'Mrs Debonair, I…'

'Call me Josephine, for Heaven's sake,' she said in an irritated voice.

'Sorry. Josephine, I didn't know you were coming. I don't know why Lizzie didn't mention it. Does she know that Roger's your brother? Does she know you owned the house when Roger lived there?'

'She knows, alright,' said Olivia, fiddling with a long, beaded necklace. 'I'm not happy with her to be honest. She should have told you, you poor thing. I felt awful for you. Mum, are you OK?'

'I suspect Lizzie is too wrapped up in her own business to have even considered it,' said Josephine. She glanced over at Lizzie, laughing loudly with her friends in the kitchen. 'Look, Julia. I won't apologise for my brother's actions – I'm not responsible for his behaviour. But I will say, I hope you and your family can move on from it. I was horrified when I heard what he'd done. But please bear in mind, he's had a terrible life. Our upbringing was not happy. He's always had mental health problems, never diagnosed, but he's struggled since school. Of course, it didn't help when his wife left him for her lover nearly 30 years ago, and he never met anyone else. I think he's been suffering more than we all imagined.'

Olivia raised her eyebrows. 'Mum, I think that's an excuse. You had a strict upbringing too, but you're not so screwed up you move into people's attics.' She hesitated for a few seconds before continuing. 'You gamble your money away instead.' She laughed, but I knew she wasn't joking. She was serious.

To hide my embarrassment, I took a sip of wine. Josephine's face drained of colour. 'Olivia …' But before she could say anything more, Lizzie interrupted her, leaning in with two plates of sausage rolls and cheese swirls, her dangly sleeves hanging across the food.

'Eat up,' she said. Then noticing she'd interrupted a serious conversation, she added, 'Oh, sorry. Didn't mean to butt in – everything OK?' Then the penny seemed to drop, and her smile disappeared. 'Oh. I've just realised. Julia. I'm sorry. I didn't think. I should have thought. Sorry. I really am – it's because I didn't know Josephine when she lived at Catcher House, I completely forgot she'd lived there, and Roger was her brother. I'm so sorry.'

To be fair, Lizzie did look guilty. The other three women now had joined the table, and with total tactfulness which I could have hugged her for, Josephine picked up her glass of wine. 'Water under the bridge, Lizzie. Can I make a toast? Here's to Julia – good luck in your new house, and welcome to the book club.'

We all picked up our glasses and my worries washed away.

Everything would be OK.

But Lizzie – I'd have words with her later. As for Olivia's revelation that her mother gambled – that came as a shock, but it at least explained why she sold Catcher House. That family really had problems. I wondered what happened in their past to make her and Roger so screwed up.

Chapter Nineteen

As I reached the school gates the next day, I spotted Lizzie in the playground talking to another mum, while Wilf bombed around on his scooter. Isla placed her hands on her hips.

'Miss Acrington will tell Wilf off; he's not allowed to scoot on the playground.'

'Miss Acrington's right,' I said. 'It's really dangerous with all these people about.' *And Lizzie should be controlling him,* but I didn't say that bit out loud, instead, I walked up to her and waited for her to finish speaking. When the other woman finally said goodbye and walked away, Lizzie touched my arm.

'Hi Jules, sorry again for last night. I honestly just forgot. Josephine never talks about her brother, and I never see her with him. I completely forgot they were related.'

'Mm, OK. But it was embarrassing.' I clutched my hands into tight fists – I hated conflict, but she needed to know she'd been thoughtless.

'Yes, I can see that now. I'm really very sorry.' Her face fell, and she knotted her eyebrows together. She did look sorry, and I had a sudden pang of guilt for making her feel bad.

'Alright, I'll forgive you.' I said with a small smile.

With a look of relief, she put her arm around me and gave me a hug. 'Thank you!' She pulled away and lowered her voice, conspiratorially. 'Did she mention her brother at all? Did she say anything about why he was in your attic?'

'No, not really. She just said what happened was awful and hoped we were OK. She's quite nice, really.'

'Yes, she is. She's more relaxed than Olivia, you wouldn't think she's her daughter. Olivia can be a bit cold sometimes. Did you notice? And it's a pity she has a problem with her weight, because she's really pretty – she has the same eyes as Josephine's – that's something they do have in common.'

I looked over my shoulder to check no one had heard Lizzie's bitchy comments, but despite being in a public place, it seemed her comments went unnoticed. 'I didn't really speak to her that much,' I replied. 'But she seemed nice.'

Before Lizzie could answer, the classroom door swung open, and the teaching assistant shouted across the playground. 'Wilfred Stevens, get off that scooter straight away and go and put it by the bike racks.'

I bent down to kiss Isla on the cheek, and she ran into class. Lizzie gritted her teeth and watched as Wilf put his scooter away. He soon came charging back with his coat hanging off his shoulders, and Lizzie blew him kiss. We both laughed and walked towards the gate.

Lizzie turned her head and spoke to me over her shoulder, her voice echoing in the narrow passageway. 'Look, Tom said you're starting work on the kitchen in the summer. I was going to say if you ever want to use our oven or anything while yours is out of action, you're free to pop over whenever.'

'Thanks, that's so kind,' I said. Then, after taking in her words, my stomach tightened. 'When did you see Tom?'

'Oh,' She went quiet for a few seconds, then all her words came out at once. 'At the park – I was with Wilf, and he was with Isla. When was it now? Last Saturday? Something like that.'

We reached the main road, and she stopped so we could walk side by side. 'Oh, OK,' I said, wondering why Tom hadn't told me he'd seen her. He normally mentioned it if he'd bumped into one of my friends.

'It was just a quick coffee,' said Lizzie in a high-pitched voice. 'Don't worry. The kids wanted milkshake and it had begun raining, so …'

'It doesn't bother me, Lizzie,' I said with a smile. 'Tom can go for a coffee whenever he likes. It's just he normally tells me if he's seen one of my friends. No matter.'

She looked relieved and began talking again, blabbering on. But I wasn't listening. The fact was, I did mind that she'd met Tom. My skin prickled with irritation; I didn't want to walk along the road with her anymore. 'I've got to go to the chemist,' I said suddenly. 'I'll catch you later.'

'Oh, OK,' she said. 'See you later.' She gave me a hug, but I didn't put my arms around her. She carried on up the high street, her long flowing skirt billowing in the wind.

With my mind elsewhere, I stepped off the pavement and didn't see the silver SUV coming towards me. The driver slammed on his brakes. My heart lurched at the screeching and the smell of burnt rubber. I jumped back, lifting my hand to apologise. He tooted his horn. Although I couldn't hear him, I knew he shouted and swore. His expression full of unnecessary hate. With blood pumping through my veins, I ran towards the chemist. A little bell jangled as I opened the door; the quietness and warmth calming me as I stepped in.

Biting my bottom lip, I stared at the shelves and pretended to look at the products. Eventually my mind cleared, and I picked up a deodorant and joined the queue to pay.

Lizzie and Tom going for coffee wasn't a big deal really. Why had I let myself get so upset? By the time I left the chemist, I'd convinced myself I'd blown it out of proportion. It was Thalia's doing; telling me to keep an eye on Lizzie – she'd put ideas in my head, and it was stupid. Totally unfounded. As for the car tooting me – well, lots of people make that mistake, the driver totally over-reacted.

I jogged back home, gripping my keys in one hand, the deodorant in the other. I had to be at work for ten o'clock, and the trip to the chemist had slowed me down.

Rushing into the house, I kicked off my trainers and hurried into the kitchen. After emptying the milk dregs from the breakfast bowls into the sink, and putting them into the dishwasher, I pinned my hair up into a bun, and then sat on the bottom of the stairs to put on smarter shoes. I shivered – the heating had gone off and an icy chill lurked in the house. But it wasn't just the temperature. Ever since the business with Roger North, it wasn't really a home, it was unwelcoming. A sensation that something wasn't quite right. I sat still, listening. But there was nothing. No odd noises. Nothing strange. Only a tap dripping in the downstairs toilet, and the dishwasher whirring.

There was that strange floral smell again, though, this time it was in the hallway. I breathed in. It was a heavy flowery smell, I recognised it, but couldn't think what it was, or why I could smell it. I stood and grabbed my handbag lying under the table. The beam of sunlight that had been shining through the hallway window suddenly disappeared, and heavy, black clouds drifted across the sky. The shadows became longer and darker, and a sense of gloom made my stomach sink. I squeezed my bag tight, and let myself out, slamming the door behind me.

Chapter Twenty

Tom was late home, and the kids and I had already eaten. Sometimes he worked late if he had a job that needed finishing. When he eventually got in, he was tired and grumpy, so I waited for him to shower and eat his supper before I mentioned the coffee he had with Lizzie. I read Isla her bedtime story and tucked her up, and when I went back down, Tom was sat on the sofa with Alex, playing one of their computer games. I sat on the chair by the window, reading my book while they finished the game, and when Alex yelled in delight that he'd won, I knew Tom would send him to bed pretty soon. I wasn't disappointed.

'Time for bed, mate.'

'Aw, Dad, come on, one more game. See if you can beat me this time.'

'Good try. But nope, up you go,' said Tom. He ruffled Alex's hair and picked up the TV remote control.

'Night, love,' I said, as Alex bent over for me to kiss the top of his head.

'Night, Mum.'

For a few minutes, Tom and I sat in silence. Then, taking a deep breath, I slipped my bookmark between the pages, and put the book down.

'I saw Lizzie today. She offered us the use of her cooker when we do the re-fit.'

'That's nice of her.'

'Yeah. She mentioned you went out for coffee with her.' I pretended to inspect my nails, while I waited for his reply.

'Well, I'd hardly say we "went out". Is that what she said?' His voice rose in pitch, almost shouting but not quite.

Raising my head, I caught him frowning. 'Well, not exactly. She said she bumped into you in the park, and you decided to go for a coffee because it was raining.'

'Right. Hardly "going out" with each other, is it? For God's sake, Julia. You're not going to get all jealous over that are you? Don't be so ridiculous.' He took a swig of beer from his bottle, and started to scroll with the remote control, randomly flicking through the channels.

The tone of his voice stabbed at me, his words sharp. 'I'm not jealous,' I said. 'I just thought you'd have told me, that's all. You wouldn't like it if I went for a coffee with, say, Mack, would you?'

Mack was Tom's friend. They used to work together at GS Plumbing before Tom left. Now and again, I saw Mack in the office when he called in between jobs. Sometimes he asked me to go to the pub with him at lunchtime, but I never did. He wasn't my friend; he was Tom's, and I didn't think it was right.

'I wouldn't give a shit if you went out with Mack, to be honest, I trust you both. And it's about bloody time you trusted me.'

'I do trust you, it's just …'

'Whatever, Julia,' he said and turned off the TV. 'I'm going to bed.' He got up and walked across the room, accidentally kicking the plate he'd left on the floor earlier. The door clicked shut – more of an act of defiance from him than anything else, but at least he didn't slam it. I stared down, blinking. His reaction had surprised me, I hadn't expected him to get so cross and wished I hadn't mentioned it at all. The lamp in the corner of the room started to flicker and I sighed – maybe the electrics were more worn than the property survey had suggested? Like most things in this house, it would need updating when we could afford it. Perhaps we shouldn't have moved here, maybe it was too much for us to cope with. All this business with Roger North had created a bad atmosphere in Catcher House, and it began to eat into our marriage too. I stood and picked up the discarded plate and cutlery and took them out to the kitchen, before turning off the lights and heading up to bed myself.

*

Thalia still hadn't seen our house properly. She'd seen photos, and seen it from the outside, but she'd never come in. There just hadn't been a good time for either of us. But that Friday evening, she was coming over for a take-away while Tom planned to go out with the lads. Alex was going for a sleepover at a friend's and Isla was no problem, she was quite happy watching a film on my laptop in her bedroom after she'd had her tea. I'd promised her fish fingers and chips followed by chocolate mousse, so easily bribed.

A little after seven o'clock, there was a knocking on the door, and I let Thalia in. In one hand she held a brown bag full of Indian takeaway, and in the other, a bag containing a bottle of pinot grigio.

'And out of heaven, an angel appeared,' I said, laughing. 'Come in!'

Isla had stayed up to say hello; she loved Thalia. She ran over and gave her a hug, her little arms reaching around Thalia's waist.

'Hello, sweetheart, how are you? Look what I've got for you and Alex.' She opened her tote bag and showed Isla two large Cadbury Easter eggs. You have to wait till Easter Sunday though.'

Isla's eyes opened wide. 'Thank you,' she said. 'Can I have the Creme Egg one?'

'Well, you and Alex can talk about that later. Anyway, are you going to show me your bedroom?'

'Yes, come on,' said Isla, bouncing up and down with excitement. 'I'll show you now.'

With a wink, Thalia gave me the bag of curry and the bottle before taking Isla's hand. 'Show me the rest of the house, Jules, after I've seen her ladyship's.'

I put the things in the kitchen and followed them upstairs. After five minutes of Isla showing Thalia her room and all her favourite toys, I managed to get her into bed, and I set up a Disney film for her.

'If you're good,' I said, 'I'll bring you up a poppadom and some mango chutney as a bedtime snack, OK?'

'Yay!' she shouted. 'Big crisps! I love Fridays. Awesome!'

'Easily pleased,' laughed Thalia. We stepped outside onto the landing, and I looked up at the attic door.

'That's where he was,' I said in a low voice. 'I take it you don't want to look up there as part of your tour?'

'Jesus, are you joking? I hate attics at the best of times,' said Thalia with a shudder.

'According to Josephine Debonair – you know, his sister – his wife left him,' I said. 'She reckons he never got over it. Apparently, they had a bad childhood as well. Not that I feel any sympathy for the man, but I suppose it does explain a few things.'

'It does. People are easily broken. Now, come on. Let me see the other rooms. Is this Alex's?' Thalia walked across the landing and into Alex's room. It was a complete mess, despite having been decorated recently. Clothes, bits of Lego and computer game boxes lay on the floor.

'Yes, it's got a good view out from here. You can see across the rooftops to the Downs.' I turned on the light and walked over to the window. 'Too dark to see now, of course.'

'Where was the writing?' said Thalia, looking around. 'The writing on the wall.'

'Over there, under the window.'

She wandered over and crouched down. 'You've done a good job painting over it. So bloody creepy.' She gave an involuntary shiver.

'Tell me about it.' I led the way out, and showed Thalia our bedroom, which also looked over the street at the front, then I took her into the bathroom. 'We'll have to replace the suite with something modern. This plastic 1970s design is revolting, isn't it?'

'Oh, I don't know … quite retro,' she said. I pulled a face and laughed, shaking my head.

'Downstairs now,' I said, leading the way. First, I showed her the dining room and where we'd be knocking the wall down, then the kitchen and the toilet, and finally, I showed her the living room.

'This is where he sat,' I said. 'Just here.' I stood in the middle of the room, with my arms out wide. 'With the lights off. Can you imagine the bloody scare he gave me?'

'So weird, Jules,' Thalia said. She gazed around the room. 'You've got a lot of work to do, Babe. That paintwork is a revolting colour. Who paints skirting boards battleship grey for fuck's sake?'

'Battleship grey!' I laughed at her description. 'And, yeah, I know. It's a bit depressing, isn't it? I always loved the idea of doing up our own place, and I was so excited by it, but now I just find the idea a bit much.'

'Yeah, I get that.' Thalia sat down on the chair. 'But you didn't have a great start, what with Roger North. Have you heard about his court case yet?'

'It's in a few weeks,' I said, sharply.

'Will you have to give evidence?' Thalia was intent on questioning me, not picking up my signals that I didn't want to speak about it.

With a sigh, I gazed down at the floor. 'No, my Witness Care Officer has discussed it with us and doesn't think we'll need to give evidence because North admitted to it. She reckons it'll be clear cut. Look, the man gives me the creeps, let's not waste our evening talking about him. I'll go and get the curries. Do you want white or red wine?'

'OK. I'll not talk about it anymore,' said Thalia, putting her hands in the air, as though surrendering. 'Can I have white please? I'll come and help, hang on.' She followed me into the kitchen, looking over her shoulder.

'Alright?' I said.

'Fine, fine. Shall we eat here instead of the living room?'

'Yeah, of course.' And really, I couldn't blame her.

Chapter Twenty-One

I lit a couple of candles instead of putting on the overhead light, and brought in a small lamp from the dining room. It was quite cosy and certainly a lot nicer than sitting in our ugly lounge. We decided to share dishes, laying the poppadoms between us on the brown paper bag. I broke off some and dunked it into the pot of mango chutney. 'I can't wait for this,' I said, putting it into my mouth.

After taking the cardboard lids off the metal containers, I spooned the coloured grains of pilau rice onto our plates, ladling the chicken dhansak, and matar paneer on top. The smell of cumin and other spices made my mouth water; I was so hungry and began eating straight away.

Thalia poured the wine, and the only sounds for a few minutes were the clink of cutlery on our plates and the whirr of the fridge. 'So good,' said Thalia at last.

I put my fork down and took a sip of wine. 'You have no idea how much I needed this.'

'Why?' she said. 'Everything OK?' She opened a foil lined bag and pulled out the naan bread, tearing it in two.

'Not really.' I told her about the business with Lizzie and Tom. 'The thing is, I think I'm getting a bit paranoid. I don't want to start accusing him of things. He was so cross.'

Thalia raised an eyebrow. 'I don't think you're in the wrong. He should have told you if he went for a coffee with another woman. And are you sure this Lizzie isn't deliberately stirring things? Is she married?'

'Yes, she is. She seems quite happy with her husband. He's called Simon, he's a lecturer at the university.'

'Mm. Well, I'd watch her if I was you. I don't want to make you more paranoid, but this is the second time you've told me something about her that's made you worried. As for Tom – I think he's got a bloody cheek getting so angry with you. '

'Do you?' I smiled and looked at her, relieved she thought I was in the right.

'Yes. He knows you get anxious and worried about things, so instead of getting angry, he should have reassured you. Seriously, Julia, you shouldn't let him off the hook. Where's he gone tonight?'

'Out to the pub with the lads.' I picked my fork back up and scooped up some rice and chicken. 'He'll probably come home drunk around half eleven.'

'Stinking of alcohol and kebabs.'

'Probably,' I laughed. 'But to be fair, I'll probably reek of garlic.'

'Such a romantic combination,' said Thalia.

'Talking of romance, how's things going with Bentley?' I smirked as I said his name, and Thalia shook her head and raised her eyebrows.

'Not bad actually, and call him, Ben, please!' she pointed her knife at me, and grinned. 'He stayed over last night. Let's just say we didn't do much talking …'

'Seriously? Love it! Do you think this one will last?'

'You know my track record, probably not. The sex is great, but I don't reckon we're that compatible. But let's see.'

I gazed at my friend across the table, the candle flame lit up her brown eyes. I envied her the thrill of the first date, the exhilaration of new love, but then I thought how Tom and I had that once; I'd been so happy in those days.

After eating, I put the plates in the dishwasher, while Thalia poured us another glass. 'Let's go in the living room,' I said. 'I know the décor is disgusting, but the sofas are more comfortable than these chairs. You never know, it might not look so bad after a few glasses of wine. I'll bring the candles through too.'

'Yeah, that's fine,' said Thalia. 'I don't mind.'

But I think she did mind, she was just being polite. The room made her feel uncomfortable; I could tell by the way her eyes darted around, and she sat with her arms and legs crossed. I put the candles down on the coffee table, and then turned on a side light. The bulb flickered for a few seconds; it was probably on its way out. Thalia shot a look at the ceiling, then she glanced at me, scrunching up her nose. 'What's that smell? It's like my aunt's perfume she keeps in some old bottle in her spare room. What's it called now?'

I sniffed. 'Yeah, I keep smelling that too. Not sure what it is. I think it's some scent that's got absorbed into the walls of the house. It oozes out now and again.' I laughed, trying to make light of it. 'Maybe it's to do with the temperature or humidity?'

'Maybe. Quite nice though. Could be worse smells,' said Thalia. Then she shivered. 'Talking of temperatures, it's a bit cold in here, Jules.'

I rubbed my hands together; she was right. It was cold. 'I'd light the fire,' I said. 'But we haven't had the chimney swept yet. I think there's been crows or something in there.' I pointed to the dried sticks lying in the grate. 'Shall I bring the electric heater in?'

'Is that OK?' said Thalia. 'You know what I'm like, I feel the cold easily.' She'd pulled her jumper sleeves over her hands and clutched the cuffs in her fingers.

'No worries, Tom's set the timer on the radiators to go off at half eight, so we'll need something. We're trying to save money on gas.'

The little electric heater was in the cupboard under the stairs, and I rummaged around the boxes and wellington boots. It smelt damp and musty in there, and cobwebs clung to the cupboard walls. The heater was right at the back, and as I grasped it, there was a terrified scream.

Stumbling out, I trod on the boots and shoes, catching my ankle on the vacuum cleaner. With a curse, I darted back to the living room. 'Thalia?' She was still on the sofa, but pressed right up against the arm, gripping a cushion. She pointed to the far corner of the room.

'Over there,' she said. 'I saw someone.'

The brightness in her face had drained, and her hands trembled.

Laughing nervously, I walked over and put my arm around her. 'What was it? What do you mean?'

'I'm serious. It was a figure. A dark, black shape.'

'A real person?' A lump started in my throat and my voice came out as a hoarse whisper.

'No, it wasn't a real person. I don't think so, no. It couldn't have been. It kind of appeared in the corner. It was so dark. Darker than anything. I'm not joking Julia. It had arms and I could see a shape of a head. It was real, Julia.'

She shook against me as I held her hand. Thalia was sensitive, I knew that, but to see something that clearly – I didn't know what to think. My jaw hurt as I gritted my teeth hard together. 'Shall we go back into the kitchen?' I said, totally unnerved and not sure what else to do or say.

She nodded, and I picked up the electric heater on the way through. She sat by the kitchen table and grasped the bottle of wine, pouring the remains into her glass. I plugged in the heater next to her and took a throw from the back of a chair and wrapped it around her shoulders. 'I'm just going to check on Isla, will you be OK for a minute?'

Thalia nodded, and I picked up the remaining poppadoms and a pot of mango chutney and went upstairs. I poked my head around the door, and found Isla fast asleep, propped up on the pillows and her head tilted to the side. The film had finished. With my spare hand, I carefully took the laptop off the duvet and kissed her cheek. I felt a little guilty that I hadn't taken up her night-time snack earlier and told myself I'd treat her to breakfast to make up for it. Glancing around the room, everything seemed the same as usual, and there certainly weren't any strange, dark shapes, but I decided to leave the little lamp on anyway.

When I got back into the kitchen, Thalia was leaning back in her chair, looking happier. 'Alright?' I said, squeezing her shoulder as I slid by to get another bottle of wine from the fridge.

'I'm fine,' she said. 'Maybe I just got the creeps? It could have been a car's headlights shining in through the window, casting a shadow in the room, couldn't it? I expect my imagination got carried away.' She gave an uneasy laugh, and I nodded.

'Yes, yes, that'll be it, car lights do shine through that window,' I smiled, unscrewed the bottle cap, and poured us both another glass. We sipped our drinks, not believing our own words – both of us knew it wasn't a car.

After a few moments, I said quietly, 'What do you think it really was, Thalia?'

She gazed at me, her eyes flashing with fright. 'I think it was a ghost,' she said. 'And that smell? I've just remembered what it is. It's Anais Anais perfume.'

Chapter Twenty-Two

I didn't tell Tom about what Thalia saw. By the time he came home, I was in bed. He climbed in next to me, smelling of alcohol as predicted. He was cold, and cuddled up behind me – at a guess, more to get warm than as a show of affection. I pretended to be asleep, and before long, I dropped off into a dreamless, heavy slumber. When I woke, my head was fuzzy, and the beginnings of a headache thudded behind my eyes. The rain hammered against the window, and I lay there, thinking about the night before. Through the gap in the curtain, the dull day hung like lead, and it was easy to believe that Thalia had seen something ghostlike.

Tom stirred. I put on my glasses and got out of bed to make a cup of tea. Isla was up, watching TV in the living room as usual. I glanced to the corner of the room, half expecting to see something, but of course, there wasn't anything. 'Hello sweetie, fancy breakfast at Gino's today?'

Isla turned away from the screen, 'Yes please Mummy, and you forgot to bring me my big crisps and mango chutney – can I have them before we go for breakfast?'

I laughed. 'No, they'll be stale. Get washed and dressed, and then we'll go.'

'Is Alex coming?'

'No, he's going to S.S. Great Britain for Zachary's birthday, remember?'

'OK,' she said dolefully. 'Can we go to there? I like ships.'

'Not today, love. Maybe another time, OK? Alex is going with all his mates, he won't want us there.'

'OK,' she said again, before turning back to watch the television.

'Washed and dressed, Isla,' I called as I headed into the kitchen. After putting on the kettle, I leant against the worktop and texted my mum.

FANCY GOING FOR BREAKFAST? WE'LL BE IN GINOS FROM AROUND 10.

Mum and Dad only lived half an hour away in Clevedon. It's where I grew up, and I had happy memories of going swimming in the sea lake and playing on the rocks. I knew they'd be up and awake – Mum always swam first thing in the morning, no matter what the weather. It only took a few minutes for her to message back.

WE'VE HAD BREAKFAST ALREADY, BUT WE'LL JOIN YOU FOR A COFFEE. WE'LL GET THERE AROUND 10:30, IS THAT OK?

I texted back, then finished making our drinks. Foggy-headed, I squeezed the teabags against the side of the cups, then watched the milk swirl, turning the black liquid brown.

Tom was sitting in bed looking at his phone when I went back upstairs. 'Alright?' I said. 'Good evening?'

'Yeah,' he said, rubbing his face with his hands. 'Got a massive hangover though.'

'What a surprise. Fancy breakfast at Ginos? I thought I'd take Isla. Mum and Dad are coming for coffee too.' I passed him his mug and got back into bed. He looked quite rough – black rings under his eyes, his bald head shiny with sweat.

'Don't think I'll manage any food until at least lunch time,' he said. 'Do you mind if I give it a miss? Your mum and dad won't mind, will they?'

'No, that's OK,' I said.

'How was your night?' he asked with a hoarse voice, indicative of too much drink the night before.

'Good. Except …'

As if to block out what I was about to say, he snapped his eyes shut.

'Nothing bad,' I said quickly. 'It's just that Thalia thinks she saw something in the living room. You won't believe it. She thinks she saw a ghost.'

Tom tutted. 'Typical Thalia. That woman is such a drama queen.'

'She was really frightened, Tom. I believe her. If you'd seen her face, you would have too. Besides, that room does have a weird feel to it, doesn't it?'

'Yeah, I'll give you that,' he said. 'But that's probably why she thought she saw something. She probably got the creeps from the room. You know what she's like.'

I sipped my tea in silence. Tom was right, Thalia was one for dramatic stories. She once thought she'd seen a dead body by the side of the road, and insisted I do a U-turn to check it out. It turned out to be a bag of oil-covered rags that some workman had dumped.

'Yeah, you're probably right,' I said. 'Anyway, I better get showered.'

'Alright, I'm going back to sleep. Any paracetamol up here?'

I opened my bedside drawer and took out a box and passed it to him. He gulped the tablets down with the remains of his tea, then rolled over and pulled the duvet up tightly around his shoulders. It irritated me that he always drank too much at the weekend – it totally ruined any plans I might have for doing something together as a family. It was becoming more and more often too – maybe taking on such a big project with the house stressed him? I sighed, and popped two pills out for myself, swigging them down with the remains of my tea. Putting my cup down, I swung my legs out of the bed. I needed to get in the shower if I had to be at Gino's for half past ten.

*

The café was buzzing, and I wished I'd booked a table. With gritted teeth, I surveyed the crowd, but then I saw Mum and Dad right at the back, waving us over. I waved back. 'Oh, Nanny and Grandad have got a table, excellent!'

Isla stood on tiptoes to see. She ran in between the chairs, and up to my parents, squeezing herself onto the bench between the two of them.

'Hiya. Sorry we're a bit late. Have you ordered coffee?' I took off my coat and draped it over the back of my chair.

'Aye, we've ordered. What are you having, Isla?' said Dad.

'Milkshake and pancakes,' said Isla, leaning against her grandad.

'Well, someone is sure of herself today,' said Mum with a laugh.

'More than I am,' I said, picking up the menu and trying to decide what to have. The waiter came over with two lattes, and I ordered our breakfasts – choosing pancakes for myself as well. As my dad chatted to Isla about what kind of Easter egg she wanted, I thought of telling mum about the ghostly figure Thalia had seen, but I didn't want Isla to overhear. It would have to wait. I didn't tell her about Tom going for a coffee with Lizzie either. Out of some loyalty to Tom, I didn't like to show him in a bad light to my parents. I'm not sure why. Silly really, because they had their ups and downs too, so she'd understand. Instead, I talked about the kids and how our house renovations were coming along. And of course, she asked about Roger North's upcoming case at the magistrate's court in a few weeks.

'What sentence do you think he'll get?' said Mum.

'Not sure. Our solicitor thinks he'll get a suspended sentence, and he'll have to continue going for therapy.'

Mum shook her head. 'I'm worried sick in case he does it again. You did change the locks, didn't you?'

'Yes, Mum, I told you we did.'

'Don't keep blethering on about it, Trish,' said Dad. 'Tom will have it all under control.'

Mum sighed, and started to fiddle with her teaspoon, scraping the creamy froth from the edges of her cup. 'I just worry, that's all.'

'I know,' I said, and put my hand on hers.

'Don't worry Nanny,' said Isla. 'Daddy said, "if that bloody man comes anywhere near our house again, I'll whack him over the head with Alex's cricket bat."' She spoke in a deep voice, mimicking Tom.

Mum's shocked face made us all laugh and Dad ruffled Isla's hair.

'That's grand then,' he said.

'He wouldn't really hit anyone,' I said, but I wasn't one hundred per cent sure of that.

When my pancakes arrived, I found I wasn't that hungry anymore. All the talk of Roger North had put me off my food. I trickled the maple syrup from the porcelain jug, watching the golden liquid forming swirls. Luckily, Dad had the sense to change the subject and soon we talked about his trips to the doctors and the hospital. He'd had a seizure a few months ago and had to have tests now and again. Then we got onto the subject of their neighbour who cut down their boundary hedge without asking – this was the kind of conversation I needed right now. Ordinary, mundane and harmless, and no mention of Roger North.

Chapter Twenty-Three

The next few weeks were filled with busy working days and sorting out where the kids would go during the Easter holidays. I swear they had better social lives than I did. Sometimes in the evening, if Tom wasn't too tired, we'd do some work on the house and at the weekends we tried to squeeze as much as we could in between family life. I wanted to start on the living room. Although I hadn't seen anything strange, it still gave me the creeps, especially after Thalia's 'vision'. But Tom said he wanted to crack on with upstairs first. We'd stripped the paper off our bedroom wall and painted it a relaxing green – it was called Tendril, and we wallpapered the chimney wall, choosing a William Morris leaf design. I'd bought some pot plants and some cushions and soon, our room looked fresh and botanical.

I wanted to trail some ivy over the curtain rails, but Tom thought that was going too far.

'It'll look like a jungle in here soon,' he said, laughing. 'You'll want to get some monkeys in here next.'

I nodded and smiled. 'Now, that's a good idea. Maybe some parrots?'

It was days like these that made me think that everything would be OK – we worked well together, listening to podcasts, and enjoying our time doing up the house. I didn't even care now that he'd gone for coffee with Lizzie, especially as the weeks went by. Although she was a good friend on the whole, sometimes she still brought up his name in conversation, and that got on my nerves. But maybe she did that with everyone's husband? It occurred to me that she was one of those people who liked being the centre of attention and needed men to like her.

But worrying about Lizzie became less important as Roger North's court case drew closer. It was making me nervous, and I wanted to draw a line under it and start afresh – enjoy our house and our new life as a family in Larkcombe.

I was sitting at my work desk making changes to the database when the call came through. Thalia had gone for lunch, and I was the only one in the office. I glanced at my mobile screen, praying it was the Witness Care Unit, and I knew as soon as I saw the number that it was. My palms were so sweaty, as I snatched up the phone it nearly slipped out of my hand.

Listening intently, the butterflies in my stomach almost hurt. With a soft, firm voice, my Care Officer explained the verdict, and I nodded, answering with perfunctory yes and no's – only interested in what she had to say. Finally, I put the phone down and took a deep breath. It was over. I didn't have to worry about Roger North anymore. The Care Officer said she would call Tom too and speak to him personally. With shaking fingers, I texted Mum to let her know.

THE CASE WENT WELL. NORTH HAS A 6 MONTH SUSPENDED SENTENCE. COURT ORDERED HIM TO HAVE TWICE WEEKLY THERAPY, INDEFINITELY. HE HAS A BAN FROM COMING UP OUR ROAD AND HE CANNOT CONTACT US. I'M HAPPY, COULDN'T HAVE EXPECTED MUCH MORE Xx

Just then, Thalia came back into the office, and she smiled when she saw me grinning from ear to ear. 'You've heard?' She dumped her bag on the desk and came towards me, holding out her arms. I stood and hugged her.

'Yes, it's over, Thalia!' I told her the verdict, and she hugged me again.

'Cause for a celebration,' she said. 'Come on, let's go out for a glass of fizz.'

'You've just had your lunch, you nutter, someone needs to mind the phones. Besides, I need to pop to the bank and post office. Let's celebrate one night instead. OK?'

'Spoil sport,' she said with mock disappointment. 'I'm so glad for you, Jules. Hopefully you and Tom can get on with your lives now. Sort out that house of yours. Paint and decorate over all the memories of Roger North.'

'Definitely; change the bad atmosphere.' I glanced down at the floor. 'I didn't tell you before, but Tom reckons that's why you thought you saw a ghost. He thinks you imagined it because you were over-sensitive to the gloomy room.'

'Tom's got a bloody cheek. I did see something, Julia,' she said, suddenly serious. 'I thought you believed me?' She looked away and sat on her chair, pretending to shuffle papers on her desk.

'I believe you *thought* you saw something.' I said, backtracking. 'Maybe you did, I don't know, but let's not fall out about it. Look, I'll see you in a while, OK?' I took my jacket off the coat hook and buttoned it up, hoping I hadn't upset her; she had her head down. As I opened the door, a gust of strong April air blew in, rattling the picture frame on a nearby wall.

'Bloody hell, shut the door, woman,' said Thalia with a smile. I laughed with relief as I stepped outside; she'd not taken what I'd said too seriously. Hopefully we could forget all this ghost business, along with Roger North.

As I hurried up the street, I took out my phone and gave Tom a call. He was in a good mood, and we talked about the verdict, both pleased. 'I'll see you later on, then,' I said.

'I'll be late. I have a job in Chippenham – won't be back until after seven.' This was one of the things I had to accept, married to a plumber. But doubts crossed my mind.

At least when he worked for the same company as me, I could check where he was – I had the worksheets.
'Jules? Alright? Did you hear me?' he said in an irritated voice.

'What? Oh, yes, I heard. No worries, I'll see you later.' I hung up and told myself to stop. If I wanted to make our house a perfect home, I had to trust him, or otherwise the same thing would happen again. Like last time. Crazy, stupid delusions, when I was convinced Tom was having an affair. History would repeat itself if I didn't take control of my stupid brain.

As I made my way down the street towards the bank, I spotted some daffodils in a bucket outside the florists. I chose a few bunches that hadn't bloomed and went inside to pay. Bringing spring flowers into our house was all that was needed to cheer the place up. As the florist wrapped them up in brown paper, someone came in behind me. I turned, and there was Josephine. My heart jumped in my chest, then I remembered to act like a normal person. 'Hi Josephine, how are you?'

'Hello, Julia. I'm fine thank you. How are you?'

She seemed calm and relaxed, so I assumed she hadn't heard the news about her brother, and I sure as hell wasn't going to tell her.

'Good, thanks. Really well,' I replied as the florist handed me my flowers. I scanned the card machine and smiled at Josephine as I made a quick exit. She nodded and smiled back, the lines around her eyes creasing as she did so.

As I stepped out of the shop, I heard her speak. 'Can you make me up a small bouquet please? They're for placing on a grave, so not too big.'

My mouth dropped open – a grave? Who was she laying flowers for? How incredibly sad. Finding out about Roger's sentence and visiting a grave all on one day was a lot for someone to contend with. Maybe Roger had known the deceased person too? Might explain a few things. I stared at the pavement as I hurried along the road – it wasn't my business. Roger North shouldn't be in my brain anymore. But somehow, I couldn't shake him off.

ROGER -2023

Chapter Twenty-Four

Roger sat on the therapist's soft sofa in the small room. He was pleased nothing had changed from the last time he'd come. The light was dimmed, and gentle, classical music played in the background. Wispy fronds from the pot plants dangled down over the window ledge, and a large rubber plant spread its branches in front of the moss-coloured walls of the room. He liked it. It was tranquil – which, he supposed, was the purpose of the room. It was certainly nicer than his place at the hostel. With his hands in his lap, Roger picked at his fingernails; they were really, quite dirty; he'd have to give them a clean once he got back.

    The therapist sat opposite him – not full-on opposite; the chair had been angled so it wasn't directly facing him. She went over the session they'd had the week before, and now she waited for him to speak. He didn't want to talk though. Just listening to the quiet tones of Air on the G String was enough therapy for him. He closed his eyes and inhaled, and after a few moments, his therapist broke the silence between them. 'Mr North?'

    He snapped open his eyes, irritated she'd interrupted his peace of mind. 'What?' he said, frowning.

    'I'd like to carry on from where we left off last week, is that OK with you?' She leant forward and spoke gently, as if to a child or someone with impaired mental capacity. Roger watched her. She was attractive, for sure. She had long, blonde hair that was so silky and straight it looked like a mirror or a piece of glass. The clothes she wore were professional – a black trouser suit with a crisp pink blouse, buttoned to the top. There was no possibility of misjudging her intentions. She was here strictly on a professional basis, and Roger understood that.

He shrugged his shoulders. 'Yes. OK.'

'Now, you were telling me about your childhood. Your father? You told me he often hit you and was very controlling. You told me he was deeply religious and expected very high standards from you. Is there anything else you wish to tell me about your relationship?'

Roger gritted his teeth. He didn't want to tell her, but he knew she was trying to help him, so he thought for a while before speaking. Then, he said: 'I was only eleven when he accused me of being possessed with the devil. At first, he thought I was having casual chats with him – yep me and Satan, sitting down for a chin wag. Then if that wasn't bad enough, he reckoned Old Nick had possessed me.'

The therapist lowered her pen, and a look of shock shadowed her face.

'I know, right? Outrageous, isn't it?' He smiled. 'Basically, he locked me in my room and called one of the church Elders to come and talk with me. He said he didn't want me in his house any longer while I was possessed with Satan.' Roger stopped talking. He licked his lips and picked up a glass of water from the glass-topped coffee table and took a sip.

The therapist nodded. 'Go on,' she said.

'That night, Mr Harris, the Elder who was most friendly with Faither – he was alright actually, I quite liked him. Anyway, Mr Harris came to talk to me and explained that Faither thought I was possessed and although he wasn't sure, he said it would be better if I went to stay with him, on account of Faither being so … distraught.'

'And your mother?'

'She came into the room and packed my bag for me. I could tell she'd been crying, and Josie came in too, she tried to persuade Mum to put my stuff back. She kept taking everything out of my bag as quick as Mum was putting it in.

But eventually, Mr Harris pulled her away, and told her that I had to go, and it would only be for a short while, until the Pastor could visit me and talk about an exorcism.'

The therapist blinked and wrote something down in her pad. 'And how did you feel at this point, Roger?'

'How did I feel?' he laughed loudly. 'I was shit scared, wasn't I? I wasn't sure how long I'd be going for. Scared at what might happen; what the exorcism would be like.'

'How did you feel towards your father?'

Roger thought for a couple of seconds, then looked down at the floor. 'I was angry,' he said. 'And upset.'

'Why upset?

'Upset? Why?' Roger glared at the therapist as if she was stupid, but she held his gaze and nodded.

'Because he didn't want me in the house anymore. He wanted to wash his hands of me.'

The therapist nodded and wrote something on her pad. Roger looked down and with the nail of his little finger, he began to scrape the dirt out from under the other nails. A few seconds passed before the therapist spoke again. 'And did the Pastor come to see you?'

Roger raised his head and gazed out of the window, watching the rain trickle down the glass. 'Yes, he did.'

'And what happened?'

He tipped his head back and gazed at the ceiling before speaking. 'I remember I'd been at Mr Harris's house for two nights before the Pastor arrived. It was the holidays, so I didn't have school, so I suppose it was easier for them to keep me under house arrest. I just sat and watched TV, while Mr Harris went to work. Mum and Josie were banned from coming to see me, and they locked me in. But it wasn't too bad. I remember watching *Why Don't You?* and repeats of the *Monkees* all morning. Then I read books or did some jigsaw puzzles that Mr Harris left out for me. I remember being chuffed that I could watch afternoon TV; programmes

I wasn't normally allowed to watch at home. I thought about Christina – she was that girl I liked, and who I sometimes saw at home – I think I told you about her, didn't I? I didn't see her at Mr Harris's though. In fact, it was her I spoke to, when Faither thought it was the devil. Talk about being far from the truth. Christina was anything but the devil.

On the third evening, Faither arrived. Mr Harris and I had just finished our tea – I remember it was sausages and mash with peas. I remember because he made the mash much nicer than Mum did – all salty and buttery. I scraped up the gravy, thinking how Mr Harris didn't mind me putting the knife in my mouth, when the doorbell rang. I knew it was Faither before he even came into the house, because he had a way of ringing a doorbell three times – short sharp rings. Mr Harris brought him and the Pastor into the dining room. I stood up so quick, thrusting my chair back it knocked against the wall. My heart was racing – I remember because the sensation made me feel sick after eating dinner. Mr Harris told the two to sit down, and he went into the kitchen to make some drinks for everyone. The Pastor sat opposite me and gestured with his hands for me to sit too.

After they'd all got their mugs of tea, Faither started waffling on. 'So, Pastor, how are we moving forward with this?' He stirred his tea slowly, the spoon going around and around – which, when I think about it now, was odd because he never took sugar.

'I would like to speak to Roger on his own, if you don't mind,' he said. 'And then I need to contact my supervisor to ask his advice. We may even need to consult a psychiatrist first, to check there isn't anything else going on in Roger's mind.'

I remember staring at him; I couldn't believe it had come to this – it was a load of old rubbish. Faither tried to control his temper, but I saw him tense up; his hands tightened into fists. 'Yes, of course,' he said.

Mr Harris must have noticed Faither was agitated. He stood up and said, 'Come on, William, let's go and sit in the lounge and let the Pastor do his good work. Roger's in safe hands, no need to worry.'

The thought that Faither worried about my well-being was hilarious. Faither let out a long sigh and followed Mr Harris. 'Shout if you need any help, Pastor, we'll only be in the next room.'

'I'll be perfectly fine,' said the Pastor, crossing his arms. He waited until the door was closed and then clasped his hands together, his forefingers raised like a steeple of a church. 'Roger, your father says your behaviour in school is extremely challenging. He also says you talk out loud every night. He has heard rather disturbing language, coming from you, followed by maniacal laughter. This all while you're sitting alone in your bedroom. He believes you are possessed with an evil spirit. I want to know your thoughts on this.'

I didn't answer straight away. I remember staring up at a cobweb hanging from the light. It swayed a little, as if it had a life of its own, but I suspect it was from a draught coming in from the windows. After a few minutes of sitting in silence, I met the Pastor's eye.

'I wasn't speaking to the devil. I was chatting to my friend.'

'Your friend? Who is this friend?'

'I can't say, I don't want to get them into trouble.'

'But, Roger, you must see this all sounds strange. Your father says there's never anyone in your room, and I don't expect you have a telephone connection upstairs, or your father would have mentioned it. So how are you actually speaking to this 'friend'?'

I shrugged, determined not to drop Christina in it.

'Roger?'

'It's just a friend. They visit me and we speak. That's all.'

'And this friend – what kind of relationship do you have? Are they special to you?'

'Yes, very.'

'So this *friend* visits you at night. No one else seems to be able to see them, and you seem, er, very fond of them. Is that right?'

I nodded.

'But you aren't prepared to tell me who it is?'

I shook my head.

The pastor shut his eyes and raised his fingers to his forehead. That's when things began to get creepy. In a soft voice, he began to speak in Latin.'

Chapter Twenty-Five

The therapist tapped her pen on her pad. 'So, let me get this straight. The Pastor also thought you were in league with the devil, is that right?'

Roger nodded. 'After he left the dining room, I could hear him talking to Faither and to Mr Harris. The next thing I knew, they came back, looking all serious. Faither couldn't look at me, and no matter how much I willed him to, he couldn't meet my eye. He despised me.'

'He probably didn't despise you, Roger. I suspect he was worried for you. He had deeply ingrained religious beliefs that affected his judgment. Is it possible he cared for your well-being?'

Roger shook his head vehemently. 'You haven't heard the half of it. He hated me, you see? He really did. Jesus, you aren't listening to me.' He rubbed his eyes, then dragged his hands through his hair, anguish etched across his face. 'All I wanted was for him to love me like other kids' parents did. But he didn't.'

'I am listening to you Roger. Tell me what happened next,' said the therapist, as she offered him a tissue from a box. Roger pulled one out and blew his nose before continuing.

'Not much happened for a few days. Well, I suppose things were going on, but no-one told me. One day, when I was still at Mr Harris's, I watched TV with a plate of spaghetti hoops on my lap. I heard tapping at the window. Josie's worried face was pressed against the glass, her hands cupping around her eyes to block out the light so she could see in. It cheered me up seeing her, and I put down my dinner and went over. I undid the catch and tried to push it open, but it was stiff, and the wood stuck. I thumped the frame a few times, and eventually it swung open. I remember there were dead flies between the frame and the window – lots of them, and spider's webs.

'Josie,' I said.

I had to look down at her because the pathway she stood on was much lower. She rested her hands and chin on the windowsill like one of those cartoon Chads with the big noses looking over a wall. I brushed the flies away, so they didn't touch her lips. That would have been horrible.

She laughed and pulled away as the dead creatures fell to the ground. 'Hi, Roger, how you doing? Mum's worried about you, she asked me to come and see if you were OK. Don't tell Faither though. He doesn't know.'

'I'm alright,' I said. 'A bit bored, but I get to watch what I like on TV. And Mr Harris is nice. Do you know what's happening? I'm not told anything.'

Josie looked over her shoulder and lowered her voice. 'I heard Mum and Faither talking in the garden last night. I'd opened the window to stop it steaming up when I had a bath, so I heard everything. Apparently, the pastor's been given permission to go ahead. His supervisor said he had to "nip it in the bud". Faither told mum that you'd seen a doctor, and he said it wasn't a physical or psychological problem.'

'I haven't seen a doctor,' I said. Anger burned inside me. Bloody Liar. Faither was a bloody liar.

Josie's eyebrows knotted together. 'It's not true, is it Roger? You aren't really possessed, are you?'

I shrugged, not quite sure what to say. 'Don't think so. I'm not sure what it's all about, Jose. I think I see people sometimes, and I've been thinking about that. I'm wondering now, if they might not really be there. Is that demonic?'

Josie frowned. She didn't understand what I was saying. 'Who? Who do you see?'

I wasn't sure if I should tell her about Christina. I didn't want her to think I was mad, because now, for the first time, I'd actually admitted it to myself – Christina *didn't* visit me in my room. She couldn't have. I'd been thinking about it over the last few days of my house arrest, and it didn't make sense. I'd began to wonder if it had all been in my head, and that frightened me. Maybe I *was* possessed by the devil? Maybe he tried to make me believe things that weren't real? Trying to control me?

I decided to tell Josie the truth. 'I used to think Christina visited me in my room. I was convinced she was there, Josie. She lay next to me and touched and kissed me and…'

Horrified, Josie drew back from the window. 'Touched you? Kissed you? Roger that's disgusting. Christina wouldn't kiss you.'

I narrowed my eyes, the fire in my chest burning with more intensity. 'Why wouldn't she?'

'You're delusional, that's what you are. Maybe you do need help? Maybe Faither's right?' She walked backwards, slowly stepping across the grass.

'Christina, don't go!'

She stopped and stared at me, then shook her head. 'I'm not Christina.' She turned and ran, her blonde plait swinging between her shoulder blades. And that was the last I saw of her.'

The therapist tilted her head to the side. 'The last you saw of her?'

'Well, the last I saw of her until after. After the exorcism,' said Roger.

'So, it actually happened?' she said in a worried voice. Then she corrected her features and smiled at him.

'Yes, it happened alright.' Roger's leg cramped as his heel repetitively lifted up and down; a nervous twitch which happened sometimes. He lay a hand on his knee to keep it still.

'Maybe that's enough for today. We'll continue this at our Friday session.' She closed her notebook with a snap. 'Is that OK, Roger?'

Roger nodded and kept his eyes shut. Just for a few minutes, that's all he needed. A few minutes to sit in peace and listen to the music before going back to the hostel. He could hear the therapist rustling her papers and standing and he knew it was a cue for him to leave, but he wasn't ready. He liked it here.

'Mr North? I'm sorry, but your session has finished now.'

He frowned. She was trying to get rid of him. Flicking his eyes open, he saw her putting his file in the cabinet and pulling out someone else's notes. She was done with him. A pain crushed his chest, and he let out a long cry, putting his head in his hands.

'Mr North? Roger? What's wrong?' She ran over to him and put her hand on his shoulder.

'I'm ok,' he said. 'It's all been too much for me. I might need more sessions, Doctor. I think two a week isn't enough.'

The therapist took a few steps back. 'Well, let's see how things go on Friday, shall we? Then proceed from there. Now, how are you feeling? Would you like a glass of water?'

Roger sniffed as he stood up. 'No, I'm OK. Thank you, Doctor. I'll make my way out. I'll see you on Friday.' He gave a weak smile and walked towards the door with his shoulders hunched.

'See you on Friday, Roger. You take care.'

Roger smiled and stepped out of the room; his shoulder still warm from where she'd touched him.

Chapter Twenty-Six

Back at the hostel, Roger lay on his bed and stared at the ceiling. He wished he could have his own place, but his therapist recommended he stay where he was until he felt better. "Less stress," she'd said. And she was probably right.

As he gazed at the hairline cracks, his mind wandered to the therapy session, and he thought about the past – Faither, his family and about Christina. He'd been completely obsessed with her. Forty-four years on, he still thought about her long black hair and slim, brown legs. She'd always be in his head. He lay his arms across his stomach, and his muscles relaxed. The cool air of the room made him aware of his breathing, and he inhaled slowly in and out, just how his therapist had taught him.

His mind drifted back to the day of the exorcism. He still remembered it vividly. Although it was summer, the day was dull grey and wet. The rain hammered against the window as he watched the morning television shows, exactly as he had done for the last week. Mr Harris told him he was taking the day off work, because "today was the day" and Roger didn't need to ask what that meant.

Mr Harris had left him a tin of ravioli on the kitchen counter, and said he'd be back around two o'clock to collect him. Roger had the ravioli on toast.

Not long after two o'clock, he heard the key in the lock.

'I'm back, Roger,' called Mr Harris cheerfully, as if he'd come to watch TV with him, rather than take him to an exorcism. 'Are you ready to go home?'

*

Faither had sent Mum and Josie out, saying they were far too sensitive to stay during the exorcism. Apparently, "strong emotion hindered the devil's banishment". Well, that's what Faither said, anyway. Sitting on the settee, Roger picked at his fingernails. It was like being in a stranger's house, not his own home. Mr Harris stood by the fireplace, wringing his hands; he seemed nervous too. As for Faither, Roger didn't have a clue where he was, not until someone knocked on the front door. Faither poked his head into the living room. 'Roger, come and say hello to the Pastor,' he ordered.

The Pastor stepped into the house and wiped his shoes on the mat.

'Good afternoon, Roger. How are you feeling? Have you had a good morning? No strange voices? No emotional mood swings?' He watched Roger's mouth, as if terrible words or expletives were about to shoot out.

'I'm alright, thank you, Pastor. Nothing has happened.'

'Would you like a cup of tea, Pastor?' said Mr Harris, taking on the role of Roger's mother. Faither nodded his head in approval.

'Yes, that would be lovely.' The pastor clasped his hands together, like he was praying or something, and followed Mr Harris and Faither into the kitchen. Roger sat back down on the settee, thinking things couldn't get any stranger. Cups of tea? How can they have cups of tea when he was meant to be possessed with the devil? Surely something about this wasn't quite right? Everything was too calm. Too dignified. He bit the inside of his cheek and stared at the brown and orange swirls on the rug.

The clock on the mantelpiece ticked in time with Roger's breath. The minutes passed, and he debated whether to put the radio on, but just as he was about to stand up, the living room door opened.

'Roger, we are about to start. Are you ready?' said the Pastor.

'I think so, can you tell me what's going to happen?'

'I think it's better if we go straight into it, that way you won't be anxious,' said the Pastor.

Roger raised his eyebrows but didn't say anything. Mr Harris came over and sat next to Roger and took his hand. 'It'll be OK, I promise,' he said. 'And once it's all over, you'll feel better. The temper tantrums, those voices you hear, all the evil the devil is trying to do to you, turning you against God – it will all stop. OK?'

Roger swallowed. His skin began to prickle as the hairs on his arms stood up. This was going to happen whether he liked it or not, and he was scared.

'Where are we doing this?' said Faither. 'In here?'

The pastor looked around. 'No, there's too many distractions. I think it's better if we go into the dining room. Come with me.' The pastor beckoned Roger and crossed the hallway. The room was stuffy, and the heavy furniture seemed particularly oppressive that day.

Faither stood in the corner of the room with his arms folded, Roger shot him a look, hoping to see a hint of tenderness in his eyes, but there was nothing. A cold determined stare was all. Mr Harris on the other hand, seemed concerned. He sat across from Roger, asking him if he was warm enough.

'I'm fine,' said Roger, although he really wasn't. His stomach clenched tight as the Pastor stood behind him and laid his hands on his shoulders.

'I will begin. Mr Harris, Mr North, if you would mind sitting quietly and only help if I ask. Shall we proceed?'

Both men nodded, and Faither sat down next to Mr Harris. Under the table, Roger clutched his hands into fists and squeezed his eyes shut. A pain burnt in his chest, as if a rope looped around his body and was tightening.

'We are here this morn to take young Roger North from the hands of Satan and to deliver him to a safe space amongst our brethren. The violent tempers, voices he hears, and his internal thoughts of evil will be extinguished along with the devil, and Roger will go forth and become a true advocate to our church.'

The pastor leant down and took out a small glass vial from his leather bag and placed it on the table, then a wooden crucifix. He passed Mr Harris a small, gold box with star shaped holes in. 'Please may you light the incense?'

Mr Harris nodded and took the matches and the incense burner from the Pastor. He placed it the centre of the table, opened the lid and struck a match to light the tiny incense pyramids inside. Soon a sweet-smelling, woody scent wafted from the holes and the smoke drifted around the room. Roger recognised the smell – it was frankincense.

The Pastor then inhaled and placed his palms on the top of Roger's head. They were heavy and he pressed down hard. In a deep, whispering voice, the Pastor began speaking in tongues – Roger was familiar with this, but on that day, it made him feel uneasy. What was he saying? The pastor mumbled and then suddenly his voice rose, and he began to speak again in English.

'May the Holy Spirit defend us in our battle against the rulers of darkness and against wickedness. Crush Satan beneath the cleansed soles of our feet so he may no longer hold Roger captive. Cast this devil into the bottomless pit of hell, amongst rabid dogs and the serpents of evil.'

Roger flicked open his eyes and stared directly at Mr Harris, who watched him transfixed. Faither had now clasped his hands together, and muttered in tongues, his eyes had rolled back into his head as if he was no longer in control of his body. Roger couldn't bear the sight; he pressed his sweaty hands to his eyes. The pastor uncorked the vial and poured three drops of the holy water onto Roger's head. The liquid trickled down into his ears, it tickled and made him itch. He tried to rub his ear on his shoulder, but the Pastor clasped his head with both hands and straightened it.

'Stay still, my son, let the holy water do its work.'

All Roger could hear was the Pastor's breath, and Faither and now Mr Harris, mumbling strange words and incantations. The incense was too intense, too strong – filling his lungs and choking him. He coughed, cleared his throat. It was too much. Roger tried to stand, but the Pastor pushed him back down.

'The devil knows we are here, Roger, he is trying to fight. Don't move, or he has won. Mr Harris, Mr North, please come over and sit on either side of the boy and hold on to him. Satan wants to reject the exorcism, so we need to be prepared. This is why Roger is coughing – his body is working with us, trying to expel the devil.'

The two men immediately stopped speaking and did as the Pastor requested. They sat on either side of Roger. Mr Harris held his hand stroking his skin with his thumb; Faither pressed down hard on his thigh.

The pastor began again. 'We drive you from us, whoever you may be. Unclean spirits, all satanic powers, all dark forces, sects and cults. In the name of the Holy Spirit, I order you to leave this boy alone.'

The pastor picked up the crucifix and held it over Roger's head. 'I cast you out, demon, in the name of Jesus Christ.' He tapped the cross, so it just touched the top of Roger's hair. 'I cast you out, Satan, in the name of God Almighty.' Again, he pressed the crucifix into Roger, harder this time. 'I cast you out, Devil, in the name of the Holy Spirit.'

Roger gasped as the Pastor thrust the top of the crucifix between his shoulder blades. A sharp, digging pain shot down his spine. Mr Harris and Faither tightened their grip – their fingers squeezing hard. Roger lost control of his breathing, it became faster and faster and soon he was panting like an anxious dog.

Speaking rapidly, again in tongues, the Pastor laid the crucifix back on the table and gripped Roger's shoulders. The room was so hot. The men's tight hold and the lack of air made Roger dizzy. He swallowed down bile, his throat was so sore. His head swam and he began to feel weak. So weak.

And then there was nothing. He felt nothing and could hear nothing.

JULIA – 2023

Chapter Twenty-Seven

Life settled down, but the house still made me uneasy. We'd finished decorating upstairs now, and we had a new bathroom suite fitted, but no matter how many walls we painted in bright, light colours and even though we'd pulled up the old, worn carpets, it still seemed to ooze bad feeling. Tom wasn't bothered by it, he said it would feel like home once we'd finished the renovations. Yet both the kids said the house gave them the creeps too – I'm not sure if they really thought that, or if they picked up on my mood. Alex spent most of his time playing football in the park, or at his friends' houses. Isla followed me around a lot of the time, colouring in at the kitchen table or 'helping' me with the housework.

One late afternoon, I was having a cup of tea in the living room when a strange sensation crept through me. My stomach sunk and a depression washed over me, like the feeling you get when you receive bad news. I'd been messaging Lizzie to see if she could pick Isla up from school the next day, when a darkness seemed to fall across the room as if a heavy cloud had rolled in front of the sun. I glanced out of the window, but the sky was blue and there wasn't a cloud in sight. The room went cold, and a sudden panic gripped my heart. That floral scent again. It prickled the inside of my nose. I lay my phone on the sofa and watched Isla, to see if she'd noticed anything, and the strange thing was, she had. At first, I thought it must have been my imagination, but within seconds, she put down her pen and came to sit next to me.

'I'm cold, Mummy,' she said and cuddled into me.

'Yes, it has got colder,' I said. 'Maybe we should put our jumpers on?' I put my arm around her and pulled her close. Having her warm body next to me made me feel better, and soon the room brightened, and it became warm again.

'It's gone,' said Isla.

I frowned and pulled away. 'What do you mean?'

'The thing that made it cold and dark has gone,' she said, matter of factly. She scrambled off the cushions and went back to kneeling by the coffee table, where she'd been drawing pictures. Picking up my tea and cradling the mug in both hands, I watched her carefully, but she seemed happy enough. I wasn't sure what had just happened, but I knew one thing – it sure as hell wasn't a cloud.

When Tom came home from work, I didn't mention it; he'd have laughed at me. But as I rinsed the bubbles down the plughole after Isla's bath, I heard her telling Alex about it. She stood by his door in her pink dressing gown, chattering away about how the room had turned 'dark and cold' and 'that scary thing was back'.

I rushed out to the landing, searching her face for clues. 'What scary thing?' I said.

'Nothing, Mum,' said Alex quickly. 'It's just a silly game Isla likes to play.' Isla opened her mouth to protest, then closed it again.

'You must tell me if anything's scaring you both.' I stroked the back of Isla's damp hair, trying to keep the concern from my voice.

'Nothing's scary, Mummy,' said Isla. 'It's just a game, just what Alex said.' Then she skipped away and into her bedroom. I raised my eyebrows in Alex's direction, but he shrugged and went back to his phone.

That night, I read Isla her bedtime story on automatic pilot, thoughts constantly playing in my head. The kids knew something, and they weren't going to tell me – not that night anyway. I decided I'd wait a bit, then casually ask Alex about it.

Once we'd finished her story, I closed the book and Isla snuggled down under the duvet. Her hair smelt of apple shampoo, and I breathed it in, kissing the top of head. 'Night night, sweetheart.'

'Night, mummy.' She put her thumb in her mouth and curled up; my heart squeezed – she was still so young. Too young to have scary things happen to her. I sighed and walked away, making sure I left her door ajar so a little light from the landing would seep into the bedroom. Alex had closed his door, but tomorrow, I told myself, I'd have a word with him.

In the kitchen, Tom was on his phone messaging someone on WhatsApp. Probably his football mates. 'Can you pick Isla up from Lizzie's tomorrow?' I said, as I put away the cups that were draining by the sink. 'I've got to take Dad for a check-up at the hospital. Mum's gone to Aunty Diana's so she can't take him.'

'Yeah, no problem. What time?'

'Around 5:30? I should be home about six, so could you get tea ready too? That'll be great. I've got those cheese and onion pies in the fridge, and we can have them with mash and peas. Alex will probably walk home with his mates as usual. He should be back when you get in.'

'OK. What's wrong with your dad?'

'Oh, just a test to check everything is OK with his medication. I really wish Mum wouldn't go away when Dad has an appointment. It means I've got to take him to hospital, now he can't drive.'

Tom frowned. 'Well, let's hope he doesn't have any more seizures, and gets his licence back soon. Anyway, does Lizzie know I'm picking up Isla?'

'I'll message her,' I said, sitting down at the table.

HI LIZZIE, THANKS FOR HAVING ISLA TOMORROW. TOM WILL PICK HER UP AROUND 5:30 IF THAT'S OK?

A few seconds later, Lizzie replied.

NO WORRIES, THAT'S FINE, IT'LL BE LOVELY TO SEE TOM, AS EVER.

I gritted my teeth. She couldn't help herself, could she? 'Lizzie says 5:30 is fine. But don't outstay your welcome, will you? She'll need to get on with their supper and get Wilf ready for bed.'

'I'm not a kid, Julia, I know how to behave.' Tom stood up, his eyebrows knotting together in irritation.

'OK, OK, just saying.' I tried to ignore the bad atmosphere brewing. Perhaps I shouldn't have said that, but there was no way I wanted Tom sitting having a cosy cuppa with Lizzie. He crossed the room in silence and placed his dirty mug in the washing up bowl.

'I'm going to watch the footie down the pub. See you later.' He sauntered out of the kitchen, grabbing his denim jacket from the coat hook in the hallway.

Gritting my teeth, I continued scrolling through my phone, knowing his quick departure was his way of making a protest. Mentioning Lizzie had been a bad move, and my eyes stung as I sat alone in the kitchen with only a dripping tap for company.

Chapter Twenty-Eight

Luckily, I had an understanding boss who didn't mind if I took the afternoon off to take Dad to hospital, as long as I worked overtime to make up for it. Thalia was a complete angel too, and said she'd sort out the post for me.

After the morning rush, I leant back in my chair and sipped the green tea Thalia had made. She leant against her desk, holding a mug of black coffee.

'I can tell you're stressed,' she said after a few minutes.

'How?'

'You've gone quiet. What's the problem? I have to say, you're not looking great. Do you think you should go back and see the doctor?'

Taking in a deep breath, I met Thalia's worried gaze. 'There's just been a lot on my plate. All that business with Roger North; and Tom's been so snappy, and then Lizzie's been way too friendly with him. Then there's the house – there's so much work that needs doing. And guess what? Isla and I had a funny experience like you did.'

Thalia leant forward and put her cup on the table. 'Seriously? What happened?'

'Well, it went all cold and dark in the room and I felt strange. Kind of depressed and overwhelmed. The odd thing though, it was sunny and there weren't any clouds. I thought I imagined it at first, but then Isla came and sat with me.'

'Did she see anything?'

'No, just felt it. But I heard her say to Alex later that night, "the scary thing is back" so obviously they've both sensed something before.'

'Oh my God.' Thalia stood up and walked over to me with a serious look on her face. 'You need to do something about it. I also think you need to go to the doctor. Get some tablets to calm you down a bit. You don't want to get ill again, do you?'

I shook my head and looked down at my hands. My eyes prickled and I blinked hard. 'I might do,' I said. 'I'll think about it.'

'Make sure you do,' said Thalia. 'And in the meantime, I'm here.'

*

Dad didn't take too long with the consultant, and we were soon out of the hospital and back in Clevedon drinking tea in the garden. It was now the beginning of May, and it was warm enough to sit on the veranda outside their summer house. Dad pointed out a chiffchaff darting in and out of a hedge, while another perched higher. Their song, although repetitive, really cheered me up.

Dad was pleased his hospital visit had gone well. He certainly looked much brighter.

'So, Mum's back tomorrow, is that right? Will you be OK until then?' I said.

'Aye, of course I will, stop fussing. I have my newspaper and my birds for company, so I'll be grand.'

'Well, if you need anything, give me a ring. I better get going, or Tom will end up burning the pies or something.' I gave him a kiss on the cheek and let myself out of the house. My drive back to Bristol was slow, it was rush-hour, so I knew there'd be hold ups, and the roadworks didn't help either. Luckily there was a parking space outside the house – I was tired and starving hungry and couldn't wait to get in. Tom's car wasn't there – but he'd probably parked further down the road.

As I let myself in, my phone pinged. A text from Alex. Callum had asked him to stay for tea and he'd get a lift back around 7. I nodded and threw my car keys into the bowl on the sideboard. I slipped off my shoes and put on my fluffy slippers and called out. 'Hiya! I'm home.' No answer. I looked at my watch. It was quarter past six. With a frown I went into the kitchen to see if Tom had been in, and whether he'd made a start on supper. There was nothing. The kitchen was just how I'd left it that morning. Cereal bowls in the sink, and two teabags all dried out on top of the work surface.

The saucepans clattered together as I took two from the cupboard. With a burning heat rising inside me, I began to peel the potatoes. He had one job. Well two jobs – pick up Isla, then get home to start supper. Why couldn't he stick to the plan? I threw each piece of potato into the pan, scooped up the peelings and threw them into the food waste bin.

Slamming the lid shut, I glanced up at the kitchen clock. It was nearly half past six and still no sign. I tapped my fingers on the kitchen table wondering what to do. If I texted him, he'd get cross. So, I decided to carry on with making the meal, and if they weren't back in time, they'd just have to warm their food up afterwards.

While the pies cooked in the oven, I texted Thalia, complaining about Tom. She replied almost straight away.

IT'S NOT THAT LATE, GO EASY ON HIM. FOR ALL YOU KNOW, LIZZIE'S HUSBAND MIGHT BE THERE TOO. STOP WORRYING.

My shoulders relaxed as I read Thalia's message. I'd got myself in a state over nothing.

The potatoes were almost cooked, and as I prodded them with a knife, a knocking sound made me stop in my tracks. Was it Tom and Isla coming home? Still holding the knife, I stepped out of the kitchen, tilting my head to one side. It seemed to be coming from upstairs.

My slippers padded across the terracotta tiles, and with my fingers curled around the knife, I crept up the stairs, gripping the banister with my free hand. There was another sound. Scraping. It radiated from the depths of the house. Could it be Roger North up in the attic again? Stopping and listening once more, I realised the sound was coming from the airing cupboard, between the bathroom and Isla's room. I yanked back the door. The noise stopped suddenly. With my heart thudding, I turned on the light and peered in. Nothing. Nothing except clothing and towels warming on the shelves. But on the floor, there were some black things, shaped like rice – droppings. It was mouse droppings. But no, way too big. It was rat shit.

Yelling, I slammed the door in disgust, then from downstairs, a key in the lock and Tom's voice came calling up. 'We're home!' He stared at me as I charged down the stairs. 'What's wrong? What's the knife for?'

Isla sat on the floor and took off her school shoes. 'We had hot chocolate and marshmallows at Wilf's,' she said.

'Nothing's wrong,' I said. 'I heard a noise upstairs, that's all. But I think we've got rats.'

'Rats? Oh my God, that's revolting. I'll get a trap tomorrow on my way to work. I hope they're not getting into the kitchen.' Tom strolled past me and started to open all the kitchen cupboard doors. 'I can't see anything. Was it droppings you saw?'

'Yes. In the airing cupboard. That's probably why I could hear them from the kitchen, because it's just above the larder, isn't it?'

Tom looked at the ceiling, as if trying to work out the layout of the rooms upstairs. 'Yes, probably.'

Isla came in and peered at the potatoes. 'Mummy, I think the water's nearly gone.'

I rushed over to the stove and whipped the pan off the heat. She was right. A few potatoes were scorched and sticking to the bottom of the pan, but the others seemed OK. 'You saved our supper, Isla, well done.'

Tom wafted his hand in front of his nose, as the smell of burnt potato filled the kitchen. 'Well, you serve up, and I'll go and take a quick look upstairs to see if I can find out where the rats are coming in.'

I nodded, too engrossed with the food to answer.

'Don't kill them, Daddy!' shouted Isla. 'Rats are cute.'

'Sit down, Isla,' I said sharply. 'Tea's ready.'

She did as she was told, and it wasn't until we were all sitting down and eating, did I think to ask why they were so late coming home. 'Did you have a nice time at Wilf's?' I said to Isla as I speared a piece of pastry.

'Yeah, it was good,' she said with her mouth full.

As if he knew what was coming, Tom pointed his knife at me. 'I know we were late. I didn't get to Lizzie's until after six. I was held up on a job at work. I texted her to let her know, so everything was OK.'

'That's alright. Thanks for picking her up,' I said in a calm voice. But I was anything but calm. Why didn't he think about texting me? And more to the point, how come he had Lizzie's telephone number?

Chapter Twenty-Nine

'Thanks for having Isla yesterday,' I said to Lizzie as the kids ran into class. It was a foul, wet day, and even though I had my hood up, I huddled close to Lizzie so I could shelter under her umbrella. She gave me a bright orange lip-sticked smile that matched her baggy ethnic trousers. How she had time to do herself up first thing in the morning was beyond me, I could barely manage to get up and dressed, let alone pull off a stylish look. But it was her job, I reminded myself for about the tenth time.

'No worries at all,' she said. 'They played really nicely together, so I managed to get on with some work.'

'Oh good. Isla couldn't stop talking about your hot chocolates.'

'I know! She loved them. She had two in the end. She had one straight after school, and then again when Tom came to pick her up. I hope you don't mind? It felt a bit mean otherwise, giving him one and not her.'

'Oh, I'm surprised Tom had one,' I said. 'He doesn't normally like sweet drinks.' I could feel my cheeks burning, and I pushed my hood back down to get some air.

'You're kidding? He didn't say that when I piled on the marshmallows.'

'Does Simon like hot chocolate too? Did he have one?' It was a silly question, but I didn't care.

'He hates them. He had a beer.'

I took a breath, relieved – So Simon had been there too. 'Well, thanks for having her anyway. I better get to work. Are you walking to the car park?'

'No, I've got to pop into the school office. I need to ask permission to take Wilf out of school next Friday. Simon and I have been going through a bit of a rough patch, and he wants to take me for a romantic break. Not that it'll be that romantic, with Wilf being there, but I suppose it's the thought that counts.'

'Oh, I'm sorry to hear that. If you ever need to talk …'

'It's fine. Nothing we can't fix – we need a bit of time away, that's all.'

I nodded and gave her a hug. 'I better go, but remember, if you need me, you know where I am.'

'Thanks, Jules.' She hugged me back, still smiling. She didn't seem too bothered about their marriage being in difficulty. Maybe she didn't really care? I pulled my hood back up and jogged out of the playground towards the car park. The rain hammered down, and the wind blew right in my face. I bent my head and ran faster, feeling the wet seeping into my shoes. As I reached the car, I opened the door and sunk into my seat. I pushed the damp hair away from my face and wiped my glasses. Staring in the mirror, my skin looked sallow and unhealthy. My teenage acne scars seemed more noticeable than usual, and I had black bags under my eyes. With a sigh, I put the keys in the ignition and started the car.

As I drove to work, I thought about how wonderful I'd imagined our life would be when we decided to move to Larkcombe. A spacious house we could make our own, good schools and a new circle of like-minded friends. But instead, I had a spooky house with rats and an attractive neighbour who seemed a little too interested in my husband. I shook my head and turned the volume up high on the radio, letting it blare out all the way until I pulled into a parking space at work.

Thalia looked taken aback as I ran into the office. She sat calmly at her desk, as I barged in with rainwater dripping from my clothes and onto the wooden floor.

'It's awful out there,' I said as I hung my coat up.

'I know! I couldn't hear the guy on the phone a minute ago, it was so heavy against the window.'

Taking a compact mirror from my handbag, I sat down to sort myself out. I looked like a drowned rat. And then at the thought of rats, I let out a groan and clipped the mirror shut.

'We've got rats,' I said. 'In the house. Can you believe it? On top of everything else.'

Thalia put a hand to her chest. 'That's horrendous! How do you know? Did you see one?'

'No, I heard scratchy noises, and then saw some droppings in the airing cupboard.'

'Jesus, Julia, you need to sort that out straight away. Revolting.'

'So vile – Tom's buying some traps today.'

'You need to get a man in. A pest control man. My mum had rats, and they're too clever for traps. They avoid them. Seriously, Julia. You need to get it sorted.'

'I know,' I said, gritting my teeth. More things to contend with. I picked up the pile of worksheets that been dumped in my in-tray and started to sort them out – although it was a tedious job, I welcomed the distraction. Soon my mind was filled with plumbing jobs, working hours and rates of pay, and that was fine by me.

Chapter Thirty

Tom spent the evening laying rat traps in the house and garden, He seemed to enjoy it – he was excited about catching one. I told him we needed to get a pest controller in, but he shook his head. 'Nah, I'll catch the bastards,' he said, as he washed his hands at the kitchen sink. 'I've put a little poison down on the floor in the airing cupboard too, so be careful not to touch it.'

Oh, how pleasant. Poison amongst the freshly washed clothes.'

'It's not on the clothes, it's on the floor,' he said with a frown.

Sometimes I wished he had a better sense of humour. 'OK, OK, I was only kidding.' I flicked him with a tea-towel. 'Are you done now, anyway? I'm going to watch the telly.'

'Yeah, yeah,' he said. 'I'll be through in a minute. Just need to send a few texts. You go.'

By nine o'clock that night, I was exhausted. I lay on the sofa, my head on a cushion watching Love Island, and Tom sat in one of the chairs with his legs stretched out, flicking through his phone. With the lamps on and a few candles lit, the living room seemed more cheerful.

My phone pinged, and I looked down at the screen. It was a text from Olivia, Josephine's daughter, letting me know about the next novel we were going to read at book club. I replied, thanking her – I didn't agree with Lizzie; she wasn't a cold person, I liked her. Then I remembered how she'd made a dig at her mum when we sat in Lizzie's kitchen; it seemed Josephine's gambling problem affected their relationship. It was a shame. I was lucky to have a good relationship with my mum.

I was about to get up and make a cup of chamomile tea before going to bed, when my phone rang. It was Mum.

'That's funny, I was just thinking about you. Did you have a nice time at Aunty Diana's? Is Everything alright?'

'No, it's not,' she sobbed down the phone. 'Your father's had another seizure; the paramedics are here and just about to take him into hospital.'

'A seizure? What happened?' I sat up and pulled my fingers through my hair. The consultant had said Dad was doing well, this couldn't be happening again. Tom tilted his head enquiringly.

'He complained he didn't feel well, and then after we'd gone upstairs, he started twitching and then thrashing around really violently. Oh, Julia, it was awful. He fell and cracked his head on the sink, and he bit his tongue and there's blood everywhere.'

'I'm coming over,' I said, standing up and fetching my shoes from the hallway.

'No, meet me at the hospital, the Royal Infirmary. The paramedics are about to put him in the ambulance.' She hesitated for a couple of seconds. 'Oh, they're needing to speak to me, I have to go.'

'OK, I'll see you there, don't worry Mum, it'll all be alright,' I said, but not really believing it myself. I pulled on my shoes while telling Tom what had happened. 'I'll go and be with her, if you stay here with the kids?'

'Of course, ring and let me know what's going on, won't you?' He stood up and rubbed my arm. 'Don't rush, I don't want you crashing. It'll take the ambulance longer to get there from Clevedon, so drive slowly, OK?'

'OK, OK.' I pulled on my coat and headed for the front door. But then out of the corner of my eye, a dark shape darted across the tiles and into the living room. I scrunched my eyes and turned my head away. *There's nothing there. Nothing there.* I refused to believe I'd seen anything. I had no time for rats or ghosts or any imaginings. With my heart thumping hard in my chest, I stepped out of the house. I needed to get to the hospital.

*

While Dad went for a scan, Mum and I were sent back to the waiting room. The strip lights were overly bright, and the hard plastic chairs, so uncomfortable. My tatty jogging bottoms and faded white trainers were so scruffy – I must have looked a right state, but there'd been no time to change out of my 'bumming around the house' clothes.

After what seemed like ages, the doctor called us into his room. 'So, we'll need to do further tests to find out why your husband had another seizure, but in the meantime, he's stable. He did have significant injury to his head after cracking it, and to his tongue, so we've patched him up and taken him along to the ward. We've given him some sedatives, so he won't be very communicative now I'm afraid, so it's better if you come and see him tomorrow.'

Mum's bottom lip trembled, and her breath was shaky. I took her hand and squeezed. 'He's in the best place, Mum. I'm sure he'll be fine.'

'We'll know more over the next couple of days, but you really shouldn't worry,' said the doctor. 'Now, I suggest you go home – that's the best thing you can do right now. Your husband is stable, and nothing bad is going to happen between now and tomorrow morning.' He smiled, and although I knew he was trying to make us feel better, it didn't really work.

'Thank you,' I said. 'What time can we come tomorrow morning?'

'Around eleven o'clock,' he said. 'Do you have any more questions? If not, I must get on.'

'No, no thank you. You get on, doctor, you must be very busy,' said Mum.

I linked my arm through Mum's and led her out of the hospital. It suddenly occurred to me that she'd gone with Dad in the ambulance and didn't have her car. 'Come home with me, Mum,' I said. 'It'll save you getting a taxi, and then tomorrow, after we've visited Dad, I'll drive you back to your place.'

She nodded, and in a daze, she allowed me to lead her towards the car park. It was now half past one in the morning, and we were both shattered. As I turned the ignition, my eyes itched with tiredness. Mum leant her head against the window. 'Let's get home,' I said.

*

After we'd got back from hospital, Mum slept in Isla's room, and I'd carried Isla into bed with me and Tom. She was delighted to wake up that morning, lying between us. It didn't take her long to wiggle out from underneath the duvet though, saying we were too hot and sweaty to share a bed with. She skipped out of the room as I pulled back the curtains, it was a dull morning, and the grey clouds hung heavy in the sky. Tom sat up, and I told him about what happened at hospital.

After a while, I went down to the kitchen to make sure Alex wasn't eating too much sugary cereal, and Isla was actually eating something, even if it was just a yogurt or piece of dry toast. She wasn't a great one for early morning breakfasts. Tom had followed me down, and he filled the kettle with water. 'I texted Lizzie, asking if she'd pick up Isla from school again,' he said. 'I'll go and collect her later, like we did yesterday. I thought you'd want to spend time with your dad.'

I shot him a look. 'You should have asked me first. Isla can come with me to visit him; he'd like to see her.'

'OK. It was just an idea. You better tell her not to bother then. Or shall I text her?'

'I will,' I said firmly. I snatched up the cereal box and folded over the plastic bag inside. 'Alex, that's enough now.'

Alex poured milk over his second bowl of cereal and started to shovel large spoonfuls into his mouth. 'I'm starving,' he said.

'I'm off then,' said Tom. 'Don't forget to text Lizzie.'

My blood boiled – he was more interested in Lizzie than he was my dad. 'Aren't you going to wish us luck at the hospital? You're more interested in that bloody woman.'

Isla and Alex looked up from their food. Tom's top lip curled into a scowl. 'Seriously? I was trying to bloody help, you stupid …' He didn't finish his sentence. He turned around and strode out of the kitchen and out of the front door, slamming it hard. Alex went back to his cereal, but Isla's face crumpled.

'Are you and Daddy going to get divorced?' she said.

'No, sweetheart,' I laughed falsely. 'Adults do argue sometimes. You don't need to worry about that.'

'Don't be stupid Isla,' said Alex.

'Alex, don't call her stupid,' I said.

'Dad called you stupid, though,' he replied as he scooped up the last bit of milk out of his bowl.

I chose to ignore him, not quite sure what to say. 'Go and get washed and dressed if you've finished, Isla,' I said, as she piled up her crusts like building bricks. She slipped off her chair and ran up the stairs, Alex followed soon after. With an ache in the pit of my stomach, I picked up their discarded plates and bowls and put them in the dishwasher. Then I sat at the table with my cup of tea and started to text Lizzie.

NO NEED TO PICK ISLA UP. I'LL FETCH HER.

I sipped my drink, and my phone pinged a few minutes later.

TOM SAID YOU'RE GOING TO HOSPITAL! HOPE ALL OK.

I sent a thumbs up emoji, and put my phone back on the table, and then within seconds, it pinged again.

TOM LEFT HIS HAT HERE YESTERDAY. SHALL I MESSAGE HIM DIRECTLY ABOUT IT? HE'S WELCOME TO COME OVER LATER TO GET IT.

I stared at the message in disbelief. Was she serious? Were her and Tom so friendly, she saw that as a sensible option, instead of giving me the hat at school? More to the point, did she honestly think I was interested in a bloody hat, when my father lay in hospital? I fired off a reply without thinking.

SINCE WHEN HAVE YOU TWO BEEN BEST BUDDIES?

My thumb hovered over the keys. Should I send it? I decided to put an exclamation mark after – that way it might seem light-hearted, but it would still get the point across. I pressed send.

By the time I'd taken Mum a cup of tea, showered and dressed, Lizzie still hadn't replied.

Chapter Thirty-One

As I walked Isla to school, I rang my boss and explained everything. He said I could take the day off in lieu. Then I texted Thalia, telling her what had happened. By the time I got into the playground, most children had gone into the classroom, and only a few parents were milling around. I gave Isla a kiss and she ran in, past the teaching assistant who held the door open.

'Oh, Mrs Harker?' she said. 'Wilf's mum asked me to give this to you.'

I reached out and took Tom's hat from her. It looked scruffier and dirtier in the teaching assistant's pale white hand, and I wondered why so much attention was being given to such an ugly-looking woolly beanie.

'Thank you,' I said before turning and walking away. A heavy weight pressed inside my head. Perhaps I shouldn't have sent the text. I should have asked Thalia what she thought first. I bit my bottom lip as I got into the car – well at least Lizzie knows I'm on to her now. I shrugged, pretending to myself that everything would be OK.

*

Mum and I spent the morning with Dad. He looked a little better than yesterday, but he was still very tired, and his tongue was so swollen and sore, he couldn't speak without being in pain. Mum held his hand tightly, and chatted cheerfully to him, although I knew it was all bravado. We were told by a nurse that he would be in hospital for at least a few more days.

I drove Mum back to Clevedon at lunchtime, leaving Dad to rest. We agreed we'd stagger the visiting – I'd go in with Isla and Alex after school, and she'd go early evening. I got home at around half past one, and although I'd not had much breakfast, I wasn't that hungry. I settled for a couple crackers and some cheese, and yet another cup of tea. I stared into space, automatically putting the food into my mouth, but not really tasting it. I was surprised to hear the front door open, and Tom came striding into the kitchen, aggressive as a thunderstorm. 'Lizzie told me about the text you sent her. Why did you do that? I can't believe it. She's really upset. So stupid.'

I sat upright in my chair and glared at him. *How dare he?* 'I'm stupid? She's been itching to get her claws into you for weeks now, and you're too dumb to see it.'

'She's a flirtatious person, she doesn't mean anything by it. Are you going to apologise to her?' He stood by my chair; his shoulders stooped to get his face closer to mine.

'No. She needed to be told. Anyway, it wasn't such a big deal. Aren't you going to ask about my dad? And why are you home?'

'How's your dad?' he said, lowering his voice and sitting in the chair opposite.

I sunk back into my seat, and told him about my visit to the hospital. My stomach churned; the smell of the cheese made me feel sick. I pushed the plate to the middle of the table, no longer hungry. 'So, why are you home?' I said.

'To check the rat traps,' he said. 'And I thought you'd be here, so I wanted to talk about the text you sent. Seriously, Julia, this jealousy has got to stop. If anything, it's going to drive me into having an affair.'

'Oh, well, that's nice to hear. My dad's lying in hospital, and now you're threatening to have an affair.' My nerves jangled; I couldn't believe what he said.

'Look, Julia, I'm not threatening to have an affair, but you're so wired. You're showing the same signs as before; imagining things that just aren't there. You need to go to the doctors and get back on medication.'

'That's what Thalia said. Look, there's so much going on at the moment; it's no wonder I'm stressed. I'll think about it, OK? Now go and check those rat traps. I could hear more scraping sounds upstairs when I came into the house.'

I followed him up the stairs, to check the trap in the airing cupboard. He pulled open the door and knelt on the floor, shining his phone torch under the shelves. I leant in, peering over the top of his head. 'Anything?'

'No. More droppings though. I think they're getting in through that hole in the skirting board. I'll block it up this evening.'

'I stepped back to let him stand, and our eyes met. 'We're going to be OK, aren't we?'

He rubbed the side of his head and sighed. 'I hope so, Julia.' He fiddled with his phone and turned off the torch, and as he was going to say something else, there was a knock on the door.

'Who's that?' I ran down the stairs. Through the glass panel, I could see a figure of a woman. I opened up and standing there in a smart trouser suit and crisp white blouse, was Josephine Debonair.

'May I come in?' she said. Her face was pale, and her eyes were darker than usual – the lightness gone.

She was the last person I wanted to see, but I opened the door wider and smiled. 'Yes, of course, come in, come into the kitchen.' I stepped back to let her pass, and then shouted up the stairs. 'Tom, Mrs Debonair is here.'

As I led Josephine through the house, Tom came down the stairs. 'Hello, Mrs Debonair.' He followed us into the kitchen, and I pulled out a chair for her.

'Call me Josephine, please,' she said.

'Tea?'

'No, I won't be long, and I don't want to disturb you. I came to ask if Roger has been keeping to his court order?'

'I think so,' said Tom, leaning against the worktop. 'We haven't seen him. Well, I haven't.'

'No, I haven't either,' I said.

Josephine nodded. 'Good. The thing is, he's disappeared. The hostel say they haven't seen him for a few days now. I'm worried.' Her right hand lay on the table, and she moved her fingertips back and forth, obsessively rubbing the wood.

I reached my hand across the table and took hers. 'I'm sure he's OK. He's probably gone away for a break somewhere.'

'No. He never goes away. He likes routine. He's missed his therapist's appointment too.'

I sat back and sighed. To be honest, I wasn't the slightest bit interested in Roger North. I didn't care he'd gone missing, and if anything, the further he was away from us, the better. I think Tom thought the same. He shrugged and raised his hands in the air. 'Sorry, Josephine, we can't help you I'm afraid. But if we see or hear anything, we'll give you a call. What's your number?'

As she picked up her leather handbag and pulled out a pen and notepad, strands of her hair became loose and slipped out of the pretty pearl grip that held it in place. She wrote down her telephone number and passed it to Tom, and he thrust it into his back pocket.

As she tucked her hair behind her ear, she let out a sigh, seeming to be weighed down with misery. I couldn't understand why she bothered with Roger – he was obviously a great burden, but for some reason, she had this overwhelming sense of responsibility for him – maybe it was to do with their past. She said he'd had a bad life. I stared at her, wondering what it could have been.

Eventually, she stood and made her way along the hallway, glancing around as she went. 'You have it looking nice in here,' she said.

'Thank you,' said Tom. 'We're getting there.'

'Slowly,' I said with a faint laugh.

Josephine nodded. 'And you're happy?'

Tom and I looked at each other. As I opened the front door, I said, 'We're getting there.'

She nodded again, and as she passed the living room, I could have sworn she shivered.

Chapter Thirty-Two

After Josephine left and Tom had gone back to work, I messaged Thalia and told her about the text I'd sent to Lizzie.

OH MY GOD, JULIA. WHY DID YOU DO THAT, YOU NUTTER! WHAT DID SHE SAY?

NOTHING. SHE HASN'T REPLIED, BUT SHE TOLD TOM, AND HE'S ANGRY WITH ME AND SAID I'M GOING TO DRIVE HIM INTO HAVING AN AFFAIR.

SHIT. OH WELL, YOU'VE DONE IT NOW, NOTHING YOU CAN DO ABOUT IT. I WISH YOU'D TEXTED ME FIRST, THOUGH. HOW'S YOUR DAD?

I WISH I'D TEXTED YOU TOO, I'M GOING CRAZY, THALIA, SERIOUSLY! MY DAD'S NOT GOOD REALLY, BUT HE'S STABLE. I'M TAKING THE KIDS TO SEE HIM LATER.

SEND HIM MY LOVE. IF YOU NEED ME, LET ME KNOW. TAKE CARE – GO AND MEDITATE OR SOMETHING. I BETTER GET BACK TO WORK – SOMEONE HAS TO!

CHEEKY BITCH! CHEERS, GORGEOUS. SPEAK SOON XX

I didn't want to go back on medication, but the way things were going, it looked as if I was heading that way, so I decided to take Thalia's advice and do a bit of relaxation before picking up Isla. I chose a play list off Spotify, and I drew the bedroom curtains. My humidifier infused the air with lavender oil, and I sat on my favourite sheepskin rug with my legs crossed and closed my eyes. Taking deep breaths, I tried to imagine myself on a beach with the waves lapping the warm sand. Breathing in. Breathing out. Breathing in. Breathing out. But it was no good. My mind whirred like a kid's clockwork toy. There was too much going on. I knew the more stressed I was, the more I should try to relax, but it didn't work like that.

I tried for a little longer, watching colours and shapes playing on my closed eyelids, but it was no good. Sighing with frustration, I turned off the music. I wandered out onto the landing and pulled open the airing cupboard door to check the rat trap again – I was becoming obsessed with the bloody thing. Nothing. Nothing, except a vague smell of something putrid. I screwed up my nose. What was it? Leaning further, I squinted into the darkness of the cupboard, wondering if there was a dead rat or mouse in the corner. It seemed to be stronger right at the top of the cupboard.

There was a gap in the ceiling where the water pipes came down from the attic, and when I leant up and sniffed around the hole, the smell seemed strongest. I shut my eyes and groaned. There must be a dead rat in the attic. But that would have to wait. I had to pick up Isla and visit Dad. Sometimes there are more important things than dead rodents in the roof.

*

After I'd fetched Isla, I drove to Alex's school to pick him up, as we'd arranged. They both sat quietly – Isla on the back seat eating a packet of crisps I'd given her, and Alex in the front, with his feet up on the dashboard, scrolling through his phone. I didn't have the energy to tell him to take his feet off.

Once we reached the hospital and paid for parking, the kids followed me along the corridors until we reached Dad's ward. I pressed the buzzer and waved to a nurse through the glass door. She smiled and let us in. 'Grandad's in the second room on the left,' I said, as Alex strode ahead. Isla held back and took my hand.

Dad was sat reading a newspaper. 'Hello, you,' I said.

'Ah!' He put his paper down and gave Isla a hug. She sat on the edge of his bed and stared at him. After saying hello, Alex leant against the wall, fiddling with the sleeves of his blazer.

I sat on a chair next to the bed, and took Dad's hand, rubbing his wrinkled skin with my thumb. 'How are you feeling?'

He nodded and pointed to his mouth. 'Tongue still sore,' he said, sounding as if he had a mouthful of boiled sweets.

'Does it hurt to speak?'

He nodded again.

'Well, shall we write messages to Grandad instead?' I said to Isla, taking out a pad and a pen from my handbag. As I'd guessed, she loved that idea, and she took the pen and began writing and drawing him pictures. After a few minutes even Alex joined in. I was pleased to see Dad smiling, and while the kids were entertaining him, I wandered over to the desk to ask how he'd been getting on.

'He's been very tired.' The nurse, who was probably in his early thirties, smiled at me sympathetically. 'He'll probably be in a little longer, while we do more tests.'

'My mother's coming in later this evening, will she be able to speak to the doctor about him? She's really worried, and I'm sure she'd feel much better once she's spoken to someone before going home.'

'I'll see what I can do,' he said, writing a note.

I chatted to him for a little longer, and then joined Dad and the kids who were now playing a game of consequences. After we'd been there for a while, a woman wearing a white apron and pushing a trolley came into the room. She smiled broadly and announced it was dinner time.

'We'll leave you then, Dad,' I said. 'You don't want us watching you eat.'

He rolled his eyes and pointed at his tongue again.

'Poor you.' I caught the auxillary's attention. 'What's he ordered?' I said.

She looked at her notes, and then pulled out a bowl from her trolley and took the lid off. It was some sort of soup. 'Try and eat as much as you can, Mr McRae, I know it's painful, but you need to build up your strength.' She placed the bowl on the side table, and he frowned.

I put an arm around him and squeezed. He leaned against me, his body frail against mine. 'See you later, Dad, make sure you eat something.' He didn't sit back up, so with a heavy weight in my chest, I pulled away, kissing the top of his head. 'We love you Dad, hurry up and get better.'

He sniffed and blinked as he lay against the pillows. Isla climbed on the bed and gave him a hug, nearly spilling the soup.

Alex waved. 'See you later, Grandad, get better soon.'

As we headed for the door, Dad picked up his spoon and used it to salute us. My stomach clenched; that spoon wasn't going to be used for anything else that night – certainly not for eating soup.

*

The kids were quiet when we got back to the car. I could tell they were worried about their Grandad. 'Who wants a McDonalds?' I said, knowing full well what the answer would be.

'Me!' they both shouted.

I smiled at them in the rearview mirror and manoeuvred out of the parking space. 'Can you text Dad, Alex? Let him know what we're doing? He might want to join us if he's in town.'

I put on the radio and joined the traffic; it was busy as people were coming out of work and making their way home. It only took Tom a few seconds to reply to Alex. 'Dad said he's on a job and can't make it.'

'Oh, OK,' I said, and straight away, my mind flicked to images of him walking up Lizzie's path. In my head, she opens the door, looking beautiful.

Chapter Thirty-Three

I drove into the McDonalds car park, telling myself to get a grip. My thoughts were out of control, and I had to stop catastrophising over and over again.

'There's a space, Mummy,' said Isla, leaning forward between the two front seats and pointing at a car as it reversed out. I indicated and pulled in. The kids got out the car quickly, nothing like a burger to get them moving, and I followed behind them, locking the car door over my shoulder.

We ordered and sat down to eat. Alex put some of his fries into his burger and took a bite. 'How's school?' I said, trying to use the opportunity to have a conversation with my son.

'It's alright,' he said.

'Are you looking forward to going up to Brookmeads?' He shrugged. 'I suppose,' he said.

He clearly wasn't interested in talking about school, so I turned to Isla. 'What about you, Isla? How are you getting on?' She picked at her fries and dunked them in ketchup, not answering. 'Isla? Is everything OK?'

'Matilda Collins keeps pulling at my knickers when we get changed for P.E. I told Miss Acrington, and she told her off, but she keeps doing it. I don't like it.'

Alex sniggered. 'Don't laugh, Alex,' I said crossly. 'I'm not surprised you don't like it, darling, I'll have a word tomorrow. No one should touch you if you don't want them to, especially your private area.'

Isla nodded. 'I told her that, but she just laughed.'

I put my hand out and calmly stroked Isla's head, but all the while I seethed inside. *How dare that little brat do this to my girl? Yet another thing for me to sort out.* My head began to hurt. A dull fuzzy ache, as if it held too much toxic information.

After we'd eaten and thrown away our mess, we got back in the car and drove home. Alex went straight upstairs, and as I hung up my jacket and slipped off my shoes, I watched Isla peering into the living room. 'OK, honey?'

'Yes, just checking the dark thing isn't there. It's all clear,' she said.

I flinched – did it bother her that much? My heart sank as I decided to speak to her again about it; but maybe later. Right now, I needed to have a cup of tea, and then get rid of that dead rat in the attic, before it stunk the whole house out.

As some crazy American cartoon blared from the television, I poured hot water on my tea bag and texted Mum. She was at the hospital and waiting to speak to the doctor. She said Dad looked weak but was dozing. I sighed and sipped at my drink, comforted by the warmth as it slipped down my throat. My index finger wavered over Tom's name as I debated whether to call him and ask him where he was, but I fought against my instincts and placed the phone on the table, face down. Facebook, Instagram and WhatsApp notifications pinged, but I ignored them. I didn't want to get lost in an hour of social media scrolling.

After I'd finished my tea, I fetched a pair of rubber gloves, a bin liner, and the head torch. Upstairs, Alex's door was closed, and loud drum and bass music thudded from inside. I sniffed. I couldn't smell anything, so I pulled open the airing cupboard door, and immediately the rotten stench hit me like a powerful wave. I cringed and exclaimed before closing the door with a bang. Only one thing for it, I'd have to go up into the attic. The smell of the rubber gloves made me shudder as I pulled them on, knowing that soon I'd be picking up dead rats with them.

The bin liner hanging from my back pocket rustled against my leg as I climbed the ladder, and I remembered the last time I'd gone up was when we'd found Roger skulking around. The odour grew stronger as I scrambled onto the attic floorboards. I tried breathing through my mouth so I didn't have to smell it, but that was a mistake; I could almost taste it now.

In the faint light, I gazed across the right-hand side of the attic. The beam from my torch crept over the boxes we'd stored up there, but there was nothing rotting. Nothing dead. I stood and stooped to avoid banging my head on the joists, and then looked in the other direction. There, lying lifeless on the floor, was an ugly, grey rat, just where the roof meets the wall. I cupped my hands over my nose and mouth in revulsion. 'Ugh, God. That's disgusting.'

With clenched teeth, I stepped over and picked up the creature by the tail and dropped it into the bin bag. Were any more around? My gaze followed the stream of torchlight to where Roger North had been sleeping. A lumpy shape was there. What was it?

I peered into the darkness, squinting to see. My heart pounded as I took a few paces towards whatever it was. Please don't let it be Roger North. Not again. A thud sounded behind me; I jumped violently. Frozen to the spot, I whipped my head around – the wind must have caught the window, it was banging against the frame – it had been forced open.

Turning once again to face the thing at the end of the attic, I took a few more steps forwards. Then, with a cry of horror, I clamped my hand over my mouth. My worst fear multiplied. It *was* Roger North. But this time, he lay curled up, with his eyes wide open. The smell came from him. Congealed blood pooled on the floorboards and his mouth hung open, distorted and grotesque. A kitchen knife lay in front of him.

There was no doubt in my mind. He was dead.

Roger – 1981-1994

Chapter Thirty-Four

As the months went by, Faither thought the exorcism had worked, but all that really happened was Roger became more secretive and more careful. Roger hadn't changed at all, but he kept his head down and avoided Faither as much as possible. It was the only way he coped.

Josephine's life was difficult too; as she got older, she wasn't allowed to go out with her friends to parties or nightclubs. Any boys she met were soon put off when they met Faither. However, Roger knew she met boyfriends in secret. He'd followed her into the woods once, but he didn't tell Faither - Josephine gave him a bag of cola cubes to keep him quiet.

She told Roger that she'd leave home as soon as she was old enough. Education was her ticket out of there, and so she worked hard at school. When she was eighteen, she moved away to university in London and only came home for the odd visit at Christmas and birthdays.

Although very bright, Roger struggled to do well at school. He lost himself in music, cataloguing his collections (which became more sophisticated as he got older) and studying nature and wildlife. He found it easier to take part in activities that didn't involve other people.

When he reached sixteen and finished school, Roger wanted to do a diploma in something like animal welfare or tree surgery. but instead, Faither forced him to do an OND in book-keeping.

At the technical college, Roger tried to fit in with the other students by sitting with them at break times and lunches. But he found it hard – his brain often hurt afterwards, and then he was too muggy-headed and confused to concentrate in lessons. Faither wasn't happy when he learnt about it at parent's evening. As a punishment, he made Roger study in his bedroom every night.

The one thing Roger did like about college, was Sue. Sue was on the same course, and he tried to sit as close as he could, so he could watch her. This was another reason he didn't do very well – she completely distracted him. Every night, after dinner and after he'd done his chores, Faither sent him upstairs to work, but Roger spent most of his time lying on his bed imagining scenarios of himself and Sue. He'd imagine her next to him; dream that she came to his room every night. He fell in love with her – her soft skin as white as a seashell, the freckles on her nose and the curves of her hips.

Sue wasn't one of the popular girls. Like Roger, she seemed to exist on the outside of social groups – probably one of the reasons why he liked her. She wasn't beautiful and didn't have a lithe body and a trendy haircut like a lot of the girls. She was short and a little rounded, but she had a cute face and a pixie haircut that Roger thought was so endearing it made his heart hurt.

One day, on his walk home, he saw Sue coming out of the corner shop with a bag of Monster Munch. He followed her for a little way, and then when she crossed the road, she turned her head and saw him. He waved and ran to catch her up.

'Hi, Sue.'

'Hi, Roger. How's it going?'

'Alright. How's you?'

'Starving. I forgot to take my lunch in today, but luckily Miss Bakari gave me one of her sandwiches.'

'I'd have shared my lunch with you, you should've come to find me,' said Roger.

Sue looked puzzled; then she smiled. 'Thanks for the offer but if Miss Bakari hadn't given me hers, I could have asked one of the girls in my tutor group. Besides, I had drama club, so had to eat fast anyway.'

She goes to drama club? Roger wondered whether he should join too, except that would involve going on stage and letting everyone stare at him, and he didn't think he'd like that. Maybe he could help backstage?

They crossed the road together and Sue opened her crisp packet and offered one to Roger. He went all hot; his hands trembling as he worried his fingernails might be dirty. She had to stop and hold the packet steady while he clumsily pulled out one of the monster's claws. 'Thanks,' he said, before licking off the pickled onion flavour and then putting it into his mouth. Sue did the same, and Roger smiled. 'They make your tongue go fizzy, don't they?'

She smiled back and nodded, and they carried walking together in companionable silence. After a few moments, Sue said: 'I'm moving away soon. After I finish college, Mum and Dad want to move to Wales. They've bought an old farm there and they're going to turn it into a bed and breakfast.' She said it as a matter of fact, not seeming to have an opinion.

Roger, on the other hand, felt as if someone had smashed a fist into his chest. He stopped walking and stared at her. 'When? When exactly are you going?'

Sue stopped too, and tipped her head to the side, surprised at his reaction. 'After the exams.'

'Do you want to go?' he said. 'Do you have to go?'

She laughed. 'I'm not going to stay here by myself, am I?'

Roger flinched at her scornful remark, but Sue didn't notice.

'I really don't mind going. Dad said I can be in charge of the accounts. It's in the middle of nowhere though, so I might get a bit bored. But Mum said she'd pay for me to have driving lessons. I might do another course too. I thought about doing the next level up – the HND.'

Roger's anger was as sharp as a dagger. He couldn't bear to look at her. How could she? Swallowing the painful lump in his throat, he stormed across the road, too full of rage to think of anything to say. Sue shouted after him. 'Roger? What's the matter? Roger?'

Roger couldn't even remember walking home, but when he reached the front door, he sank onto the doorstep and put his head in his hands. She was leaving him. He couldn't bear it. What had he done to make her want to leave? Hot tears rolled down his cheeks. His mother must have heard him sobbing because she opened the front door and peered out. 'Roger? What on earth is the matter?'

'Nothing. You wouldn't understand.' He took hold of the railings and hauled himself up, rubbing the back of his hand across his nose.

'You're not getting into one of your states again, are you?' she said. 'Faither will have to try and speak to the pastor about this. It's getting too often.'

'Please don't tell him. I'm OK, I just don't feel well. Please leave me alone, Mum.' Roger tried to swallow and calm his breathing. He didn't want his mum to involve Faither and the church. He had to stay calm until he got to the safety of his bedroom. He gave a false smile, one that didn't reach his eyes, and then walked up the stairs clenching his fists.

All the while his mind raced with angry thoughts. He'd never forgive Sue.

NEVER.

Chapter Thirty-Five

Sue did move to Wales after she'd finished her course, and Roger was heartbroken. He didn't feel happy again until he left college and started work at Millwood Accountancy as a clerk. It only took him a few days before he fell for a secretary called Kay. She wasn't like Sue. She was tall and had long, curly hair that bounced as she walked.

Unfortunately for Roger, his time at the company was short-lived. He quite enjoyed the routine and the work, but things went wrong when Kay found out that Roger liked her. It didn't take her long to work it out, because he was always staring at her, and would blush every time she spoke to him. Kay was cruel, and he sometimes overheard her bitching about him when she was in the kitchen with her friend. One day after work, he walked behind them as they headed towards Temple Meads railway station. He heard their whole conversation.

'Bloody hell, Carys, I wouldn't touch him with a barge pole. He gives me the creeps.'

'And me. He's so ugly too, can you imagine that red face peering down to kiss you?'

They linked arms and sniggered. Roger felt as if a knife had slashed his heart. His temper boiled up so high, he charged after them and rammed into the back of Kay, sending her flying to the ground. She let out a yell as her knees smacked onto the pavement, making gaping holes in her black tights. Roger stood back. 'You bloody bitches,' he said.

Carys bent down and put her arm around her friend. Kay was sobbing; her hands and knees bloodied. Roger baulked at the sight of the red fluid oozing from her pale skin. 'You bastard!' yelled Kay. 'I'll report you to Mr Millwood.'

Carys glared at him. 'Fuck off, you weirdo. Leave us alone.'

Roger backed away, and as he turned to run, he yelled, 'You deserved it!'

He was sacked the next day.

After, he got a job at a garden centre, and it suited him well. He enjoyed the routine of watering and tending to the plants in the morning. Occasionally he would talk to the customers and advise them on what type of plant to buy. Sometimes he stocked the shelves in the shop and sometimes he placed orders from the office. He never worked on the tills, but he didn't want to, anyway.

When Roger was 29 in the year of 1993, his mother, Moira, died after a long and painful bout of breast cancer. It was a tough time for him. He missed her, especially because it meant Faither's focus was entirely on him; he was always watching, waiting for Roger to make a mistake.

After he'd retired from teaching, Faither spent most of his time at church or working on church business. Roger found it easier not to talk to him, and quite often, they'd go the whole week without speaking.

Roger still went to church most Sundays, and on a glorious day in September, when the church was full of people who didn't have anything better to do while the sun shone, he saw Sue.

He wasn't sure if it was her at first. He sat in his usual seat at the back. A few rows in front of him were two women, one had a short pixie haircut. He squinted, trying to see if he could work out if it was her or not. It certainly looked like her – the shape of her head, the curve of her shoulders. It was over ten years since he last saw her though – would she look the same?

It wasn't until the end of the service and people were turning to shake hands and wishing each other the joy of God, that he saw her face. His heart leapt. She looked exactly the same. Well, maybe not exactly – she was older, of course, and she had put on a little weight around the jawline, but overall, she looked the same. Roger's stomach was in knots, and as soon as people stood to leave, he leapt up and hurried outside. He didn't want to be distracted by anyone else, so he moved away from the door and leant against the archway leading to the main road.

Pleased to get out of the cold church and into the warmth of the day, most people congregated by the porch. Some walked out onto the street, greeting Roger as they passed by, and others went around the church to go into the garden where the ladies were serving morning coffee. Almost trembling with excitement, Roger waited to see which way Sue would go. His mind was full of questions. Who was she with? Why was she back in Bristol? Why was she at his church? She'd never come to church when she was younger.

Sue stepped out and shook hands with the Pastor, Mr Harris and Faither who was now an Elder. She spoke with them for a moment, and then she and her companion (an elderly lady who Roger hadn't seen before) were ushered by two regular members towards the garden.

Roger waited for everyone to disappear from the front of the church, then he rushed along the side path, catching his T-shirt on a rambling rose as he entered the garden. He tugged the stem away and looked around. Where was she? As he took a few steps in, he felt a tap on his shoulder.

'It is you, isn't it? Roger?'

Roger spun around. His mouth agape. He could feel blood rushing to his head, and he knew his red face would be turning even more scarlet. Sue laughed. 'How are you?'

'Sue!' he said, pretending it was the first time he'd seen her. 'What are you doing here?'

'I'm back in Bristol now,' she said. 'I came back about six months ago. My dad died and Mum and I decided we didn't want to be stuck out in the middle of nowhere anymore. My gran needs looking after too.' She pointed to the elderly lady sitting on a wooden bench, holding a cup and saucer, and talking to one of the Elders. Her head shook a little, and Roger guessed she had Parkinson's or something similar.

'Well, that's great news.' he said. 'Where are you working? And where do you live?'

'I'm working for JG Ballards Accountancy in Clifton. We're living in Broadmead, with Gran. What about you?'

'I'm still in Larkcombe with Faither,' Roger nodded his head in the direction of his father. 'My mum died a while back of breast cancer.'

'Oh, I'm so sorry,' said Sue, looking genuinely sad.

'It's OK. We're OK. As for work, I'm at Drewmore Garden Centre. I've been there for about ten years now. It's alright. I quite like it.'

Sue nodded. 'Well, it's lovely seeing you again,' she said. 'I better go and check on Gran. Will you be coming next week?'

Roger felt a pang of disappointment, as she took a few steps away. 'Yes, probably,' he said. 'Will you come again?'

'I think so, Gran seems to have enjoyed herself. She used to go to the church near her house, but she doesn't like the new vicar. She seems happy here though. I expect we'll come back.'

'Good,' he said. 'Good.'

*

Roger spent that evening in his room, lying on his bed thinking of Sue. She hadn't changed one bit. He imagined her lying with him, and he closed his eyes and unzipped his trousers. Faither was downstairs and would often barge into his bedroom without knocking, so Roger knew he had to listen out in case he came up the stairs. Faither wouldn't approve. It didn't take long, and after he'd finished, he pulled a tissue from the coloured box on his bedside table and cleaned himself up.

He lay back content, images of Sue flashing in his mind. The sound of music rose through the floorboards. It was worship music. Faither would be doing some church administration in the living room – he always did that on Sunday evenings. Roger allowed the well-known tunes to weave into his mind, and he imagined Sue dancing to them – her smile and her hips swaying. He closed his eyes and sighed, before drifting into a happy sleep.

Chapter Thirty-Six

Roger had worked himself up so much that when the next Sunday came, he was almost shaking with anticipation. Sue waved and smiled at him as she entered the church, and he spent the whole service watching her shoulders and the back of her head. She wore a pretty russet coloured blouse, and Roger passed the time by counting the leaves that were printed on it.

The smile she'd given him had boosted his confidence, and he decided he'd ask her out when they were having coffee. The weather had changed since the week before. There was a biting wind and it was too cold to go out in the garden, so the ladies had set up a table at the back of the church.

After the service, he hurried to the table and picked up two cups of tea. One for Sue and one for her Gran. He wanted to make a good impression. Once he'd handed them their drinks and made polite conversation, he managed to get Sue on her own for a few minutes.

'Would you like to come out to the cinema one night, Sue?'

Sue didn't answer straight away. His blood began to rise, and his skin turned hot, but before he made a fool of himself, she patted him on the arm, and said, 'Yes, I'd love to.'

*

When the big night arrived, Roger stood in front of the mirror on the landing and inspected his reflection. He'd bought a new shirt for the occasion – a blue and white check with a button-down collar, and he'd polished his shoes. He couldn't decide what trousers to wear. Should he go casual and wear jeans? Or should he make more of an effort? In the end, he plumped for a pair of navy cotton trousers, they went nicely with the shirt. He ran downstairs and picked up his wallet and keys from the dresser in the hallway.

Faither stepped out of the living room, just as Roger put his hand on the front door. 'Off out?' he said, with a cigarette dangling from his lips. 'Where are you going?'

'I'm taking Sue to the cinema,' said Roger.

Faither nodded. 'No girls back in the bedroom though,' he said. 'Remember this is a Christian house.'

Roger raised his eyebrows and nearly said something, but he bit his tongue. Turning and opening the door, he left Faither on the doormat, watching him walk away. Roger muttered to himself as he walked towards the bus stop… *I'm bloody 29! Stupid old bastard.*

On the number 8 bus into town, he practised different ways of smiling for when he met Sue. The woman opposite kept glancing up and staring, so he turned towards the window instead, gazing at his distorted reflection grinning back.

He'd agreed to meet Sue outside the Odeon, and when he arrived, she stood on the steps looking at the posters. He was pleased; she must really like him if she was already there waiting. He ended up smiling naturally, forgetting all his practised grins.

He waved as he drew closer. 'Hi Sue.'

'Hiya, I've bought us some popcorn from Woolworths, It's cheaper than the cinema's.' She held up a pack of Butterkist toffee-flavoured popcorn. Roger crumpled like a deflated balloon. He wanted salted popcorn and enjoyed eating it out of the cardboard boxes – it tasted better. It was such a disappointment for him, but Sue beamed, so he decided not to say anything. He didn't want her to get upset and storm off, leaving him there on his own. Instead, he went through the motions and put his arm through hers, thanking her for bringing the popcorn. He paid for the tickets and bought them both a large coke each, and his heart swelled with pride as she said how gentlemanly he was.

Jurassic Park was still showing, and Roger was delighted that she was just as keen to see it again, even though they'd both seen it when it first came out. He really couldn't believe he'd found someone at last who liked the same things as he did. His stomach bubbled with excitement as he looked sideways at her, in between watching the film. Every time he turned his head, she squeezed his hand.

That day had been one of Roger's favourite ever days. They'd gone to McDonald's afterwards and both had a quarter pounder with cheese, and he'd treated her to a large Triple Thick Milkshake even though he thought it was a bit expensive at £1.14.

They walked hand in hand to the bus stop, and although he wanted to accompany her back home, she said there was no need, and his heart fell. Once she was on the bus, she'd waved down at him from the grimy window, and as it pulled away from the kerb, he ran along beside it, looking up and blowing her kisses. She laughed and waved back, and he tried to tell himself that she really did like him.

*

As the months went on, Roger and Sue got closer, even though he nearly blew it countless times. Despite telling him repeatedly that she loved him, he still couldn't get it out of his head that she would leave him.

Sue's mother and grandma didn't mind Roger staying overnight, 'as long as they were discreet' but Faither still wouldn't allow Sue to stay. However, she often came over for their evening meal. One cold January evening, Sue came to make Roger and Faither a stew with dumplings. Faither approved – it was the kind of meal Moira would've made. Sue spent quite a while preparing it, and she laid the table with a pretty white lace cloth she'd found in the drawer and had also baked some small wholemeal rolls for mopping up the gravy.

Roger drew his chair up to the table and rubbed his hands together in glee. 'I've been looking forward to this all day,' he said.

Faither sat at the table. He ran a finger across the cloth and looked up at Sue with a frown. 'We normally save this cloth for special occasions only, Susan.'

Sue, who was ladling stew into bowls, stopped midway, and her face fell. 'Oh, I'm so sorry, William. I didn't realise. Shall I take it off?'

Roger glared at his father. 'No,' he said. 'It's absolutely fine. Leave it, Faither. Sue's gone to a lot of trouble.'

Faither rolled his eyes but didn't pursue the matter. Instead, he put his hands together to say a prayer. Sue placed the ladle into the pot, and sat down, clasping her hands together too, as did Roger.

Faither cleared his throat, and started to speak in a loud, authoritative voice. 'My Lord, thank you for the day you have given us, and for the delicious food that is on our table. Please bless my friends at church and everyone around me. May Roger be blessed with humility and a sense of respect, and please give Susan the courtesy she needs to make her way through life. Amen.'

Roger banged his hand on the table, and Sue jumped. 'That's it,' he yelled as he stood up. 'Get out of the kitchen. You don't deserve Sue's meal.'

Faither didn't open his eyes and kept his hands together.

'It's OK, Roger, it really is,' said Sue in a panicked voice. 'Come on, let's eat.' She placed a bowl in front of him. 'Please let's not spoil the meal.' She squeezed his hand in the way she'd always done, and Roger shut his eyes and tried to think of nice things.

Sue put Faither's meal in front of him, and he picked up his fork and started to tuck in, as if nothing had happened. They ate in silence for a few minutes. The only sound was the tinkling of cutlery against crockery. After a few moments, Faither pointed his knife at Sue. 'Not a bad meal, my girl.'

'Thank you.' Sue brightened, and she patted Roger's knee under the table. Roger refused to acknowledge Faither's comment, instead he chose to stare at the food he ate.

As Faither tore a piece from his roll and started to wipe it around his bowl, he spoke again. 'Will you be making anything for the church's Winter Supper, Susan? Remember the Pastor asked all the women to make something. It's on Saturday evening.'

'Yes, of course,' said Sue, holding her knife and fork tightly. 'I thought I'd make some of those sugar-free fruit slices – you know, the ones Jamie Scott went on about a few weeks ago during coffee time.'

'Ah, yes. Most delicious,' said Faither, nodding with approval.

Roger's fork dropped from his hand. 'Why are you making those?'

'Because people liked them,' said Sue in surprise. 'And they're easy to make – I'm busy at work Roger, so I need something quick to bake.'

Roger pushed back his chair and stood up, leaning on the table with both hands, glaring at Sue. 'Oh, so it's nothing to do with Jamie Scott liking them then?' He knew he was raging It was Faither's fault for setting him on edge to start with, but he couldn't stop himself. The thought of that Scott bloke making moves on his girlfriend drove him crazy. He'd seen the way he looked at her, and Roger had tried to control himself, but with her mentioning his name tonight, she'd gone too far. He tried to keep his shaking hands still. Both Sue and Faither were staring at him in shock.

Sue placed down her knife and fork and dabbed her mouth on a cheap, white serviette. 'I suggest you take a long, hard look at yourself, Roger. Think about how you're behaving.' Although her cheeks had coloured, she spoke in a calm tone. Rising from the table, and without acknowledging either man, she left the room and left the house, silently closing the door.

Chapter Thirty-Seven

Despite Roger's silly tempers, Sue remained in love with him and took everything in her stride. Yes, he had faults, he could be possessive, jealous, and over emotional, but he had good points too. He was often very thoughtful – he'd bought her some Anais Anais perfume as a surprise a few months before; remembering it was her favourite. He was also faithful; she never went into work complaining he'd been flirting at a party or such like. Some of her colleagues did, and she'd hate that. He was kind and said the sweetest of things. She had to accept it; she wasn't getting any younger. If she wanted children, she'd left it a bit late to meet anyone else. Roger was the man for her, and she was resigned to the fact that his volatile nature would always be there between them, like a delicate porcelain vase she mustn't upset.

*

Two years later, Faither became seriously ill with Creutzfeldt-Jakob disease – Mad Cow's Disease, as people called it. It scared the life out of Roger; not just because the disease was so awful, but also because Faither's death was imminent. Sue was sure it was Roger's fear of being left alone that made him propose to her one evening as they sat in a quiet corner of Pizza Hut. She'd accepted immediately, although some of the reason was because she felt sorry for him.

Roger slipped the ring onto her finger; it was a perfect fit. She grinned at him as they held hands across the table. 'I wasn't expecting that,' said Sue. She was happy, but half wished he'd proposed somewhere a little more romantic. She put her hand to his face and pinched his cheek with affection. 'You're so sweet, Roger.'

'I thought it was a good time to do it,' he said as they both began eating again. 'I know you like pizzas, and I wanted to ask you before Faither becomes too ill and … you know. I don't want to be left on my own when that happens.'

'Oh,' she said, feeling her cheeks burn. 'But Roger, you don't even like Faither. You're always saying how much he ruins your life.' She took hold of his hand which he'd formed into a tight fist on top of the table. Her blue-stone engagement ring looking out of place on her finger, like a new child in a classroom.

'But when he's gone, I'll be the only one left.' He sniffed and prodded his fork into a cherry tomato from the salad bowl sitting between them.

Sue frowned. 'No, you won't. What about Josie?'

'She doesn't live at Catcher House. She's not a North anymore, is she? She's a Debonair.'

'Oh, well, that's stupid. She's still your family.'

He shot her a look and took his hand away from hers. 'She never bloody visits,' he said sulkily, looking into his coke glass and stirring the ice around with a plastic straw. 'She hates Faither more than I do. When I rang and told her that he was ill, she said he deserved it. And maybe he does, Sue? Maybe it's God's way of punishing him for all the nasty things he's done.' He stopped to think for a minute. 'But I don't think anyone deserves to get that Mad Cow Disease he's got, do they?'

'No. They don't,' said Sue, bending her head. 'But *you* can still see Josie though. Visit London and meet her new husband. We could both go; it'll be a little trip away. Why don't you ask her?' Sue looked up, her eyes shone, and she shuffled excitedly in her seat. 'We could do all the sights; Buckingham Palace, Tower of London, Madame Tussauds…'

Roger sniffed and rubbed his nose with the back of his hand. 'Maybe,' he said. 'She probably won't want us to come though. She didn't even invite us to her and Colin's wedding. Never even met the bloke.'

'Don't be so stupid, Roger, she'll love to see you. She's your sister.'

Roger shot her a look. 'Right, I'm going home.'

Sue blinked, and to her surprise, he stood up, scraping his chair across the floor and chucking his serviette onto his plate of half-eaten food.

'What? Why? What's wrong? You haven't finished your meal' She reached out, grasping for his hand with her fingers, but he shook her off.

'Think about it, Sue. Think how you speak sometimes. You need to consider your words more carefully.' He put his mouth right up against her ear and whispered, 'Twice you said it. If I'm that bloody stupid, maybe you shouldn't have agreed to marry me.'

He stood up straight and stormed out of the restaurant, leaving her with tears welling up in her eyes, twisting the ring on her finger. She stared at the pizza crusts piled up on the side of her plate and pushed it into the middle of the table. Gulping down the remains of her glass of wine, she raised her hand and ushered the waiter over. 'Another glass of white please,' she said. 'A large one.'

*

When Roger got back home, he went straight to his bedroom, like a teenage boy with secrets. Faither was in the kitchen, banging pans around, and there was a smash as if he'd dropped a plate or something. He should really go downstairs and help him, but Roger couldn't face it. Instead, he threw himself onto the bed and closed his eyes, thinking about Sue and how much he loved her. He couldn't bear it if she left him. Did she really think he was stupid? Did she prefer Jamie Scott? She never mentioned him in conversation, but he watched her at church and although she didn't really talk much to Jamie, he noticed her looking at him sometimes. And Jamie had been ogling her for weeks – it took all of Roger's willpower not to go up to the man and thump him. But he knew if he did that, Sue would definitely leave him. So, whenever he felt his emotions getting the better of him, Roger would take himself to the church toilets. He'd lock himself in a cubicle and sit on the loo seat, rolled up bits of toilet paper in his hand and squeezing them as if they were pieces of Jamie's body.

Roger opened his eyes and tried to quell the thoughts of Jamie Scott. At least she was wearing the engagement ring he'd bought her now – surely that accounted for something? Once his breathing was steady and his heart no longer strained to burst, he went downstairs to tell his Faither the good news about the engagement. As he went into the kitchen, Faither was huddled over the table, trying to raise a soup spoon to his mouth, but failing. The steaming liquid split onto the table and down his shirt. Roger leant against the doorframe. 'Sue and I are getting married.'

Faither didn't look up. He didn't even acknowledge Roger. He lay the spoon on the table. His shoulders were hunched, and his hands shaking. Then, with a laboured breath, he stared directly at Roger, with pale watery eyes. A whining sound slipped from his lips, and with a sudden, involuntary judder, Faither tilted to the side and fell to the floor.

The soup bowl tipped and clattered against the table leg, before smashing on the terracotta tiles. The old man followed suit, with a crack to his head – a sound Roger would never forget. He twitched a few times, before his body lay motionless. With a yell, Roger rushed over. He knelt and cradled Faither's head on his lap. 'No!' he cried. 'No Faither, you're not to bloody leave me like Mum did.'

He reached out a hand and felt for a pulse. At first, he thought he could feel something, but then he realised it was his own palpitations tapping hard against his bones. There was nothing. No inhalation, no heartbeat. Faither had gone.

Julia - 2023

Chapter Thirty-Eight

Finding Roger North's body was the worst thing that had ever happened to me. As I slumped on the sofa, Tom reached out to hold my hand; I was still shaking. On the other settee sat PC Jamac and PC Hinchcliffe, both sipping mugs of tea that Tom had made. On the chair by the window, sat Josephine Debonair.

Roger North had been pronounced dead by the paramedics, but they left without their patient; the ambulance silently moving down the road like an empty funeral hearse. PC Hinchcliffe had arranged for the coroner's funeral director to collect the body, and she'd called a professional cleaning company to come and sort out the attic.

'So, can you run through everything that happened,' said PC Jamac, taking out a notebook from his protective vest. He must have been roasting because it had been a sweltering day for June. PC Hinchcliffe nodded and smiled, encouraging me to speak.

The kids sat on the floor – both listening intently. I decided not to send them upstairs, I figured it was better they knew the truth and hear it first-hand rather than a distorted version from someone at school. 'Well, over the last few days, we'd been hearing noises, and then I found rat droppings in the cupboard. Then it started to smell, so I thought one of the rats must have died after eating the poison Tom put down. I thought it was rotting up in the attic.'

'OK,' said PC Jamac. 'Carry on – I will need to know what poison you used, Tom, and where you placed it, if that's alright, but finish off your statement first please, Julia.'

Tom looked up, defensively. 'The poison? You don't think North ingested some, do you? He cut his wrists, didn't he?'

'It's procedure, Tom, nothing to worry about. Carry on, Julia.'

I picked at my nails and carried on speaking. 'So, when I got back from McDonalds with the kids, I decided to go and look in the attic. The smell … it was awful.' I gulped and caught my breath before continuing. ''I found a dead rat and put it into a bin liner.' I hesitated as I remembered that I'd dropped the bag when I saw North. I turned to Tom. 'The dead rat's still up there actually, can you get it later? I'm not going up.'

Tom nodded.

'Then I saw him lying there. Dead. Quite obviously dead, I didn't touch him. Blood was everywhere. I rushed down the ladder, screaming. Alex and Isla came to see what was wrong. I told Alex to ring Tom, and I phoned the police. That's about it.'

'What about you, Mrs Debonair? How did you find out about your brother?'

Josephine had been staring out of the window, and on hearing her name, she started. 'Tom phoned me,' she said. 'I came straight over.'

My chest tightened as I watched her. She seemed quite composed, but incredibly sad.

'We know your brother had mental health issues and saw a counsellor,' said PC Hinchcliffe. 'Had there been any changes to his state of mind over the last few weeks that may have led him to … sorry to be blunt … take his own life?'

Josephine took a deep breath. 'Officer, you must understand, Roger was vulnerable. He self-harmed regularly and he's taken an overdose in the past. It wouldn't surprise me in the slightest if this was suicide.'

I put a hand to my mouth, and Isla came and cuddled into me on the sofa. 'Would you like to go and play upstairs, now Isla? I think you've probably heard enough.'

Isla nodded and scooted up the stairs. Alex on the other hand, leant back on his elbows, and stretched out his legs as if he was preparing to watch a good film.

'What about this week, though? Was there anything in particular that could have triggered him?' PC Jamac tapped his pen on his pad and tilted his head enquiringly.

Josephine thought for a few moments. 'Yes,' she said. 'It would have been his wife's birthday. Remember I'd told you about her at the book club evening, Julia? 'It would have been … let me think …28 years ago she left him. The night before she'd left him, they'd been arguing about something silly – Roger often got jealous, and they'd fall out. But she must have had enough. He got back from work the next day, and she'd gone. No one knew where. Her suitcase was gone, and some clothes and jewellery, but that was all. He was devastated. He adored her. Her mother received a postcard from Brighton saying she was well, but Roger received nothing. It drove him crazy. After that, he marked her birthday every year. He always hoped she'd return.'

'And what day would Sue's birthday have been?' said PC Hinchcliffe.

She thought for a few moments. 'I think, three days ago.'

PC Jamac nodded and closed his book. 'I think that's all for now, but one more question; do you have any idea why he killed himself in Catcher House attic?'

I glanced at Josephine, interested to hear her reply.

'It's always been his home,' she said with a shrug. 'He didn't want me to sell up, but I needed the money. The house was almost part of him. If he was going to kill himself, it would have been in the security of Catcher House. I wouldn't be surprised if he did it out of spite too –

his way of laying a claim to the property. I suppose the attic was the only place he could do it, without being seen by Tom and Julia.'

'I see,' said PC Jamac. 'Well, thank you for your cooperation. If you can think of anything else, please phone on the number we gave you. In the meantime, don't go in the attic. The funeral directors will be here very shortly.'

Blood rushed to my head and my breath grew faster. When would all this end?

'Mr Harker, how about you come and show us now where you laid that poison?' The police walked towards the door, Tom followed, his forehead creased with worry lines. Josephine caught his eye, before turning back to the window. Alex scrambled up and ran after them, keen not to miss anything of importance. No doubt he'd be messaging his school mates all about it as soon as the police left.

Josephine stood too. 'I better be going.' She picked up her handbag from the floor. I couldn't begin to imagine what went through her mind. Surely, she didn't think Tom and I had anything to do with Roger's death?

'Will you be OK?' I walked her to the front door, and put my hand on her arm, and squeezed gently.

'My dear, I've been living with Roger and his issues for over fifty years, I'm sure I'll be alright now.'

'Shall I phone Olivia?' I said. 'You don't want to drive home while upset.'

'No,' she said firmly, reaching into her pocket and pulling out her sunglasses. 'I'll be fine.'

She walked down the stone steps and along the street as if she'd popped out for an early evening stroll. The shock would hit her later, I was sure of it. Slamming the door shut, I shivered at the coldness of the house in contrast to the heat outside. I walked along a beam of sunlight shining across the terracotta tiles, and even then, I couldn't warm up.

Chapter Thirty-Nine

In the days that followed, I tried to carry on as usual, but really, I was a mess inside. If it was only one or two things going wrong, I'd have been alright, but it seemed everything was falling apart. Thank God I had good friends, and not just Thalia. I was really touched that Olivia came around one evening with a bunch of flowers. I'd been out at the supermarket at the time, but she'd handed them to Tom. He said she'd been really upset about Roger; after all, he was her uncle. Apparently, she felt bad for me too, that I found his body. She'd started to cry on the doorstep, so he'd asked her in for a glass of wine. I was sorry to have missed her, and it helped knowing I had friends who were looking out for me.

The attic had been cleaned, but I refused to go up there again. It filled me with horror every time I thought about it. Roger's face, all contorted, and the stench of decay and the metallic smell of blood. The police seemed satisfied that the poison Tom put down in the attic had nothing to do with Roger's death. The pink lump of bait was still in the same place Tom had left it, and besides, Roger had died by slitting his wrists.

We still had rats, and in the end, Tom agreed to phone the pest control. They were going to come on Monday, but in the meantime, we had to shut the food away in cupboards – nothing could be left out, or the little bastards would eat it. Every morning, I came down to find a greasy film on the kitchen tiles, all grubby from where they'd been crawling around. It was so gross.

I'd gone into school to speak to Isla's teacher about Matilda Collins and the issue with the knicker-pulling. She said she'd speak to Matilda, and her mum. This led to Matilida's mum ignoring me in the playground the next day, when normally she'd at least smile and wave. Lizzie was there too, turning her back on me. Both of them, whispering and no doubt, talking about me. It really wasn't what I needed, and it stung.

On Thursday after work, I was cleaning some bird mess off my car window, when Thalia ran out of the office, calling me. 'Hey, hold on Jules.'

'Alright?' I said, looking up at her. 'Bloody birds – shitting on a girl when she's down.'

'Are you coming to choir tonight? It'll do you good. It'll take you mind off everything.' She leant against my car, watching me as I tipped a water bottle upside down onto some tissue for one final scrub at the window.

'Well, I was going to give it a miss. I can't think straight at the moment, Thalia. I've got too much to think about.'

'Exactly. Which is why you need to get out. Have you been to see the doctor yet about getting back on medication?'

I shook my head. 'I've booked an appointment for tomorrow.'

'Good. How about we go for a glass of wine after choir? Then you can talk everything through, and maybe that'll help?'

I walked a couple of paces over to the skip in the corner of the car park, and tossed the bottle and dirty tissue in. It gave me enough time to consider Thalia's invitation. I could do with someone to talk to – work had been so busy; we hadn't been able to chat properly. And I needed to get out of the house. 'OK, that'll be great,' I said. 'I've got to visit Dad in hospital later, but that shouldn't be a problem.'

Thalia smiled. 'Brilliant. See you at 7, I think we're practising for that charity concert. Irie texted me yesterday to say she's got a list of songs she wants us to vote on. So, you *have* to be there.' She walked to her car, waving her arm in the air as she went, looking good in her tight pencil skirt and heels. I wished I could get away with wearing that, but I'd look ridiculous.

*

As I did my hair in front of my bedroom mirror that evening, Tom came in and sat on the bed, looking all sulky. 'Do you have to go out? Mack just texted to see if I could meet him down the pub.'

I gritted my teeth and counted to five before answering. 'Yes, I do. It's my choir night, and I haven't been for ages. Don't make me feel guilty, Tom, I really need a change of scenery.'

'So do I,' he muttered under his breath.

Before I could think, I swung around and threw my hairbrush onto the duvet. It bounced off and landed on the floor by his foot. 'Tom, Thursday is my only night out in the week. I *need* to go out. Everything is getting too much. First there's Dad in hospital, and I'm worried sick about him, and about how Mum's coping. Then there's all this business with Roger North and all the hows and whys. Then there's the rats, and Matilda Collins bullying Isla. And I'm worried about that weird thing the kids keep seeing in the living room. I'm going mad with it all. It's too much …' I sat next to him on the bed, gripping my fists in tight balls of anger.

'Hey!' he put his arm around me. 'I'm sorry, love. I didn't realise it was so important to you. It's OK. Your dad will be fine, he's made of strong stuff. As for the rats, we're dealing with that aren't we? Roger North is no more; we won't have any problems now. As for that 'dark thing' I reckon Thalia put the idea into the kids' heads – it's nothing, except for being in a new house, and their imaginations.'

I sniffed and wiped my nose with the back of my hand. 'And then there's Matilda's mum who's not speaking to me now, and Lizzie.'

Tom tensed as I mentioned Lizzie's name. 'Who cares about Matilda's mum? She's not really one of your friends. And as for Lizzie – she'll soon forgive you. I know her. She has a good heart.'

'How do you know?' I looked up and glared at him, and then wished I hadn't.

'Oh, for God's sake, you're not going to start all that nonsense again about us having an affair, are you?' He pulled away from me, letting his arm drop.

'Affair? I never said you were having an affair. I said she fancied you. But maybe I was right all along?' I could hear myself speaking, and told myself to stop, but I couldn't. I was out of control.

Tom stood and shook his head. 'I hope that doctor gives you some strong pills tomorrow, Julia because, to be honest, you bloody need them.' He left the bedroom, shouting as he went downstairs. 'I'm going to call Mack and ask him around for a few beers in the garden, I hope that's to your satisfaction?'

As a lump formed in my throat, I swallowed hard and bent to pick up the hairbrush. Holding it tight, I closed my eyes and wished I'd kept my mouth shut.

Chapter Forty

Choir was held in a church hall. A large space with high ceilings and long windows. Although it was old-fashioned, it was comforting, reminding me of my childhood. There was a stage at one end, with big velvet curtains; a little kitchen with a hatch, where teacups and saucers were stored for coffee mornings, fetes and jumble sales. The walls were painted a light blue, and flecks of paint had chipped off where no doubt the local scout group, and probably the Brownies, had given it their fair share of wear and tear.

It was great seeing everyone again; I'd not seen them since our meal out. After all the hugs and welcoming chatter, Irie gave us a quick summary of the songs she suggested for our concert. Her pink, fluorescent T-shirt was pulled tight across her large chest, and it read, *'I don't do drugs – I am drugs.'*

We sang everything through once. I controlled my breathing so I could reach the notes I needed. My mind slowed down; my shoulders relaxed. 'Gorgeous.' called Irie. 'Just gorgeous!'

During a quick break, we chose the songs we liked best. Not surprisingly, we all agreed – I think Irie planned it that way, giving the illusion we had chosen them by suggesting some dodgy songs she knew we'd reject. Irie was wonderful, but she did like to be in control. That suited me fine – it meant my brain could switch off at choir. All I had to do was sing.

When the evening was over, Thalia and I walked across the road and past the nearest pub. The rest of the choir were going in there for a drink, but I wanted somewhere quiet so we could talk in private. Irie's cackling laughter echoed in the passageway leading out of the church hall. The girls were in for a fun night – Irie was full of beans, and everyone was on a high, recharged by her continuous energy. Not me though, my energy levels were practically zero.

The Old Red Lion was on the corner of the next road, and we found a small table away from the bar. Thalia sat down and I got us both a large glass of white wine.

'How's it going with Bentley?' I said with a slight smile. I was dying to open up about my problems, but felt bad diving straight in. Most of our recent conversations were about me, hardly the makings of a good friendship.

She narrowed her eyes but smiled too. '*Ben* is OK thank you. Not sure how long it will last though, I'm getting a bit bored. Besides, someone else has been showing an interest in me, so…'

'Ooh, tell me more.' I took a large gulp of wine and leaned forwards.

She laughed. 'Nothing to tell really. Anyway, my love life is boring – let's talk about you. How are you getting on?'

Like an uncorked bottle of fizz, everything burst out of me. I told Thalia everything. All the things that had been piling up, how I was struggling.

'It's not surprising,' she said. 'That's a hell of a lot on your plate. What's the latest on your dad?'

I sighed and swirled my wine around in the glass. 'He's coming out tomorrow, which is good, but mum is terrified he'll have another fit. And of course, he can't drive.'

'They'll be fine Jules, don't worry. Your dad's made of strong stuff.'

'That's what Tom said.' I went quiet as I thought about the disagreement we had earlier, and I told Thalia what I'd said to him. 'I couldn't help myself. In the back of my head, I'm convinced he's having an affair.'

'But why? I reckon Lizzie's just a flirt, like Tom is. You need to give him a bit of space, Jules. You don't want to drive him into having a fling. He hasn't actually done anything wrong, has he?'

I shook my head as tears pricked my eyes. Thalia's words hurt, but I knew there was a lot of sense in what she said.

'And has your attic been cleaned now? When's the inquest into North's death? I wonder why he did it? It was suicide, wasn't it?'

'One question at a time,' I said with a smile. 'Yes, a professional company spent a whole morning up there. The police and Josephine – his sister – think it was suicide, but the inquest should confirm it. They reckon it'll be a few weeks at least. He had terrible mental health problems, Thalia – Now he's dead, I actually feel a bit sorry for him.'

'You're kidding me?' said Thalia. 'After all those weird things he did?'

'Yeah, I know, it's just … he had a mental health condition, and I do too, don't I? I shouldn't really judge others.'

Thalia snorted. 'But Jules. You're completely different. You had post-natal depression and have anxiety. It's not the same at all. What he has… had … is something on a different scale completely. He was nuts.'

I shook my head adamantly. 'No, Thalia, don't say that. He was ill. I'm sure of it now. I might try and find out a bit more actually, to give me a sense of closure.'

Thalia raised an eyebrow. 'Well, that's not a good idea. Concentrate on getting better first, OK?'

'Alright, alright.' I knocked back the rest of my wine. 'Your round,' I said. 'And then you can tell me more about this mystery man.'

Chapter Forty-One

Thank God it was Friday. Tom was barely speaking to me when he left for work that morning, but at least he shouted 'bye' as he left the house. Alex had gone to school with his friend, and I'd dropped Isla off. I was going to work later that day, because I had the doctors, so as I tidied up the breakfast dishes, I gave Mum a call. 'So, are you sure you don't need me to give you a lift?' I said.

'No,' said Mum. 'Jean from across the road has to go into hospital this morning, so she said she'll take me and bring us home.'

'Well, if you're sure. If you find you're hanging around waiting for him to be discharged, then give me a ring. No point Jean hanging around needlessly.'

'Between you and me,' said Mum, lowering her voice as if Jean was in her house, 'I think she likes going to hospital. She likes the company. So really, we're doing her favour.'

I gave a small laugh. 'If you say so, Mum. Look I have to go now, so I'll phone later to see how he is.'

'OK, have a good day, bye bye.'

A good day? I really hoped so. Once I'd got the medication from the doctors, I was sure I'd feel much better. As it was, I had a head as thick as cardboard, and nausea that nagged angrily in my guts. I stepped into the living room to get my handbag, and immediately a cold chill gripped me. I glanced at the window, and the sun shone brightly outside. In fact, the rest of the house was stuffy and hot. I told myself it was my imagination, but I knew that wasn't true. The kids knew it, and I knew it. There was something in the living room – a spirit, a ghost, an entity of some sort, and no medication would make that disappear. I wondered who it was? Did Roger and Josephine's parents die in the house? – maybe one of them came back to haunt the place? And then I had an awful thought. Now Roger was dead, would *he* come back too?

My handbag lay on the floor by the sofa, and I shuddered as I rushed across the room to get it. I couldn't wait to get out of the house, and into the warmth of the street. As soon as I slammed the front door, the smell of coffee drifted down the road from a local café, and I longed to go and sit there on one of the squashy sofas and have a large mug of milky latte. But, of course, I had to go to the doctors. I unlocked my car door and set off to the surgery.

*

As soon as I got into the office, Thalia told me Mr Sullens, our boss, wanted to have a word with me. 'What's he want?' I said, not meaning to snap at her.

'I don't know,' she said, as she bent over a filing cabinet. 'He said that as soon as you got in, you have to go and see him.'

Clenching my fists, I walked over to Mr Sullens' office and knocked.

'Come in.'

Immediately I smelt stale smoke, as I poke my head around the door. 'Hello, Mr Sullens, you wanted to see me?'

'Yes, Julia, please close the door and take a seat.' Mr Sullens was in his early sixties, a large man with a red face. He had built up the company with his father, who had since died. As bosses go, he was nice enough. Always fair, and treated the staff well, but he was old fashioned, both in his values and his appearance. He wore a shirt and tie to work, whatever the weather. It didn't really make him look any smarter; his shirt always hung out of his trousers.

The stuffiness of the room hit me, even though the window was open, and a fan was whirring in the corner. On the desk were piles of job sheets. I could never figure out why he didn't use a computer to update things. But I suppose he was old school. He leant forward. 'Nothing to worry about, but...'

Straight away, I knew that meant there *was* something to worry about.

'... But I've noticed you've been taking a lot of time off recently, some paid, some unpaid, or in lieu. I appreciate you've had a lot on at the moment with your ... with your father being in hospital, and I wanted to check everything's OK?'

I could tell he was struggling to say what he wanted – he wasn't particularly good on the personal side of the business, and as he stuttered and rolled his thumbs, I shuffled awkwardly in my chair. 'I'm fine, really,' I said.

'Er, do you need to take a longer period off work? I noticed you seem very, er, er, stressed over the last few days, and wondered if you, er, if you think you aren't coping with your work, alongside your personal problems.' He cleared his throat, and sat back in his chair, relieved that he'd finished. I was relieved too.

'Thank you, Mr Sullens, but my father's coming out of hospital today, and I think everything will be OK now. It has been a stressful few weeks, and I really appreciate you giving me time off, but really, I'm alright.' I smiled, to prove to him that I really didn't need time off. That was the last thing I wanted – sitting at home in the house dwelling on my thoughts.

'Well, I'm not sure,' he said, clasping his fingers together and leaning on top of the job sheets. 'Nasty business with that man in your attic.'

I nodded and looked down at my lap. Now he was getting to what was really bothering him.

'I'd like you to take a week off,' he said. 'No arguments. Thalia told me you were at the doctors this morning. Are you having episodes like before?'

Thanks a lot, Thalia. 'The doctor has given me some medication, like last time. It'll take about two weeks before I feel better.' I cringed as I said it because I knew exactly what was coming next.

'Take two weeks off, then Julia. If you rest, you won't need to take a long period off like last time. Hopefully, we can knock it on the head, now we know what to expect.'

We? He began to get on my nerves. I really didn't want to take time off. I was better keeping busy. But he was pretty adamant.

'Is that settled then? Two weeks sick leave – and you'll be paid. I can't have one of my best staff members struggling.'

I nodded and stood up. 'Thank you, Mr Sullens, I appreciate it.' And I did appreciate his kindness. I was flattered by his words. Maybe he was right? Maybe I wasn't aware of how bad things were? After wishing me well, he said goodbye and I left the room. With a sinking feeling in my stomach, I walked back into the office. Thalia was on the phone.

'Got to go now, Julia's come out,' she said. 'Bye.' She looked up and smiled sheepishly.

'I suppose you know I've been told to take two weeks off?' I said, opening my drawer and taking out two bananas that were going brown.

'He asked me how you were. Sorry, I didn't tell him anything personal, I promise. I think he's concerned about you,' said Thalia.

'Yeah, I know, don't worry.'

'Tom's concerned too, you know,' she said, shuffling her things around on her desk.

'What do you mean?' I shot her a look.

'He's just been on the phone, wanting to know how you'd got on at the doctors. He seemed a bit pissed off you hadn't messaged him.'

I laughed loudly. 'He's got a nerve. He barely spoke to me this morning.'

Thalia shrugged. 'Whatever.'

I thrust the bananas in my bag and moved towards the door. 'Look. I'll see you in two weeks.'

'I'll see you before then, silly.' she said. 'I'll pop over to see you one night, OK?'

'Whatever,' I said, and I left the office without looking back.

Once I got into my car and started the engine, I started to mull over what Thalia had said. Why was Tom phoning her at work? I drove out of the car park, not really concentrating on the road. All I kept thinking about was Thalia's words last night ... "Someone else has been showing an interest ..."

A burning heat rushed through me, and my stomach flipped. No! Surely not Thalia?

Chapter Forty-Two

Not concentrating on the road, my mind raced as I drove home. All those times Tom had gone out to see "Mack" – had he been seeing Thalia all along? Had I been wrong, and it was never Lizzie in the first place?

It was odd getting home at 11 in the morning, and I pushed my work things into the hallway cupboard – I wouldn't need them for a while. Next week would be half term. We'd planned for the kids to stay with Tom's mum so I wouldn't have to take time off work. Should I go with them, now I had time off?

I sat on the sofa, thinking. Spending a week with Tom's mum wasn't that appealing. We got on OK, but she'd planned a week of activities with the kids, and she wouldn't want me around. No. I'd stay here. I could help Mum out with Dad and keep an eye on him. I could also do some detective work. Find out if Tom was having an affair. I sat up straight as an idea occurred to me. I could research into Roger North's family, and find out who, or what, haunted the house. If you *could* call it a haunting.

I remembered the medication was still in my handbag; I should have taken it that morning. As I stood, an icy breeze swept up behind me – cold on the back of my head. I spun around. As I rubbed the nape of my neck, the warmth of my hand became apparent. Like before, the room turned dark, and the air was heavy with sadness. With shallow breaths, I backed out of the room on high alert for anything strange. But there was nothing.

Maybe it was all in my brain? The sad, dark atmosphere – was it my anxiety, tied up with a kind of depression? I didn't know. I didn't seem to know my own mind. Yet the kids had felt and seen things too, hadn't they? Or had they picked it up from my neuroses? I reached for my bag and pulled out the packet of tablets. Fumbling to open the box, I eventually found the blister pack of fourteen little white tablets. I popped one out and put it in my mouth. The taste was bitter, but I swallowed and then sat on the stairs. All these thoughts weren't good for me, I had to get better.

I leant against the wall; it was cool and soothing against my cheek. Closing my eyes, I breathed in slowly, taking a few moments to calm myself down.

*

That evening, while we were all sitting around the kitchen table having tea, I decided it was a good time to tell everyone I was taking two weeks off work. Tom immediately put down his cutlery. 'Seriously? Why didn't you tell me?'

'I'm telling you now,' I said. Simple.

'Aren't you well, Mummy?' Isla gazed at me with her big, hazel eyes.

I tried to smile. 'I'm fine, darling. Mummy is a bit stressed with everything that's happened, and she needs a bit of time off. I'll be fine.' I reached out and patted her hand.

She seemed happy enough with my explanation and carried on eating her supper.

'Does that mean we're not going to Gran's now?' said Alex. 'Cool! I'll be able to meet up at with my mates, instead.'

'Alex!' said Tom, his eyebrows knotting together. 'That's such a horrible thing to say. I thought you liked going to your Gran's? You're definitely going – she's planned all sorts of things for you.'

Alex looked down at his food. 'Sorry,' he said. 'I do like going there. It would've been nice to hang out at the park, that's all.'

I did get what Alex, was saying. He was nearly twelve, of course he didn't want to go and stay a week with his kid sister and his gran. But I knew I had to have time on my own. Things to sort out. 'Well, how about you arrange something for the weekend when you come back? You can have some mates around to stay and get a take-away.'

Alex nodded. He still looked fed up.

'It's only five days, for God's sake. You'd think we were sending you to outer Mongolia for a year or something.' Tom let his irritation show; his words were clipped, and his voice raised. 'Anyway, did the doctor give you the same medication as last time, Jules?'

Both kids glanced up, enquiringly. Isla hadn't known I'd been ill before, and although Alex knew something had been up, he didn't know exactly what. I frowned at Tom, cross at him for speaking so openly in front of the children.

'Yes, but let's talk about it later, OK?'

He shrugged. Isla cocked her head and looked up at me, as if she was trying to work something out. I ruffled her hair. 'Sometimes people aren't well, but you can't see it,' I said. 'Sometimes I need special tablets to help me be less anxious. That's all. Nothing to worry about.'

After everyone had finished eating, the kids went to their bedrooms; Tom and I cleaned up the kitchen. 'So, did you ask Sullens for time off, or did he tell you to take it off?' Tom loaded the dishwasher carefully, keeping the plates in regimented formation. He was trying to avoid eye contact with me; he found it difficult talking about mental health.

'He asked how I was,' I said. 'He noticed I wasn't myself and he'd also spoken to Thalia, and she told him I was struggling, I think.' I watched him closely to see if he reacted to her name, but there was nothing.

'Thalia said she's worried about you,' he said. 'I've been worried too. Look, have the two weeks off, relax, sort out your parents and then everything should be fine. OK?'

I nodded and sighed. He put his arm around me and hugged me close. 'We'll get through this, like we did before.'

He kissed me on the cheek, and I leant in, enjoying his touch and his sympathy. Maybe everything would be alright after all?

Chapter Forty-Three

That evening, as I tucked Isla up in bed, I vowed to myself we'd have the next day together as a family and do something nice. It would be good to remind us that we were a closeknit family, even if things went wrong sometimes.

'What would you like to do tomorrow, Sweetheart?' I said as I sat on the bed next to her, with a copy of her latest reading book on my lap. 'Shall we all do something nice? Go to the lido or a museum or something?'

'The Wild Place,' she shouted, bouncing up and down, her eyes shining bright.

I smiled. I knew she loved the animals there, and I had to admit, I always liked going too. 'OK, that's a deal.' I said, giving her a tight squeeze. Now, shall we start the story?'

Isla went quiet.

'What's wrong?'

'Matty's invited the whole class to her party at the leisure centre, but she didn't invite me. She said we're not friends anymore.'

A knot of anger tightened in my guts. How dare Matty's mum take out her grievances on a little girl? Isla hadn't done anything wrong. I painted on a smile. 'Oh, don't worry, I don't expect everyone will go, anyway. You've been invited to Ruby's party, haven't you? So, everyone likes you still. It's only Matty, and you don't particularly like her either. Don't worry, darling.' I kissed the top of her head, and she snuggled into me. 'That's life, sometimes people don't like each other, and that's OK. Now, let's get a chapter read, shall we?'

*

The next day, we had a successful trip out at *The Wild Place*. I'd packed a picnic and the sun had shone. Both kids got on well with each other and Tom and I managed to put all our problems behind us and enjoyed ourselves; or at least pretended to, in my case. It had upset me, seeing families out with their grandparents, and I thought of Mum stuck inside, nursing poor old Dad. I'd wished they could have joined us too.

On the way home, we picked up some pizzas and ate them in front of the television, watching a movie that all of us agreed on. Tom had a beer, and my glass of pinot grigio worked like a potion, soon turning into three glasses. The nagging doubts about Tom were still there though, especially when he took out his phone to check his messages with a secretive smile on his face. Of course, whenever I relaxed, negativity slinked into my brain like a mugger creeping up behind me.

I can't say I was sad to see the kids go on Sunday morning. As much as I loved them, I was relieved I didn't have to keep pretending to be cheerful. I'd have time to get my head together. As soon as Tom chased them out of the house, my shoulders slumped like a beanstalk having its supporting pole removed.

Tom planned to stay overnight at his Mum's, so I went to my parents for lunch, which gave me the chance to check all was OK with them. By the time I'd got back home I was exhausted. Dad had been weak, and his mood was very low. He hardly ate a thing, and Mum was desperately worried. Going there hadn't calmed my fears, it had made them worse. I made a cup of tea and sat at the kitchen table, wondering what to have for supper, when my phone rang. I glanced at the screen.

Thalia. I put my phone on speaker. 'Hello.'

'Julia? It's me. Look, I hope I didn't piss you off yesterday in the office. You seemed angry when you left. Did I upset you? I wasn't siding with Tom, I promise. I just want what's best for you.'

I ran my thumb up and down against the mug, my stomach lurching. I knew I had to tell her the truth, but I hated confrontation. Besides, could I trust anything she said? 'Well, to be honest, Thalia, you did piss me off. You seem to think it's my fault that Tom and I are having problems. I know I'm getting edgy, but he's really difficult to speak to at the moment. He gets cross and goes out a lot; I'm sure he's having an affair. Basically Thalia, I want you to believe me and listen to me – that's what friends are for.'

There was silence at the other end of the phone, until eventually Thalia said, 'I know. I'm sorry. I just try to be objective – see things from both sides so I can give you the best advice – that's what friends are really for. To be honest with each other.'

'Honest, yes, but loyal too.' I wasn't sure if I meant loyal as in "she should stick up for me", or loyal and "not sleep with my husband". Either way, I could tell Thalia was upset by my comment. There was another brief silence where I could almost feel her glare.

'I am loyal,' she said with a hoarse voice.

'I know, but …'

'Julia, if you really need to question my loyalty after all the years we've been friends, then I really don't know what to say…'

I cringed. Maybe I'd been too harsh? 'I'm sorry, look Thalia, shall we begin this conversation again?'

'I'm not in the mood now. I rang to clear the waters, but it seems I've made things murkier. Let's talk another time. Speak later.'

She hung up before I could even say goodbye. I sat still. A sharp pain shot through my chest, and before I knew it, tears ran down my cheeks. I gasped between sobs, trying to catch my breath. Swallowing. My head hurt, my cheeks stung, and my insides were breaking into pieces. I wanted to trust her, I really did, but my head refused to believe it.

Chapter Forty-Four

I woke up on Monday with my head throbbing. Reaching over to the bedside drawer, I pulled out a packet of paracetamol and downed two tablets. I lay there, staring at the ceiling, thinking of the conversation I'd had with Thalia, and I groaned.

Under the duvet, it was so warm and secure; I had to force myself to get out of bed and into the shower. I needed to make good use of the day. Tom was going straight to work from his mum's and would be back home that evening. It wasn't an option for him to see me in the same state I was in last night – I had to get it together.

Luckily, I was distracted by the pest control guy who arrived just after nine o'clock. I opened the door to a funny-looking man in his fifties, clutching a dirty looking holdall. His combed-over hair was obviously dyed chestnut brown. He wore thick rimmed glasses, a polo shirt, and trousers that hung from his hips – absolutely not in a fashionable way.

'Mrs Harker?'

'Yes, hello, are you Mr Churchill? The pest control?'

'That's me,' he said.

I stepped back and let him into the house.

'I've been here before, you know. Years ago.' he said, looking around. 'With my dad when he used to run the company. I was still learning the ropes back then. But I remember it well. They had a terrible rat infestation – getting in through a tiny hole and under the kitchen cupboards.'

'Horrible,' I said. 'Ours seem to be everywhere. Even in the attic.'

'I'll catch 'em, don't worry about that. First things first, we have to find out where they're coming in.'

'Who lived here when you came before?' I said.

'A married couple; quite young they were, about the same age as I was. Nice lady. He was a bit weird though, that's why I remember it. He kept looking at me funny. I remember he gave me the heebie jeebies. I got the impression he thought I was going to make a play for his bird. Ha Ha! I was a bit of a catch in those days.'

I smiled and nodded politely, not quite believing he could ever have been a catch. But I knew as soon as he described the man that he must have been talking about Roger and his wife. It made sense that he was 'weird' even then.

'Right,' he said. 'Show me all the places you've found droppings.'

We went into the kitchen first. He pulled back the kick board under the cupboards and shone his torch about. He did a lot of nodding and saying, 'Ah, right.' I showed him upstairs and where the droppings had been in the airing cupboard. Then I stood under the attic.

'They're up there too,' I said. 'Do you need to look?' I hoped he'd say no, and he could deal with it from downstairs, but he nodded.

'Yes please.'

I gritted my teeth and fetched the pole to pull down the hatch. The ladder slid down the rails and thumped as it hit the carpet; my heart jumped. I couldn't go up. My palms were sweating, and my head began to spin. 'I'll wait down here, if it's OK?'

'No worries,' he said, then, with his torch between his teeth, he hoisted himself up into the attic. My fingers pressed hard against the side of the ladder; I was sure I could still smell decay and blood. Swallowing hard, I tried to stop myself from retching. A few moments later, he peered down through the hole. 'There're loads of droppings. I wouldn't be surprised if they've made their nest up here. They're probably getting in under the eaves. Good climbers, rats are.'

I shuddered at the thought of a nest up there. Mr Churchill clambered back down. 'Cardboard and insulation's been chewed up. Might be a good idea to get your electrical wires checked, they often have a good chew on them. Have you had any electrical faults? Lights flickering or anything?'

I tilted my head to the side, thinking. There had been some flickering in the living room when Thalia saw the dark 'thing'. Maybe that's what it had been all along? Damaged electrics. A feeling of hope rushed through me. 'Yes, sometimes,' I said.

'Well, get it checked out as soon as you can. I'm just goin' to the van to get some bait boxes and stuff, then we'll get rid of the bastards.' He laughed as he walked down the stairs, and I followed after. Getting the electrics checked was yet *another* thing to worry about. Was the house safe? I made a mental note to google some electricians as soon as the pest man had gone.

He moved around the house setting his bait boxes in various positions, while I sat in the living room, wondering if the flickering lights had been caused by rat-chewed wires. Or was it something more sinister? I stiffened as my spine tingled at the thought.

'Bloody, creepy house,' I said out loud, then I turned my head to check Mr Churchill hadn't heard me. He'd think I was nuts. Maybe I was nuts? I suspected I was.

'Is anyone there?' As soon as I said it, I laughed at myself. What a total cliché. Did I think I was in a horror film or something? I really was going crazy. And of course, no one replied. The darkness didn't descend on the room, and it didn't turn cold. I shook my head and picked up the novel we had begun to read for book club. I hadn't gone to the last meeting because of my disagreement with Lizzie, but I figured I might as well read it anyway.

After about fifteen minutes, Mr Churchill tapped on the door. 'All done,' he said.

'Wonderful,' I said. 'How long do you think it'll take?'

'Well, I'll come back on Wednesday to check they're taking the bait. Then I'll leave it for a week to put some more poison down. But we're on to them now, so don't worry.'

'Thank you so much,' I said. 'How much do I owe you?'

'Nothing for now, I'll invoice you.'

As I walked him to the front door, I wondered if he remembered anything else about Roger North. 'You know that woman who lived here before? The one you met? She left her husband. Apparently disappeared with her lover.'

'Not surprised,' he said. 'I told you he was weird.'

'Yeah, I met him a few times. We bought the house from him; well, his sister anyway. He was odd. Seemed to be very lonely.'

'Did she take the baby with her then? No wonder he was lonely.'

'Baby?' I frowned. *What baby?*

'When I came, she had a baby. It wouldn't stop crying. She held it to her the whole time.'

'Oh,' I said. 'I don't know. How strange. No one's mentioned there was a baby. I didn't think Roger North had any children. Maybe his wife took it when she left?'

'Maybe. Can't blame her to be honest.'

We both laughed, but I didn't think it was funny. Maybe that's why Roger was so bitter? Had his wife taken his only child? That would send anyone mad. I showed Mr Churchill out and went to sit back in the living room.

I picked up my book – just one chapter before I got on with something useful. I curled my legs up and found the page I was on. But then, out of nowhere, there was a shooting pain against my cheek. It was as if someone had pinched me. With a gasp, I swung my head around and dropped the book on the sofa. No one was there. Of course not. Was there a wasp or bee in the room? But there was nothing. Nothing I could see, anyway. I rubbed my cheek and reached for my book again, but the pages were already turning. Very slowly. As if someone was flicking through it.

With panicked breath, I leapt off the sofa. The smell of perfume caught in my throat, that ugly floral scent turning putrid. As I charged into the hallway, the change in temperature hit me like a fist. It was as if I'd walked out of an icehouse into the heat of a summer's day. Grabbing my keys, I raced out. The door slammed behind me, and I stood on the step for just a moment, waiting for my head to stop spinning.

Chapter Forty-Five

I stumbled to my car and slumped into the seat. An onslaught of traffic zipped by – that's what it felt like, but in reality, it was probably just one or two vehicles. It made my head thump. I closed my eyes and rubbed my temples. What the hell was happening in that house? Was I losing my mind? It would take a few weeks for my medication to kick in, so I had to keep my cool. Everything would be OK. I said to myself over and over, like a mantra.

The sweet scent of the air freshener was cloying as I breathed in and out, trying to calm myself down. Classical music drifted from the radio speakers, and after a few minutes I felt a little better. More rational.

I twisted the key in the ignition. Where could I go? I drummed my fingers on the steering wheel. Could I drive to Josephine's house, go and pay her a visit, under the pretext of checking if she's OK?

But the truth was, my real plan was to find out more about her and Roger's past. There had to be a reason for the strange happenings in our house. Or at least I could discover why Roger was so screwed up – if I could find an answer to that, I'd certainly feel more comfortable. I'd hate to think I was responsible for Roger's death by forcing him out of his lifelong home. Of course, I knew it wasn't really my fault – Josephine made that decision. But maybe I could have been a little more caring when he was upset about moving out. I cringed and went red as I remembered how I'd spoken to him: *'I don't get what your problem is.'* – I didn't know his history, what right did I have to judge him?

I wasn't sure where Josephine lived. I knew roughly which area, but not the address. I scrolled through my phone, looking for a solicitor's email to see if I could find an attached copy of the contract.

After about five minutes, I found it. I typed the address into the sat nav and set off. I had no clear plan, and I didn't know what I was going to say to her, but I didn't care. My brain was anything but clear.

The city centre was busy, and I wished I'd taken the longer route which avoided the main roads. After twenty-five minutes, the sat nav told me I had 'reached my destination'. The street was rammed with cars, and there was nowhere to park, so I drove around the block and squeezed in between a battered escort and a white van.

As I walked along the road, I took in my surroundings. A number of trendy cafes and boutiques were dotted between the shabby houses, and at a guess, there'd been an attempt at gentrification. I always assumed Josephine was wealthy and would be living somewhere swanky, because she had a posh accent and dressed classily. But then I'd remembered she had a gambling problem. That's probably why she had to sell the family home.

Josephine's house was a tiny terrace with bins in the front garden. Although the neighbour's house had paint peeling off the woodwork and tatty net curtains hanging in the window, Josephine's was well kept. I opened the wooden gate, walked up to the doorstep, and rang the bell. Not hearing any ringing sound, I knocked on the frosted glass panel of the front door.

It didn't take long. Josephine answered almost immediately. She had a light blue blazer on, her handbag hanging off her shoulder. 'Oh, Julia,' she said. 'I'm about to go out. What can I do for you?'

I stood back, aware she must think it strange, me turning up on her doorstep. 'Oh, I don't want to hold you up. I was only passing and thought I'd pop in to check you were OK. You know, after Roger and all that.'

She smiled. 'Oh, that's sweet of you. I'm fine, honestly. Look, why don't you walk with me? We can perhaps get a coffee up the road?'

I nodded. 'OK, that sounds like a plan, as long as I'm not getting in your way.'

'Not at all,' she said as she clicked her door shut. 'I'm heading for the cemetery. I go every week.'

'Ah, I saw you buying flowers for a grave, didn't I? From the high street near where I live.'

She nodded, not seeming to mind my direct question. 'Yes,' she said. 'I always buy my flowers from that florist; she's the best in Bristol.'

I struggled to keep up with her. She had long legs and walked fast, but still managed to look elegant. Unlike me, as I trotted along beside her.

'I lost a child. It's for her grave.'

With a gasp, I turned to look at her, touching her arm gently. 'Oh, Josephine, I'm so sorry, I didn't know.'

'No reason for you to know. Besides, it was a long time ago now. I'd moved to Bristol when I was a few months pregnant after I'd split up from my husband you see. I didn't want him to be around when the baby was born – he was violent. Ironically, if I hadn't moved to Bristol, Clementine wouldn't have died.'

'I'm so sorry,' I said again. 'How did she die? You don't have to tell me if you don't want to, sorry, perhaps I shouldn't have asked?'

'I don't mind. It's good to talk about her. I don't like to deny her existence. She was only three. My little Clementine. She was killed by a car that lost control. Running ahead of me, she was, on the way back from the park, and the car mounted the pavement and …'

I swallowed. 'That's shocking. Josephine, I don't know what to say. Look, you don't want me tagging on. You go and visit your daughter, and I'll catch up with you another time.'

I could hardly ask her about Roger's mental health after what she'd just told me. I decided it would have to wait. We both stopped and I put my hand on her arm again. 'I only came around to see how you were.'

Josephine nodded. 'Thank you, Julia. Maybe we can have a coffee another time?'

'That would be nice.' I smiled in an attempt to be compassionate, and her smile in return brightened her sad, beautiful face. We said goodbye and I retraced my steps – passing her house on my way back to the car.

Josephine and her baby played on my mind. How awful for her. I couldn't think of anything worse. If Roger was prone to mental health problems, maybe the death of his niece could have exacerbated things? What with his wife and child leaving him too. But would that be enough to lead him to kill himself in our attic? Or was the odd atmosphere in the house related to Clementine's death? No. There was definitely more to it, and I needed to find out what.

ROGER - 1995

Chapter Forty-Six

Despite hating Faither, Roger was distraught in the months after his death. Paradoxically, it made Roger feel even more rejected by Faither than when he was alive. Especially as he'd left the house to Josephine in his will, and not to Roger. That had hurt – why hadn't Faither thought he was good enough to inherit the house? But Sue was such a tower of strength. In the autumn of 1995, they got married at the church. It was a small affair. The only guests were members of the congregation, a couple of friends from Sue's work and Josephine, who had come back permanently to Bristol a few weeks before the wedding, with bruises on her arms and a baby in her belly. Sue's mother refused to come. She disapproved of Roger, thinking her daughter was far too good for him.

The wedding reception was a humble one. Sue and Roger decided to hold it in a small hotel, not far from the church. They had a buffet meal in a meeting room, where the church guitarist and the choir sang afterwards. It was a happy occasion. While Sue danced with friends, Roger sipped his third cava (because now Faither was dead, he chose to drink alcohol). The pastor came up to him and lay a hand on Roger's elbow. 'I'm proud of you, my son,' he said. 'Your father would've been too. All those years ago, when we had to … er … sort out your problems, I didn't think you'd ever get to this point in your life. But here you are.'

'Thank you, Pastor,' said Roger. 'I am lucky to have a good woman who understands me.'

'You're very lucky. Don't blow it, my boy, remember, God is always here to guide you. Follow his lead and you won't go wrong.'

'Yes,' said Roger, nodding. 'I'll try.'

The pastor took the glass from Roger's hand. 'I think in the circumstances and going by your previous behaviour, it's a good idea for you to stop drinking now, don't you think?' Being smaller than the man, Roger had to bend his neck to look up at him. His mouth fell open in surprise. *It's my bloody wedding! I can't drink at my own bloody wedding?* His face burned as a furious heat seared through him.

Josephine marched over. 'Excuse me, but it's Roger's big day, I'm sure he can have a few glasses of fizz to celebrate. Don't you think?'

With her height and her abundance of ash-blonde hair, Roger thought Josephine looked like a Viking warrior. The pastor gritted his teeth as Josephine took the glass from his hand and passed it back to Roger.

'Remember, the devil can always return once it has visited before,' said the pastor, his voice ice-cold.

Roger put the glass to his lips and downed the drink in one. His hands were shaking, and it wasn't until Josephine linked her arm through his, did he feel calmer. A muscle in the pastor's jaw twitched, then he walked away, tightening his tie as he went.

'Roger, you do know you never had the devil in you, don't you?' said Josephine. 'They were trying to control you. You should have left that bloody church years ago and found another congregation.'

Roger studied his sister's face, as if her words were a revelation. 'I was pretty bad, though, Josephine. My temper …'

'You have your problems, Rog', that's for sure. But possessed with the devil? I don't think so. Why do you think I left and didn't come home? Our parents were the bad ones. Not you.'

Roger couldn't believe his sister was saying such things about his mother. Maybe Faither, yes, but Mum?

She'd been so kind to him. 'But mum was lovely,' he said, squeezing the stem of his glass tightly.

'She should've left him. She shouldn't have allowed us to live in the way he made us live. Why do you think I left Colin in London? He was a terrible husband, and I didn't want him treating my child in the same way Faither treated us.' Josephine brought her hand up to her cheekbone and stroked it, as if remembering a wound from the past. 'Let's be honest,' she said, 'we were never happy as kids, they were awful parents.'

Roger nodded. He gazed at Sue with a tenderness in his heart, and vowed he would never, ever hurt her or cause her pain. Not to her, or to any children they planned to have.

'Thanks for sticking up for me. Let me get you another drink, we need to celebrate.' Roger squeezed his sister's arm and led her to the bar.

*

Roger and Sue settled down in Catcher House, and were happy, despite Roger's mood swings and insecurities. Roger continued to work at the garden centre and Sue at her accountancy firm. Sue had stopped speaking entirely to her mother, refusing to engage with someone who disliked her new husband.

Sue had suggested Josephine moved into Catcher House with them, but she'd refused. With her savings and a settlement from Colin, Josephine could afford to rent a small place. She insisted Roger and Sue must carry on living at Catcher House and make the home a happy one.

Occasionally, Roger and Sue saw Josephine for Sunday lunch. Sometimes they popped in to see her at the small café where she was a waiter. She worked long hours, needing to keep her mind busy after her divorce. Sue often told her to slow down. Once, she saw Josephine doing a whole lunchtime shift by herself. 'You'll make yourself ill, working so hard – you need to rest now you're carrying a child,' she'd said.

Josephine just laughed at Sue; she thought her sister-in-law was a little old fashioned. But that's one of the reasons why Roger loved her. Sue didn't even mind his strange collections that he kept in the house. After they got married, he'd started to collect springs. He liked the way they expanded when he pulled them. His favourite one was a brass spring from an old piano he'd found in a skip.

After two months of marriage, Sue fell pregnant. Roger was overjoyed – he saw this as a chance to become a better dad than Faither. Life was good. He was happy, his wife and his sister were happy. Roger was calmer and more settled than he'd ever been in his entire life.

Then one afternoon in early June, Roger got a phone call from Josephine. He and Sue were in the kitchen preparing their lunch. Sue had two pieces of toast under the grill and Roger was mashing up some tinned sardines to put on top of the toast. He laid down the fork and hurried into the hallway to answer the phone.

'Roger North speaking.'

A sob came down the phone. At first, he didn't know who it was, until a small voice finally whispered, 'There's so much blood.'

Roger swallowed. 'What? Josephine, is that you?'

Through uncontrolled gulps, Josephine tried to speak. 'I had a horrible pain in my belly. I went to the toilet and …'

'I'll get Sue,' said Roger. He couldn't handle this conversation. He wiped the sweat away from his forehead and rushed into the kitchen. Sue had heard Roger's end of the call and knew something was wrong. She turned off the grill and wiped her hands on the tea towel before heading into the hall. 'She's lost the baby,' said Roger as he began to mash the sardines again. He pressed hard; so hard the tomato sauce splattered up the side of the bowl.

After a few moments, Sue came back in. 'I'm going around to Josephine's. She's had a miscarriage. She'll need to go to hospital. You stay here, it might be too much for her if we both go.'

'But she's my sister, I want to come.'

'It's not about you, Roger, you stay here.' Sue picked up her car keys and headed towards the front door.

'But what about your sardines?' said Roger. 'Sue, don't go. Your sardines … Why don't you wait for me, and I can come with you?'

'No, I'm going now. Stop it, Roger. Josephine needs me.' She left the house, shutting the door with a sharp bang, the floral scent of Anais Anais perfume was all that was left of her.

Roger pulled the toast from under the grill and slapped the fish on top. He threw the empty bowl into the sink, and it landed on top of a dirty plate with a crack, breaking both pieces of crockery. Roger turned away and picked up the toast, beginning to munch, shovelling the food into his mouth. He needed to occupy his hands and mind to fill the emptiness inside him. Anything to take his thoughts away from the loss of the baby; to stop him thinking about how his sister and wife hadn't included him.

Chapter Forty-Seven

When Sue came back, Roger was sitting in the living room, watching Match of the Day. He didn't like football, so Sue guessed straight away that he wasn't happy. He stared at the screen with a blank expression on his face, a muscle twitching in his jaw.

Sue leant against the doorframe and glared at him; she tapped her fingernails against the wood. But he didn't speak.

'I took her to hospital,' she said after a few moments. 'She's home now, and once I've picked up a few things, I'll go back to be with her. I'm going to stay the night.'

Roger shrugged.

'Don't you want to know what happened? Or how she is?'

He turned to look at her. 'So, you're including me now, are you?'

Sue shook her head and exclaimed in exasperation, 'You have a serious problem, Roger, do you know that? I'm wondering if you need to get some help from a doctor. Your behaviour isn't normal sometimes, do you know that?'

Roger looked up. He shook. 'Tell me then, what happened?'

'They've given her something to make sure all the tissues are passed out, and then the miscarriage will be complete. She's not in a good place, Roger.'

'Can I come and see her?'

'She said she doesn't want to see anyone except me at the moment. She's too upset.'

Roger stood and barged past Sue, knocking her shoulder as he went. He knew he was behaving badly, but he couldn't help himself. Couldn't bear to be left out. And now the baby was dead too, it was too much for him to cope with. He ran out of the house and down the street, leaving the front door swinging open.

*

Poor Josephine struggled to come to terms with the loss of her baby. It had been the only thing that kept her going after the break-up from her husband. But whereas some people might have been jealous of Roger and Sue's pregnancy, Josephine found it brought her joy. She worried terribly when a heavily pregnant Sue went into hospital in early January with intense labour pains. But after a long delivery, they came back to Catcher House a few days later with a tiny little girl.

'We don't know what to call her yet,' said Roger, as he sat on the settee, cradling his daughter protectively in his arms. 'I suggested Moira, after mum, but Sue doesn't like that.'

Josephine crouched down next to him and stroked the top of the little girl's head. Her body tingled with warmth as she looked at the tiny creature in his arms. 'She's just beautiful,' she said. 'So soft.'

Sue sat next to Roger and leant her head on his shoulder. She had black rings under her tired eyes, but she smiled. 'I'm not sure about a name. We don't have to decide now, do we?'

'No, but soon,' said Roger. 'I like the name Celestine. Or how about Clementine?'

Sue laughed. 'That sounds like an orange.'

'I think it's pretty,' said Josephine. Clementine, wasn't Winston Churchill's wife called that?'

'Yes,' said Roger. 'That's where I got it from. I was watching a documentary the other night and thought it a beautiful name.'

Sue nodded. 'OK, Clementine it is, as long as I can call her Clemmy.'

*

So, Clementine it was, and Clemmy proved to be quite a difficult baby. She'd cry every night, and both Sue and Roger were exhausted. Josephine helped most days and sometimes into the evening. If it wasn't for her, there was no way the two parents could have coped.

Time seemed to pass without anyone noticing, and by the time Clementine was two, Roger began to wonder when things would start getting easier. Sue was shattered, still being woken up most nights, and Josephine even suggested the little girl might have something wrong with her, even though the doctors said everything was as it should be.

Then one evening, Roger and Sue were in the living room, listening to Clementine crying in the bedroom overhead. It was past ten o'clock, and she'd been crying non-stop. Roger turned the television up and Sue knitted furiously, her hands twisting the wool manically between the needles. Roger's jaw ached as he clenched his teeth together.

'It's no good,' said Sue finally. 'You'll have to go up again, Roger. She doesn't listen to me.'

'I'm not going up again,' said Roger. 'I've tried. I can't bear the crying, it's too loud for my ears. Just go up, Sue.'

'I was trying to see if she'd wear herself out, but it hasn't worked. She keeps on and on,' she said with tears of exhaustion in her eyes. 'You need to help me out more at bedtimes. I can't do it all the time.'

'I do help out,' he shouted. 'But don't forget I work full-time. You get to sleep in the mornings. I don't.'

'Sleep? Are you joking? I never get to sleep in the mornings. At least you have a lie-in during the weekend. It's never-ending for me.'

Roger stood, his fists on his hips. 'I work,' he said again. 'I can't turn up tired, I have to deal with customers. Please Sue. Get her to sleep so we can go to bed. I can't bear it anymore. It's doing my head in.'

Sue turned red and her lips pursed together. She stood and flung her knitting in anger. It spiralled in the air and hit Roger on the chin. He yelled as the needle penetrated his skin like a dart.

'Sorry, sorry, I didn't mean to throw it at *you*. I didn't know the needle would come loose. Are you ok?' Sue rushed over and held onto his arm.

A rage burned inside him as he touched the wound. He stared at his hand; the red stickiness coating his fingers, and a feeling of nausea rose in his throat. Blood: he hated blood. The screams from upstairs grew louder and Sue's high-pitched voice stung his ears. He pushed her. Shoved her hard. She fell back, knocking into the settee arm, which sent her ricocheting towards the fireplace. It happened so quickly. Roger would always remember the thud.

Her head cracked against the sharp iron hook that was fixed into the fire surround, and she slumped to the ground.

'Sue!' he knelt next to her. The blood disgusted him, but now there was so much more. Clementine yelled upstairs, a cry that pierced his brain, sharp like the needle. 'Sue, Clementine's crying.'

Sue didn't move.

Blood pulsated around his body, in his head. He rushed into the hall and snatched up the phone. Josephine would know what to do.

Josephine picked up on the third ring. 'Hello?'

Roger sobbed into the receiver. 'There's so much blood,' he said.

Chapter Forty-Eight

Twenty minutes later, Roger threw the door open to Josephine and pulled her by the arm into the living room. Clementine had stopped crying by now; she'd bawled herself to sleep.

'What shall I do? What shall I do? I don't think she's breathing. Should I ring for an ambulance? Is that a good idea?' He gabbled; his words coming out quicker than his racing pulse.

'I think it's too late,' interrupted Josephine as she yanked her woollen coat off and threw it on a nearby chair. She crouched and felt Sue's wrist. 'She's dead.'

Roger let out a high-pitched moan and bent to hold Sue's hand. 'I didn't mean to, she banged into the settee and that sent her flying against the hook. I only gave a little push. Josie. What shall I do?'

Josephine clasped a hand over her mouth, eyes wide with horror. 'Oh God. What have you done?'

He wrung his hands as a scorching heat burnt through his insides and up to his face. 'Are you sure? Are you sure she's dead?' He glanced down at Sue, the pale skin on her cheekbone laced with scarlet blood.

'She's dead, Roger. You pushed her. That's murder. Or manslaughter at the very least. You'll go to prison.'

Roger paced the room like an animal in a slaughterhouse – the scent of death triggering fear. Eventually, he slumped into a chair, putting his head in his hands. Josephine took a paisley blanket off the back of the settee and draped it over the body. 'I can't … I can't bear it.' Her voice choked on the words; stifled with emotion. She stared at Sue for a few seconds, blinking. Then as if a switch had been flicked, she straightened her shoulders and took a deep breath. 'Let's go into the kitchen. Come with me.'

In a daze, Roger followed her. The heating was off, and the kitchen was freezing; he trembled uncontrollably. 'Bugger sweet tea,' she said. 'We need something stronger.' She opened a kitchen cabinet and hunted for a bottle of brandy. It was right at the back, only used for lighting the pudding on Christmas Day. She poured them both a double measure and sat down opposite Roger. 'We need to decide what to do,' she said.

'It was an accident.' said Roger, his eyelids blinking so quickly as if they were automated.

'Of course. It was an accident. I know that; you know that. But the police won't see it that way. Especially with your record of violent behaviour.' She sipped her drink and thought for a while. 'You can't go to prison, Roger. You won't cope, and we need to think about Clementine.'

Roger nodded.

Josephine knocked back her brandy and poured herself another. Her eyes brightened, the alcohol charging her with energy. 'We could tell people that she's left you, because she was having an affair.'

'An affair? I don't want people thinking she had an affair. Sue loved me.' He wiped the sweat off his forehead and then across his jumper.

'It's better people think she's an adulteress than think you're a murderer.' Josephine snapped. 'We need to have a decent reason for her to leave you. She wouldn't leave you and Clementine for no reason, now, would she?'

Roger shook his head. 'She wouldn't actually leave Clementine at all. No one will believe us.'

'They will if you say her lover didn't want to take Clementine.' Josephine put her thumbnail to her mouth as she thought out her plan. 'He wanted Sue to travel with him because he's a ... hang on a second, er ... a salesman? No. A photographer. He wanted to take Sue to exciting places, and her young daughter would get in the way. And besides, we'll say you refused to let your daughter go and live with a strange man.'

'But what about Sue? What are we going to do with her, with her … body?' Roger's voice shook, he could barely get the words out. The word 'body' sounded too final. Too dead.

'Roger, I…' Josephine faltered. She lowered her head and rubbed her eyes. 'Later tonight, you'll have to bury her in the garden.'

Roger stared at her; memories of childhood flashed through his mind. How he'd been forced by Faither to dig the earth with a spoon and bury his bone collection. He shuddered. 'The ground will be solid,' he said.

'You'll have to dig hard, then, won't you?' Although harsh, Josephine's words were spiked with emotion. Her eyes became glassy as she stood up and pushed her chair in. 'Use the pickaxe. This is all your fault Roger; you need to sort it out. Now, I'll take Clementine back to my house. We don't want to take the chance that she might see you. I know she's only two, but we can't risk it. We don't want her to grow up with tainted memories.'

Roger nodded. 'How will I cope with Clemmy, though? I have to go to work. I can't bring her up on my own. Will you help me?'

'We don't need to discuss that now, do we? Besides, I think Clementine would be better off with me, at my house. I can take care of her. Of course, you can visit whenever you want, and pay for her clothes and things, but it's better if she has a mother.'

Roger slammed his glass on the table. 'No. She's not living with you. She's my daughter. Why can't you come and live here with us?'

'I'm not living with you. I need my independence. I'm not living in this bloody house either. Too many bad memories. I don't know how you bear it.'

'I like it here. I'll find a way to look after her.'

'How can you possibly look after her? You have a temper. Imagine if you pushed her like you did Sue? Jesus Christ, Roger, we don't need to speak about this now; we have a bloody body in the living room.' Josephine peered over her shoulder and shivered.

Roger shook as he raised the brandy glass to his dry lips. 'What have I done?' he said. 'Josephine?'

Josephine put a hand on his shoulder and squeezed. 'I'll go and fetch the little mite, pack her a suitcase, and then you can get on with … '

Roger put his head in his hands. 'I can't do it.'

Josephine gripped both of his shoulders, pinching hard. She whispered viciously into his ear. 'You must. You have no choice. You will bury her. Then you must go to work tomorrow and tell them that Sue has left you.'

Roger leapt up and shrugged off her tight grip. Anger and fear burning inside his gut. 'No, we can't do this, we just can't.'

She headed for the kitchen door. 'It's happening Roger. That temper of yours has finally got the better of you, and you can't back out now. Finish your brandy, then go and look for your spade and pickaxe in the greenhouse. It needs to be done and done quickly.' She ignored his outstretched hand and marched up the stairs.

Roger stared at her retreating figure until he could no longer see her, then he rushed to the sink and vomited.

Julia - 2023

Chapter Forty-Nine

After leaving Josephine, I walked for a while, before coming across a small café in a park. There were only a few tables and chairs, and it was busy, but I managed to find a spot under a tree. I sat down and a pretty girl in tight jeans and a halter neck top took my order. I ordered a latte and a piece of coffee and walnut cake. I needed a treat, and coffee icing was just the thing.

An elderly couple shuffled along the path, with their arms linked. It reminded me to ring Mum. I reached for my phone. 'Hi Mum. It's me. How's things?'

'Well, your father isn't brilliant. He's very down about not being able to drive still. I'm taking him to the doctors tomorrow. He's so weak too. I don't know, Julia … I …'

'It's just going to take time,' I said as I picked absent mindedly at a flake of chipped paint on the table. 'If you need any help, I'm off work for a few weeks.'

'Why?' My Mum's voice was laced with concern and suspicion.

'Nothing to worry about. Just thought I could do with a break. I'm back on some anxiety medication, but you don't need to worry. I've caught it before it gets too bad. Not like last time.'

'Well, you should have told me before. You're taking on too much. Don't worry about me and your dad. We're fine. You concentrate on getting yourself better. Is Tom helping out?'

'Yes, yes,' I said. 'And remember the kids have gone to Tom's mum's for half term? So, I've got nice relaxing week planned.' I didn't tell her about all the things I was worried about – especially my suspicions about Tom having an affair. There was no point in worrying her. She had enough to think about.

'Good, well, I better go and get his lordship his morning espresso. He's sitting in the summer house at the moment, trying to do The Times crossword – so he might be there for a while.'

'Alright, look after yourselves, OK? I'll pop over sometime this week to see you.'

'OK, love. See you later.'

'Bye.'

I hung up just as the server brought over my coffee and cake. The coffee tasted delicious – hot and strong with milk that had been steamed well. A perfect, velvety texture. Picking up my pastry fork, I scooped off a little of the cake icing, and sat back into my chair, finally relaxing for the first time in ages.

When I'd finished, I paid up and headed back to the car, thinking about what I should do next. It was getting on for lunchtime, so maybe there was a chance I could find out if Tom was meeting a woman in his break. He was definitely up to something, there was no question.

Tom had been contracted to work on a big job that week; he'd pointed the house out to me when we'd driven by a few days before. It only took me ten minutes to get there. I parked a little way down, on the other side of the street, but near enough for me to see when he came in or out. The house was a new build, and there were roofers fixing tiles and another workman going in with a toolbox. I wasn't in a hurry; quite happy to wait. I put Audible on my phone and listened to my latest story.

I waited three quarters of an hour, but just as I was thinking of giving up and heading home, something made me start. I slid down into my seat. It was Thalia. Despite her high heels, she hurried along the path with a tote bag hanging off her shoulder. Was she going into the same house as Tom? I licked my dry lips, waiting to see what would happen next.

The two men on the roof leant over the scaffolding to look at her. And y*es. She was going in.* Not taking my eyes off her, I opened the door, and stepped out, peering cautiously over the top of my car. With prickling nerves, I waited. Nothing happened. The two roofers went back to their work, but Tom and Thalia didn't come out. Surely, they wouldn't be up to anything in the house with other people about? Should I go straight in and confront them? But the thought of those roofers watching, put me off. I didn't want to come over as some neurotic wife, or even worse, being the focus of their pity.

I waited a few more moments, then suddenly, the men on the roof began caterwauling as Thalia rushed out of the house. She looked up. 'You're cheeky sods,' she said with a laugh.

'You just can't put him down, can you, love?' said one of the men.

'I'm not your love,' she shouted over her shoulder, and then she looked at her watch, and walked back the way she'd come.

I felt sick. My stomach lurched as I got back into the car and slammed the door. So, I'd been right all along. What do I do now? Should I confront her? Or him? I started up the car, did a three-point turn and drove in the opposite direction.

As soon as I got home, I went straight to the kitchen cupboard and stared at the bottles of gin, vodka and Jack Daniels. I put my hand around the gin, the cool, clear glass was reassuring to touch. But no. I'd just started medication, and alcohol would stop it working properly. And God, did I need it to work properly.

But would one drink hurt?

I scrunched up my face, fighting my inner turmoil, then pushed the bottle back into the cupboard. My shaking hand gripped the kettle, and I filled it up with water from the tap. As I waited for it to come to the boil, I leant against the worktop and took a deep breath. My mouth was dry, my tongue rough as sandpaper, and although I knew that was a side effect of the medication, it didn't stop the panic burning in my gut.

My husband and my best friend.

They'd been seeing each other behind my back, and the thought killed me. Nothing would make that better.

Chapter Fifty

I decided not to confront Thalia, I thought I'd wait until Tom came home from work and have it out with him. After ringing an electrician to come and check our wiring, I sat down to read in the living room. My heart palpitated in my chest from the medication and from thinking about Thalia and Tom together.

The darkness fell pretty much straight away, nothing tangible, only a sense of sorrow. What had happened in this house? Something terrible for sure. I tried to focus on my book but kept imagining Thalia and Tom having sex in our bed. After reading the same page over and over again without anything sinking in, I closed my book with a snap and went into the kitchen.

Trying to keep busy, I raked through the cupboards, pulling out ingredients to make some brownies. It was therapeutic, sifting flour and whisking the eggs, it took my mind off everything for a while. It wouldn't be long until Tom was home, and I could finally confront him with my evidence.

At six o'clock, I decided it was perfectly acceptable to have some wine. One glass would be ok with my medication, I wasn't going to down the whole bottle. I gratefully poured myself a large glass, and flicked through a cookery book, waiting for Tom to come in.

The slam of the front door. He was here. 'Hiya,' he yelled out.

'In the kitchen,' I said.

His toolbox clanked on the hallway tiles, and then he wandered through, and went straight to the sink and poured himself a glass of water. 'You've started early,' he said, nodding at my wine glass.

'Not really, it's six o'clock.' I wouldn't let him make me feel guilty. 'Did you drop off the kids OK? Alex texted this morning and said your mum took them to the water park.'

'Yeah, all good. Mum has a whole week of things for them to do, Alex shouldn't have worried – he'll be coming back boasting to all his mates about it.'

I smiled, pleased. At least the kids were happy, that made things easier.

He peered into the open cake tin and licked his lips. 'Nice brownies! What else have you been doing? Were you ok on your own all day?' He sat down at the table, took out his phone and scrolled as he spoke to me.

'I've been fine. I went to visit Josephine in the morning to see how she was, and to see if she wanted to go for a coffee, but she was on the way to the cemetery. I walked with her for a bit. Did you know, she had a little girl who died. How sad is that?'

Tom lowered his phone. He looked genuinely shocked. 'Seriously? That's so sad.'

I nodded, pleased to have got his attention, even if it was because of someone else's bad fortune. 'Then I went for a coffee and a cake in a really lovely park – Hambledon Park, we'll have to take Isla there some time, it had a fab playground.'

'Cool,' he said, glancing at his phone again.

'Then I took the car and sat outside the house where you're working.'

His head shot up, and he glared at me, his eyebrows knotting together. 'What are you talking about?'

'I watched Thalia going in. I was right all along, wasn't I? You're having an affair. The guys on the roof confirmed it with their disgusting comments – they obviously know what's going on.'

Tom stood up. 'You've really lost your mind this time. You are fucking crazy, woman. Seriously Julia. When the hell is this medication going to start working? I'm not listening to this shit. I'm going to Mack's. In fact, I'm going upstairs now to pack a bag. I'll come back on Friday when the kids are home.' He stormed out and stomped up the stairs.

I leant back in my chair and took a large gulp of wine. As I expected, he totally denied it all, trying to gaslight me, and make me look stupid. Although tears pricked my eyes, I was relieved. At least it was out in the open. I waited. Five minutes later, the front door slammed. He was gone.

The house suddenly seemed incredibly quiet. The only sound was the hum of the fridge. When my mobile buzzed, I jumped out of my skin. I looked down at the screen. Thalia. What the hell did she want? No doubt Tom had told her that I knew, and she rang to suck up to me. I let it ring a few times, then picked it up.

'What do you want?' I said.

'Tom's just phoned me,' she said. 'Julia, you really are a nutter. You've got it all wrong. Totally wrong. Look, I'm coming to yours. Get me a wine glass ready, we need to talk.'

I went upstairs and paced around our bedroom wandering what the hell Thalia meant. Was she lying? I was half pleased that I might have got it wrong, but half disappointed that maybe I hadn't got to the truth. I leant on the window ledge and peered out, waiting to see Thalia's Mazda screeching to a halt outside, but a lack of parking spaces put a stop to anything that dramatic. Instead, there was a knock at the door a few minutes later. I rushed downstairs and saw Thalia's silhouette through the frosted glass.

My hands shook as I opened the door, and stood back to let her in. To my surprise, she put down her bag and hugged me.

'You silly thing,' she whispered in my ear. She then took my arm and led me into the kitchen. I poured her a glass of wine, and we both leant against the worktop. She took a sip. 'It's not Tom I was seeing,' she said with a smile. 'It's Carl. You know, Carl Winsgate? He's the electrician from Hall's Electrics. I couldn't tell you because it's a bit of a secret. He's just started divorce proceedings with his wife and doesn't want her to know about it. It's all quite new, I went to see him at lunchtime to give him his wallet – he dropped it in my car this morning before I dropped him off at work.'

My eyes widened and I'm sure my mouth dropped open too. I didn't know what to say. In the end I hung my head and apologised. 'I am so sorry,' I said, feeling the heat rise in my face. 'I got it totally wrong, didn't I? I should have trusted you. Thalia, I'm so sorry.'

'I'll forgive you, but seriously Julia, you're losing the plot.'

'But I know he's having an affair, I'm sure of it.'

'What proof do you have? Why are you so sure?'

'Well, at first, I thought it was Lizzie, because of the way she behaved, and because he went around there a few times. Then he was really defensive when I asked him, and he keeps checking messages on his phone. Then I got caught up with the idea, and it kind of shifted into thinking it was you.'

Thalia bit her lip before speaking, 'You need to stop imagining things. Seriously, Julia, you're going to lose Tom if you're not careful.'

'I know. I think everything has got on top of me.' Tears started to trickle down the side of my nose, and I wiped them away angrily with my sleeve.

'I know, love,' said Thalia. She put down her glass and wrapped her arms around me. I leant my forehead against her shoulder and hugged her back. What on earth had I done to deserve such a good friend?

Chapter Fifty-One

Having Thalia back on side was so good. I'd hated not having her around; not being able to text and phone her. I was one hundred per cent sure she wasn't involved with Tom now. My mind drifted back to Lizzie, but I shook that thought away – Thalia said I had to stop. She was right. I tried to phone Tom to apologise, but it went straight to voice mail, so I left a message saying Thalia had told me about her and Carl. Tom must have known about them seeing each other, I don't know why he just didn't tell me. He didn't reply. I began to think I'd really blown it. On Tuesday evening, I even went around to Mack's house, but they weren't in. Probably drowning Tom's sorrows in a pub somewhere; or else picking up women.

It was important to get Tom out of my head; there was nothing I could do to repair the mess I'd made. To take my mind off him, I ignored the decorating and spent a few hours in the library, scrolling through old copies of the local newspaper to see if there were any reports about Catcher House. Something *must* have happened there. Why else did Roger keep returning to our attic? And was there a connection between him and the haunted atmosphere in the living room?

But there was nothing. Nothing I could find anyway. I'd have to come back another day to search further back in the archives.

On Wednesday, two days before the children came home, Mr Churchill, the pest controller, returned. When I answered the door, a smile spread across his face. Seeing he killed animals for a living, he was infuriatingly cheerful.

I followed him around as he inspected the bait boxes. 'Have you heard anything or seen anything?' he said.

'Yes, a little scratching.'

'Mm, well it's bit early really, to see any improvement, but we can check if they've taken the bait.' He lay on the tiles and crawled as far as he could under the kitchen cupboards. 'Yep, they've had a good go at this one. I'll put some more down.'

He wiggled back out, then went to fetch something from his van. Strolling back in with a bucket hung over his arm, he pulled on rubber gloves like a surgeon going into an operation theatre. He lay back down to lace the bait box. When he'd finished, I glanced at his hands, hoping he wasn't going to touch my kitchen cupboards, but to my relief, he took the gloves off and put them in his bucket. 'Right, let us go and check the airing cupboard and the attic,' he said.

I wasn't exactly thrilled with his use of the word 'us', but I followed him upstairs anyway and watched as he checked the airing cupboard. 'No sign of the buggers here,' he said. 'Can you open the attic for me please?'

Opening the hatch again was the last thing I wanted to do. But with gritted teeth, I did as I was asked and unfastened the latch. The creak of the hinges sounded like something from a horror movie, and I shook my head at the irony.

Mr Churchill climbed the ladder with the torch between his teeth. 'Would you mind bringing up my bucket?' he said.

Surely, it wasn't normal for a customer to help a pest controller – It had to be against regulations. 'Yes, of course,' I said, minding very much.

'There's a box of latex gloves on top of the poison, you can put some on if you like,' he said.

'How kind,' I said under my breath. In the bucket was a battered cardboard box, and I pulled out two blue gloves before carefully climbing the ladder. Mr Churchill shone his torch around, and I placed the bucket on the floorboards. No way was I going in, so I stood on the third to last rung, with only my head and shoulders poking up through the attic space.

He stooped low and shone his torch onto the bait boxes, crouching down to examine one in particular. 'This one's moved, they've had a really good go at it,' He unlocked it and peered inside. 'It's all gone. This must be where they're hanging out.' He scurried over, not unlike the movement of a rat, and got some poison from the bucket to reload the bait box. When he'd finished, he shone his torch around. 'I think they're getting in there,' he said, shining the beam into a gap where the floorboards met the roof. 'The insulation's been chewed, can you see?'

'Not really,' I said. 'Not from here.'

'Come on, up you come. I can't show you otherwise. We'll need to block this hole after we've got rid of them.'

I sighed, and reluctantly climbed up. What was it with this man, always trying to involve me with his bloody job? Bending low, I moved towards him and knelt down about a metre away. I saw what he meant. There was a small hole in one of the floorboards. He reached in his toolbelt and pulled out a chisel, then he stuck it into the gap and forced up two of the boards.

He leant closer, shining his torch in, and I watched him for a reaction, tensing my body in the fear that hundreds of rats would scurry out; adults and babies, squealing and scratching, like the James Herbert novel.

'Well, I'll be buggered.' He put his torch down and reached in with both hands. The torch beam shone on his pale skin. It made his face look like a skull. Within seconds he'd pulled something out. Something long and thin. Something greyish white in colour. He held it in his outstretched hands as if making an offering. 'It's a bone. A human bone if I'm not mistaken, and there's more in there.'

'A bone? Are you sure it's human? How do you know?' I scooted forward on my knees and picked up his torch. I shone it at the bone and grimaced. Peering down into the hole, I knew he was right. Partially covered in sticky, see-through plastic there were lots of bones. And there was no doubt they were human, because among them there was a skull.

'Oh Jesus,' I said.

Next to the bones was a tatty toy rabbit and a book, thick with dust. In embossed gold, the title of the book glinted in the torchlight. *Jane Ayre*. I leant back on my heels, swallowing. It was so sad. Just really sad. My heart squeezed tight. Fancy being stuck up in this attic for God knows how many years? And who was it? I peered around the attic as Mr Churchill examined the bone in his hand. The spot where Roger North had been lying was parallel to the hole. *He knew.* He must have known. Did that mean he had something to do with it?

Was it murder?

Chapter Fifty-Two

'Make sure you phone the police,' said Mr Churchill on his way out. 'If they want a statement from me, you can give them my phone number. I'd have stayed around but I'm enrolled on a speed awareness course.' He rolled his eyes. 'You'll let me know what happens, won't you?'

'Yes, of course,' I said. 'You're back next week, anyway, aren't you?'

'Back next week, yes. Same time, next Wednesday, OK?'

'Yes, that's fine.'

'Great. I'm off to phone everyone about my find now – still can't believe it.' He walked down the steps, waving his hand in the air. Finding the bones seemed to have made his day.

As soon as he'd gone, I *had* to speak to someone. I nearly phoned Tom but decided not to – he wouldn't pick up. Instead, I called Thalia and told her what we'd found.

'I can't believe it,' she said. 'Who is it do you think? It might even be before Roger and Josephine's time.'

'It might be, but I doubt it, I think it's related to Roger North. I reckon that's why he was up in the attic.'

'Are you phoning the police?'

'Yeah, I will, but I'm going to phone Josephine first to see what she says about it.'

'Is that a good idea?' said Thalia doubtfully.

'Yeah, why not?'

'I'd phone the police first if I were you. Anyway, it's up to you.'

We arranged for Thalia to come around the next night, and after hanging up, I still wasn't sure what to do; whether to phone Josephine or not. So instead, I rang Mum and told her. She was half excited, half worried about it. 'It might dig up old memories for someone, be careful,' she said. 'By the way, your father and I are going to the solicitors today. He wants to alter his will, after all this business at the hospital.'

'Oh,' I said. 'Is he OK though?'

'He's alright. He's decided he wants to leave some money to The Brain Charity. After his seizures, I think it's made him more aware of …' she hesitated. 'of his mortality.'

Poor Dad, and I could tell Mum was upset about it all. I promised to go and see them later in the week. I wished them good luck for their visit to the solicitor, and then finished the call. The thought of my father writing his final wishes, broke my heart, especially after finding bones in the attic. He would soon be bones – that's what happens to us all. But it was so bloody unfair. So sad that my lovely dad was suffering.

Dejected, I stared at my phone. I had to focus. Should I phone the police or Josephine first?

It had to be Josephine.

As soon as I'd told her, she went silent. So quiet. 'Josephine?'

She inhaled sharply. 'I'm waiting for a cake to bake. I'll be straight over as soon as it's out of the oven. Don't ring the police, Julia. Please. Let me talk to you first.'

I agreed. I'd phone the police once Josephine had explained herself. Needing to keep busy, I cleaned and put things away in the kitchen, then I messaged the kids to see how they were getting on. Waiting for Josephine seemed like ages, but really, it was only about half an hour.

My heart thudded as I swung open the door, and she marched in without saying anything. Her eyes locked on mine. 'Let's sit in here,' I said, showing her into the living room.

'Do you mind if we sit in the kitchen instead?' she said.

With a shrug, I led the way to the back of the house. 'Coffee?'

'Yes please.' She sat down and leant across the table with desperation etched on her face. 'I can't believe you've found the bones. In the attic you say?'

Taken aback at how direct she was, I swallowed hard before speaking, attempting to get my thoughts in order. 'Yes, in the attic. Are you telling me you didn't know they were there?'

'No. I didn't know. Well, I knew there were bones, but I didn't think they were in the attic.'

My stomach turned as I poured boiling water over the coffee granules. 'Who is it?' I said. 'Whose bones are they?'

She sat in silence as I put the mug in front of her.

'Milk and sugar?'

'Just milk please.'

While I waited for her to tell me about the bones, she watched the milk flow from the carton into our coffee. She bowed her head and swirled her drink around, but still remained silent. So, like a police officer interrogating a suspect, I sat down opposite and stared straight at her. Intimidation wasn't my style, and my heart beat fast, but after a moment, she began to speak. 'It's Sue,' she said, her words coming out in a long sigh. 'Roger's wife.'

'Sue? So, she didn't leave Roger? Why did you say she'd left him? What happened to her?' I pushed my chair away from the table, trying to get a bit of distance between the two of us.

'It wasn't murder, you don't need to worry,' she said with a cruel laugh.

'What was it then? Because if it wasn't murder, why did you and Roger hide her death?'

'I'll tell you,' she said. 'I'll tell you on one condition. After I've explained everything, you're not to go to the police and you'll let me take the bones. I'll bury them near

Roger when the coroner releases his body, and he's had his funeral.'

'Roger?' I began to feel incredibly uneasy. 'I can't promise that, Josephine, you know I can't.'

'I won't tell you then,' she said. 'Call the police, but I'll deny all knowledge of everything. You'll have no proof I was involved, and Roger is dead, so ...'

I narrowed my eyes. I really wanted to know the truth. If a crime had been committed, it would hardly matter if I broke my promise later. 'OK, I swear,' I said. 'I won't say a word.'

Josephine nodded and stood up. She walked over to the back door and gazed out. For the first time since I'd known her, her slim frame seemed fragile. She crossed her arms, and her jumper pulled tight across her bony shoulder blades.

'It all started when Roger and Sue had a little girl called Clementine,' she said.

I gasped and put my hand to my mouth. *Roger and Sue's little girl?* 'But you said she was *your* daughter.'

'I know, and in a way she was. But you mustn't interrupt. Let me tell you the story all the way through, and then you can ask questions afterwards. I can't keep stopping and starting. I need to get the whole thing out before I change my mind.'

'OK, OK,' I said. 'Carry on.' I sat with my hands clasped on the table as I listened to her story – and that's what it was like, just a story. It was so fantastical I couldn't believe it was true.

'Roger and Sue had been arguing. He pushed her. Oh, he didn't mean her any serious harm, but she stumbled and banged her head on the iron hook. Roger phoned me in a right state, he didn't know what to do. When I arrived, she was dead. We decided it was best to bury Sue. We didn't want Roger going to prison, he wouldn't have coped, you see. I left with Clementine, he asked me to take her, said he wouldn't be able to manage her on his own.

What could I do?'

She paused to catch her breath. 'He was going to bury Sue in the garden. I don't know why he didn't. I always thought he'd buried her near the apple tree, because not long after, he'd planted a rose bush down there. I don't know why her bones were up in the attic.' She turned to look at me, and she leant against the back door as if for support. 'I brought up Clementine like my own child. Roger's mental health was so bad, he couldn't take her back, but he came to see us all the time. He said he didn't want her to visit him at Catcher House – he said it wasn't right for the child to go there after Sue's death.'

'Did you tell people Clementine was your child? What about the doctors? Or anything official?'

'I didn't tell anyone anything, but most people assumed she was mine, and I was happy to let them think it. Those that might have known she was Roger's soon came to think of her as my daughter. I'd miscarried before, so I was more than happy to take on a child. If I took her to the doctors or the dentist or anything official, I told them, of course, that she was Roger's daughter. Everything seemed to take care of itself.'

'But she died…' I said. 'Is that true? Knocked over by a car?'

Josephine rubbed her eyes with the ball of her hands, making her mascara smudge. 'Yes, that was all true. I sometimes wonder if it was God's way of punishing us for what we did. We should have told the police right from the beginning about Sue, but we did what was best for Clementine.'

I nodded. I kind of understood where she was coming from.

'Afterwards, he went to pieces. A complete wreck. He nearly confessed to the police about what he'd done. But when Clementine died, it was as if nothing could ever be put right. From then on, he was never the same again. He became a recluse.'

'And what did you do once Clementine died?'

'Nothing. I got another job, I started gambling. It was a way of coping. I also slept around quite a lot.'

I was surprised at her candour, but she mistook my shocked expression for something else.

'Yes, you might not believe it now to look at me,' she laughed. 'but I never had any trouble picking up men. And sex helped me cope.'

Josephine was a stunning woman even in her sixties, I could well believe it.

'That's how Olivia came along. Of course, she was just what I needed to get my life on track.' She came and sat back down at the table.

'Does Olivia know about Clementine?' I said. 'And about Sue?'

'No, she knows nothing about what happened to Sue. She knew about Clemmy but didn't know she had been Roger's daughter; she thought she was my daughter. It all happened so long ago when Clemmy came to live with me, you see? I think she's a bit jealous of the love I had for her – does that sound catty? But it's true. I've never been close to Olivia. I found it hard to love another daughter, after Clementine.'

I nod and shift in my seat, not quite sure what to say.

'I blame myself really, because I think that's why Olivia finds it hard to settle into a relationship. She's always flitting from man to man; sleeping around. A bit like I did after Clemmy died. Ironic really.' Josephine rested her chin in her hand. 'So, that's the story.

You'll keep your promise, won't you? You won't go to the police?'

I didn't answer for a while. We locked eyes; her expression was full of remorse and pleading. 'Yes,' I said. 'I will.'

And I meant it. I wasn't going to tell the police.

Roger - 1995

Chapter Fifty-Three

Josephine walked out of the house with a sleeping Clementine in her arms. After taking her to the car, she came back for the suitcase, but before leaving, she'd put a hand on Roger's shoulder. 'Wait a few hours,' she said. 'Don't start until all the neighbours have gone to bed. But do it before it starts to get light. I'll come and see you tomorrow.'

And then she left without saying goodbye. Roger lay down, huddled on the parquet floor next to Sue's body. He wasn't sure how long he'd been there, but when he woke up, his arm was stiff, and his eyes were sore. For a few seconds there was a sweet moment when he'd forgotten what had happened. In that split second, Sue was alive, and Clementine was asleep upstairs.

When reality hit him, Roger scrambled to his feet panting and crying like a man who had lost his mind. He marched into the kitchen, threw open the back door and stumbled into the garden. As if they were his accomplices, heavy clouds scudded across the sky concealing the glow from the stars and moon. He squinted up at the house on the left – no lights were on. Of course there wasn't, they were in their nineties, they'd not be up after ten o'clock. Roger peered through the darkness and realised if he dug the grave under the apple tree by the light of his torch, the young couple in the house on the right wouldn't see him either. The branches were far too thick and would block any view they might have. He nodded. *Good*.

With his heart thudding, he went back inside to fetch a torch, there was one in the sideboard drawer in the dining room. But as he passed the door to the lounge, he halted.

The shock of seeing Sue hit him like a sledgehammer. Guilt and grief made his head spin, and he gripped the doorframe to steady himself.

After catching his breath, he walked over and knelt by her. An icy draught on the back of his neck made him shiver; he couldn't bury her outside in the hard earth. Not his Sue. He took her hand. 'I'm so sorry, love. I'm so sorry.' He bent his head and pressed her fingers close to his face; her manicured nails scratched his cheek.

No, he just couldn't bury her. He stumbled to his feet and rushed to the back door, slamming it shut and locking it behind him.

He hurried upstairs to the bathroom and began running a bath, adding two capfuls of Sue's lavender oil. His body shook with adrenaline as he ran back downstairs and put his arms under Sue's knees and shoulder blades to lift her. He tried to be careful, but she was heavy; he cursed every time her ankles or head knocked against the wall. At last, he made it. He stumbled into the bathroom and lay her on the linoleum tiles, swallowing the rising nausea in his throat. Gently, he undressed her, silent tears leaving tracks on his cheekbones. Her naked body looked vulnerable, and her skin seemed whiter than normal - like the inside of a delicate oyster shell. He turned off the taps, tested the temperature, and then lifted her up again.

It was difficult to lower her into the water without banging her body, but he managed the best he could. Reaching for a flannel from the side of the bath, He soaked it and gently dabbed at the blood crusted on her face and neck. In one hand he cupped some water and ladled it over her hair, like a priest at a font baptising a child. He kissed the top of her head when she was clean, and then pulled out the plug. The bath water had turned a light red colour, and it twisted down the plughole like pink sugar spinning in a candyfloss machine.

Once she was dry, he sprayed her behind the ears with her Anais Anais perfume. Then he fetched her best white linen nightdress from her bedside cabinet and slipped it over her head. The steam swirled around like a stifling mist; he cleared his throat and sat back on his heels, staring at her. She looked quite beautiful if it wasn't for the deep purple gash on her head, and that made him cry again.

He wiped his eyes. Where was the best place to lay her to rest? He couldn't put her in the spare room, someone would see her eventually – maybe Clementine when she visited, or Josephine. Josephine would be so cross. No, he had to hide her. The only place was the attic. That way, she'd be near him all the time and he could visit her whenever he wanted. No one else would ever find her.

Roger pulled down the hatch door and climbed up the ladder. He twisted himself around and sat on the floorboards with his feet dangling down through the hole. How on earth would he get her body up there? But before he tried, he needed to find a place to rest her. The attic was dark; he couldn't see a thing, there was only a very faint glow from the streetlight coming through the window. He was cross with himself for not replacing the lightbulb. He felt about on the floor with his fingertips – he had a torch up here somewhere. A while ago, he'd put it by the hatch, always ready for him to use. Brushing away dust and bits of fallen grouting from the wall, he groped around and soon found the torch. Switching it on, a faint glow lit up the room. He stood and walked along the length of the attic. He couldn't lie her down anywhere. For a start, it would be disrespectful, and he had to think about Josephine – she might need to go up there to fetch something.

Maybe he could put her in the void between the floorboards and the bedroom ceilings? *Yes. Perfect.* He'd need something to prise the planks up. With his insides twisting with excitement and nerves, he clambered back down the ladder to fetch a chisel from his toolbox in the cupboard under the stairs.

As he ran back up, he smiled at Sue. 'Don't worry, my love, I've got just the place for you.' He went into his bedroom and pulled a waterproof sheet from the top of the wardrobe – the one Faither had used on his bed when he was very ill. Then he tugged the thin nylon eiderdown off their bed. He bundled them up under his arm, and then climbed back up the ladder.

With the chisel, he forced two of the boards up, and he smiled. It was just as he thought. There was enough space to lay Sue. He spread the waterproof sheet down first, and then the eiderdown, making sure all the fibre glass insulation was pushed aside so she wouldn't be scratched. There wouldn't be much room between her and the floorboards, but that didn't matter. She did need some important things in there though. Her favourite book, and her old cuddly rabbit she used to have as a child – it would be a comfort to her. Once he'd fetched her belongings, and placed them at the foot of the cavity, he sat back and admired his work. It looked so comfortable and snug. Sue would be pleased.

As he sat there thinking, he decided the best way for him to bring her up was to wrap her in a sheet and hoist her. It would be hard work, and he knew he'd have to use all his strength to lift her, but there was no alternative. It had to be done.

First, he needed to wrap her up in clingfilm. He had plenty of it, left over from his days when he wrapped up his dead animals. He was under no illusion that Sue's poor decomposing body would smell, but at least the clingfilm might help to contain some of the fluids. Roger worked hard. Once he had wrapped her up, not forgetting to kiss her before covering her completely, he cloaked a sheet around her and twisted the corners together to make a handle. 'I'm so sorry, my love, this won't be very dignified, but I'll try my best.' He climbed on the first two steps of the ladder, holding on with one hand, and with the other, he pulled her up behind him. He'd never really understood the term 'dead weight' before. With a groan and his palms burning, he took one step at a time, leaning back onto the ladder to stop himself from falling. Finally, he managed to raise her up into the attic. He sat down next to her for a few minutes to get his breath, rubbing his shoulder where he'd pulled a muscle.

When he was ready, he dragged her over to the open grave, rolled her out of the sheet and into the hole. She fell with a thud onto her front, and Roger winced. He hoped the ceiling wouldn't collapse, or even crack. Later, he'd have to check it from downstairs. The next five minutes he spent trying to lever her over so she could lie on her back. Sue never slept on her tummy. Not ever.

He covered her with the sheet and patted it gently. Then he sunk to his knees and put his hands together. 'May God protect you. Keep your spirit safe and at peace. Please forgive me.'

Trying to control his sobs, his shoulders heaved as he picked up the floorboards and slotted them back into place. He'd come up the next day, with some nails and a hammer and fix them in properly.

With the chisel in his hand, he climbed back down the ladder and slammed the hatch shut. He slumped against the wall and closed his eyes. The whole sordid evening was over.

Now, he had to live with it for the rest of his life.

Chapter Fifty-Four

Josephine came around with Clementine early the next day. The little girl didn't seem bothered by waking up in her auntie's house, and after giving Roger a hug, she'd gone up to her room to play. Josephine took Roger's arm and led him outside. She tilted up her chin as if surveying the garden, then nodded. Putting her head close to his, she whispered; 'Have you done it?'

'Yes,' said Roger. 'I don't want to talk about it.'

She sighed, and then took a few steps onto the grass. Roger glared at her as she walked all around. Would she notice that none of the soil or grass had been removed? Eventually, she came back to the patio and gestured Roger into the kitchen. 'You've done a great job, I wouldn't have noticed anything at all. Where is she?'

'Under the apple tree,' he said. 'I told you I don't want to talk about it.' He sat down on a chair and gripped the edge of the table. Josephine shut the back door and leant against it with her arms crossed.

'OK. Now we just need to keep calm. As far as we're concerned, she's run off with her lover. You need to get ready for work, what time do you start?'

'Nine.'

'Right, before you leave, you're to phone Sue's work and tell them she's left you. I will type out a resignation letter from her and forge her signature at the bottom. Now, you go into work and tell them the same thing. It won't matter if you're upset, it'll be more convincing.'

'What about Clemmy?'

'She's more than happy with me. I told her mummy had gone away for a while, and she accepted it. She's so young, she'll soon forget Sue. Besides, she likes Tabitha – she even helped me feed her this morning. You can visit any time you like, Roger, and I'll bring Clemmy to visit you too.

OK? I'll collect all her things at some point, then she'll feel more at home in my place.'

Roger nodded, but he wasn't totally convinced about the plan. His head was a complete mess, and he couldn't think straight. But it helped that his sister was in control, and he decided the best thing to do for the time being was to follow her lead. At least Clementine was happy, even if it was because of some old mangy cat.

*

Over the next few weeks, Roger barely functioned. Everyone seemed to accept their story. Roger saw the way people looked at him, some with sympathy, but most nodded as if Sue leaving Roger was perfectly understandable. He even overheard the work cafe ladies talking about him. 'I'm not surprised his wife left him. Are you?'

'Nope, he's a bit weird, isn't he? And she was quite nice. I met her once. I'm surprised she left the little girl though. Apparently, Roger's sister is looking after her at the moment.'

'Mm, yes, I'm surprised Sue left the little girl. Apparently, she went off with a travel photographer though. You can't really take a small child on jobs like that.'

'I suppose. Maybe she'll come back once all the excitement has worn off?'

'I wouldn't be surprised.'

Over the top of his baked potato, Roger stared at the blank wall in front of him. Little did those gossiping bitches know – Sue hadn't gone away at all. She was at home with him, and always would be.

The only problem was the smell – it got worse over time. Despite opening the dormer window in the attic and trying to keep the house as cold as possible, it became unbearable. As soon as he got home from work and opened the front door, the stench made him retch. He tried sprays and air fresheners, and breathing through his mouth instead of his nose, but nothing worked. It was horrendous. The fluids and gases must have leaked, and every time he went to bed, he'd lie there, staring up at the ceiling, imagining Sue's body gradually seeping into the plaster. He knew he'd have to go up and clean, or the smell wouldn't go away.

He'd told Josephine not to come around. If she did, she'd know straight away what he'd done, the smell was that bad. He told her he wanted privacy, and she seemed to understand that. So instead, Roger picked Clementine up every other day and took her to Hambledon Park. Sometimes she asked about her Mummy, but she was so young it was easy to gloss over everything. She adored Josephine, and Roger was thankful for that. Josephine had even taken her to Brighton for a few days for a little holiday. She said she had a little business to take care of, and she sent him a postcard of the pier. Clementine had loved it, and Roger was pleased his little girl was happy. She didn't seem to miss Catcher House either, which was just as well, because no one was allowed inside. No-one but him and Sue. They could have some quality time together at last – if only he could get rid of the smell. The damn clingfilm wasn't working.

Roger told himself the foul odour was his punishment. He put up with it for a while, willing to accept his penance, but soon, the smell got so bad, his retching led to vomiting. As he knelt on the bathroom floor in front of the toilet bowl, he wondered if the bodily gases would make him seriously ill. Was it a biohazard? He wiped the vomit from the toilet seat, his throat burning. Even though he'd just got in from work, he stumbled out of the house and took the car to B & Q. He bought the strongest disinfectant and cleaning materials he could find, along with a face mask, gloves, plastic overalls, and some sealant too, so he could decorate the ceiling. He hoped that would be enough. If not, he'd have to live with it.

That evening, he laid all the equipment on the landing carpet. He stripped off his clothes, and put on the overalls, gloves and mask. With his hands shaking and his stomach churning, he pulled down the attic hatch once again.

JULIA - 2023

Chapter Fifty-Five

It was gone 2 o'clock by the time Josephine left, and I rang Thalia to tell her everything while I made myself a sandwich. I was starving. 'So, you're not telling the police?' she said.

Hesitating, I cradled the phone between my shoulder and ear so I could cut some cheese. 'Well, no. I think she deserves a chance, don't you? She wasn't the one who killed Sue, and she was only trying to do the right thing. To be honest, those bones have been in the attic for years. It doesn't really matter, does it? As long as they're buried again.'

'Well, I think you should tell the police,' she said. 'That woman, what's her name? Sue? She deserves a proper burial. Not her bloody sister-in-law digging up a churchyard or a cemetery or whatever, in the middle of the night.' Thalia spoke slowly, trying to control herself, but she was failing big time. It was clear she disapproved.

'It's a bit difficult now,' I said. 'I kind of told her that I'd not tell anyone.'

'You don't have to keep your word, for God's sake. No matter what, a crime's been committed. You *have* to tell the police. Seriously, Julia, sometimes I worry about you.'

Sighing with frustration, I wanted to argue my point, but didn't want to fall out with her again. My head was buzzing, and the medication was only making my brain fog worse. 'I tell you what,' I said, as I put the salad bag back in the fridge. 'I'll think about it today, OK?'

'OK, but don't spend too long about it. Anyway, on a different subject, I spoke to Carl this morning and asked him if Tom goes out at lunchtime or if anyone comes to visit him at all …'

'Oh, really? Well done. What did he say?'

'He said something interesting,' Thalia lowered her voice, even though I knew she was probably sitting in the office on her own. 'He said that Tom used to have his lunch in his van, but these last two weeks, he's been going out for a whole hour. Apparently one day he came back an hour and a half later, and the boss had to have words with him.'

'Seriously?' An intense nausea surged through me, and I swallowed hard. I'd been right all along. 'I'm going to follow him tomorrow, then,' I said. 'I've got to find out where he's going.'

'Well, be careful,' said Thalia. 'Don't make any hasty decisions or do anything you'll regret, OK?'

'I won't. I must find out though, Thalia, you've got to admit.'

'Definitely. Well, take care, and ring me as soon as you find out anything, OK? And think about going to the police too, about that other matter.'

'OK, OK. I speak to you later,' I said.

'Bye, gorgeous.' Thalia hung up and I sat there with the phone in my hand staring at the screen. Tom *was* having an affair. Absolutely no doubt. My body became numb, as if all the feeling had been sucked out. The phone slipped from my fingers and fell onto the terracotta tiles with a thud. I jumped and bent to pick it up. It jolted me into getting out of the chair.

My thoughts were foggy. I couldn't think. A walk would do me good, so I took the car and headed out to the downs. Parking up, I walked across to the Clifton Suspension Bridge. I often came here when I was struggling a few years back, and now here I was again, to think and get my head together.

I pushed down the thoughts of Tom and tried to focus on what Josephine had told me. Was Thalia right? Should I tell the police? If Josephine takes Sue's remains, I'd be complicit. I didn't know who I was trying to kid, because it was pretty obvious that Sue's death was a police matter. I'd be breaking the law if I didn't tell the police, I'd be covering up a killing – even if it was accidental. And how did I know it *was* accidental? The hair on my arms stood on end; my skin tingling at the thought – could it have been murder? I clung on to the sides of the bridge, and stared down at the river below, my head ringing. The banks were muddy, the water low. There wouldn't be much of a current to carry anyone away if they fell in.

*

12 o'clock the next day, I sat in my car, a few metres down from the house where Tom was working. I gripped the steering wheel hard, as if holding on for my own safety. Thalia texted around half past twelve to get an update. Mum rang, but I didn't answer – I couldn't be distracted, or I might miss him.

Then just after quarter past one, the front door opened, and there he was. He raised a hand, shouted at the roofers, and with a grin, he walked to his van and got in. My hands trembled as I started up the engine. If it wasn't such a serious situation, I'd have laughed at myself. I'd watched enough films to know how to tail people. But the truth was, I didn't. In my attempt to keep a distance, I nearly lost him twice. Why do lights never go red in the films? But even though the traffic lights were against me, I managed to catch him up. Where was he going? He drove in the direction of our house, and I wondered again if it was Lizzie he was meeting. Or someone else from our area. After a ten-minute drive, he pulled onto the dual carriageway. He was now heading towards the M5. Odd. Was he going out of town? I carried on following; switching off the music so I could concentrate. After a while, he pulled into Cribbs Causeway mall, right outside the Travelodge. So that's his game. I parked a safe distance away, and watched as he got out of his car, glancing over his shoulder. He walked across the carpark towards the hotel, but instead of going straight into reception, he crossed the lawn and gave a wave to someone in a ground floor room. I was too far away to see who it was, but they'd pulled back the net curtain. He went straight up to the window and wiggled his fingers in a playful way, before turning to walk towards the entrance.

My whole body was on high alert; the car keys dropped from my hand as I fumbled to lock the door. I marched over, but then stopped myself. I had to give him time to get into the room. It was the longest five minutes of my life. My lips bled from where I'd bitten them. My throat was so dry, I had to keep swallowing. When I was sure enough time had passed, I took a deep breath and walked over the grass. I leant against the brick wall to the left of the window and counted to ten. I didn't want to walk straight up to the glass, I had to peer in from the side, so they didn't see me.

From that moment, my actions would change my life, and I was scared. I took off my glasses and rubbed my eyes with the heels of my hands. One last deep breath, pressing my fingers into the brick wall, I twisted around and watched.

Bile rose from my stomach, I turned, fell to my knees, and retched. Tom had been standing wide legged at the end of the bed, his trouser zip down, his head thrown back.

Kneeling on the bed naked, except for a pair of high heels, was Josephine, with her lipsticked mouth in the shape of an 'O', performing oral on my husband.

Chapter Fifty-Six

How I got back to the car, I don't know. It was a complete blur, but as soon as I sat behind the wheel, I grabbed my phone and rang Thalia. Between sobs, I managed to tell her what I'd seen.

'What shall I do? What shall I do?' I ran a forefinger under my eyes, my nose ran, and I must have looked a right mess. Two men walked past and stared in at me. I turned away. 'Thalia, What shall I do?'

'Nothing right now. You need to think. You don't want them to have the upper hand. Go home, and as soon as I've finished work, I'll come around and we can talk about it, OK?'

I nodded, then remembered I was on the phone, and she couldn't see me. 'OK,' I said. 'Thank you.'

Glancing over at the hotel, I was tempted to stay and wait for them to come out, but I remembered Thalia's words. I put the key in the ignition and drove home on auto pilot. All I could think about was Josephine. Her eyes and her lips. She was double his age for Christ's sake. She was old enough to be his mother. In fact, she *was* older than his mother.

Once I got home, I went straight upstairs, took off my leggings and T-shirt and hid under the duvet. I cried myself to sleep, and didn't wake until my phone started to ring, and someone rapped the knocker hard against the door.

Thalia. I ran down the stairs and let her in. She took one look at me and my half naked body, and she stepped in, closed the door, and enveloped me in her arms. As I sobbed against her shoulder, I remembered how I'd thought she was the one having an affair with Tom, and I held her all the more tightly. She'd never been my enemy; she was my very best friend.

After lots of crying and some laughter, we'd formulated a plan. The kids were due back the next day, as was Tom. The thought of seeing him made my stomach turn. My main concern was the children. I didn't want them to hear any arguments or pick up on anything, but I also didn't want them to stay longer at Tom's mum's – she'd know something was up, and Alex would be disappointed not to come back to see his friends. Especially as I'd promised him a sleepover – Jesus, why on earth had I done that? A houseful of noisy boys was the last thing I needed. But eventually, the two of us came up with a solution, and I couldn't wait to see Tom's face, and Josephine's, when they realised they'd been caught out.

*

The kids were pleased to be home the next day and were full of stories about their week away. Tom's mum had spoilt them rotten, and they were excited but tired. By the time five o'clock came around, I started to make them an early tea. Mac and cheese – something I knew neither would complain about, and something they'd both eat quickly. I needed them to be finished before six.

True to her word, Thalia texted me just as the kids were sitting down to eat. I read the message and smiled. 'Hey, you two, guess what? Thalia's niece and nephew have come down with a sick bug and can't go ice skating this evening. She wants to know if you two want to go instead?'

Both looked absolutely ecstatic – it had been something they'd been asking about for ages, and I knew it was just the thing to get them out of the house. 'Yes,' shouted Alex, punching the air. He shovelled the food into his mouth, and Isla wasn't far behind.

'She's coming in half an hour,' I said. 'So as soon as you've eaten, go and get changed, she's going to take you to that new ice cream parlour first.'

'Oh my God, could it get any better?' said Alex. He rushed upstairs, texting his friends as he went. 'Josh is going tonight too, so I'll be able to see him,' he shouted.

'Good,' said Isla. 'That means me and Thalia can have girly time together.'

I smiled at her and ruffled her hair. 'Absolutely, so go upstairs and get changed then.'

When I answered the door to Thalia, Tom came up the path too.

'Hi guys,' he said, as if he'd not been living away for the last week.

'Hello, Tom,' said Thalia. 'I'm about to take your kids off ice skating.'

'Oh,' he said, sounding disappointed. He sidled past her and put his bags down next to the hall table. 'OK.'

'Hi, Daddy,' Isla ran up and gave Tom a hug, and Alex stood in front of him smiling.

'We're going skating,' said Alex.

'So I hear,' said Tom. 'I was looking forward to hearing about your week away, and snuggling up with a movie tonight, but I'm sure you'd rather go skating. No worries, Mum will have to do.' He glanced over at me, with a sheepish smile.

'I'm sure we'll have a super time,' I said. I leant down and gave Isla a kiss and Alex a quick hug. 'Be good.'

The two charged down the path in front of Thalia, who blew me a kiss. 'See you later, good luck,' she whispered.

I nodded, blinking my eyes so tears didn't well up. After shutting the door, I followed Tom into the kitchen, where he got himself a beer from the fridge. 'Look, it's been a long week, hasn't it? Shall we try and sort things out tonight? We let things get out of hand, didn't we?' He lay the bottle opener on the table and put an arm around me. He swigged his beer as he hugged me. 'How are things? Are the tablets beginning to work?'

My skin crawled. I pulled away from him and opened the fridge to get the white wine out. 'Yes, they are. Things are much clearer now.'

'Good! What's for tea? Shall we get a takeaway if you haven't anything planned?'

'Yes, I was going to suggest that too,' I said. 'But let's have a drink for half an hour or so first, shall we?' I looked at the kitchen clock. Just a few more minutes.

He followed me into the living room. Although it was warm outside, the room was as cold as usual, and I shivered as I sat on the sofa. 'So,' he said. 'Are you going back to work next week?"

'No, I have one more week off. But that's good. I'm going to get some decorating done and spend some time with Mum and Dad.'

'How are they? How's your dad?'

'Not good really.' I gazed down at my glass and swilled the wine around. Just then, there was the sharp thud of the doorknocker. 'I'll get it,' I said.

Tom picked up his phone, not expecting the caller to be anything to do with him. Little did he know it was everything to do with him. As I swung open the front door, the setting sun cast a path of light straight along our hallway.

'Hello Josephine, thanks for coming.'

'I'm so glad you've decided to give me the bones,' she said, as she followed me into the living room. When she saw Tom, she stopped suddenly. 'Oh, hello Tom.'

He stood up. Shock flashed across his face before he corrected himself and held out his hand for her to shake. 'Hello, Josephine, how are you?'

'Very well, thank you,' she said, and I inwardly rejoiced at their inability to look at each other; the uncomfortable way they held their bodies. She turned and looked at me quizzically. I knew what she was thinking. She wasn't sure if I'd told Tom about Sue's remains. She was worried.

'Sit down, Josephine,' I said. 'Would you like a glass of wine? Beer?'

'Oh, a glass of white would be lovely, if it's no trouble.'

'No trouble at all, Tom, do you mind getting Josephine a glass?'

'Of course,' he said, and he left the room, glancing at me suspiciously.

'Well, Josephine, I expect you're wondering if I've told Tom?'

'I'm hoping you haven't,' she said. 'It is a rather delicate matter, and one I'd rather keep between the two of us.'

'I bet. And no, I haven't told him.' I said.

Her face lit up.

'But I am going to. I think he'd like to know his mistress has been covering up a killing for the last twenty-five years.'

Chapter Fifty-Seven

It was timed to perfection. Tom walked back into the room, holding a glass of wine in his hand. He came to a halt by the doorway, as if he'd smashed into an invisible barrier. Although my insides churned, I forced a smile. 'Yep, I know all about it. In fact, I watched you both through the hotel window yesterday. Next time, you must ask for a top floor room, if you want to keep your seedy sex-life a secret.'

His mouth dropped open, and his Adam's apple rose up and down in his throat as he swallowed. They glanced at each other, and Josephine's cheeks turned red. Tom slumped onto the sofa next to Josephine and passed her the glass of wine. He picked up his beer with a trembling hand, completely lost for words.

'You can't lie your way out of that one.' My voice was hoarse and my throat dry, but my words were confident. 'You can hardly say, "it's not how it looks," can you?' I mock.

'Julia, sweetheart, I …'

Josephine took a large gulp of wine, 'What can I say? I'm so sorry, Julia. Tom told me you were on the verge of separating. I thought things weren't good between you.'

'I didn't say that,' shouted Tom. He leant away from her and rubbed his hand over his face. 'I said we'd been having trouble. I didn't say we were going to separate. Where did you get that from? And bloody hell, what's all this about a killing?'

Josephine stood and put her glass on the window ledge. 'It's something that happened a long time ago. Roger had an accident, and his wife died. That's all. There was no "killing". You do exaggerate Julia.' She leant against the wall, acting as if she didn't care, but I knew she was terrified – the muscle in her jaw twitched and her eyes darted around trying to avoid my glare.

Anger burned inside me. How dare she try to gaslight me? 'Tom, you've got to hear this. Roger hit Sue and she fell and died. Josephine knew about it, and the two covered up her death. And do you want to know what the icing on the cake is?'

'No, Julia, please,' begged Josephine, her face turning pale.

Tom stood and walked towards the door, clenching his fists. 'No, but I'm sure you're going to tell me.'

'The bones are in the house. They're up in the attic.'

We stared at each other. Horror sketched on his face, quickly changing to disgust. He turned to Josephine. 'Get out of my house,' he said in a low tone.

'Tom, it wasn't me. It was Roger.' She hurriedly picked up her handbag from the floor and looked over at me. 'Julia, shall I take the bones now, before I leave? I promise I'll not see Tom again.'

She was behaving like a naughty child, I half expected her to say, "pinky promise" and offer me her little finger, like Isla did. I tilted my head back and laughed; a genuine laugh – I couldn't believe she honestly thought I'd give her Sue's remains after everything. 'You're kidding, aren't you? As soon as you and Tom have left, I'm going to phone the police. Now, get out.'

'Please don't,' She walked towards me, crouching next to my chair, and laid a hand on my arm. 'I'm so sorry about sleeping with Tom. I honestly thought you two were over. Please don't tell the police. You promised you wouldn't.'

'And you think I owe you anything?' I shook off her arm as if her touch was poisonous. 'Get out.' I walked towards the window and gazed at life passing by on the street below. A child on a scooter, an old man walking his dog.

Tom marched over to join me, as if we were a team. He pointed at Josephine. 'You heard her, get out,' he said. 'I seriously can't believe what you've done.'

Screwing up my nose in disgust, I stepped away from him. 'And you, Tom. You can piss off too. I don't want to see either of you again.' I took a large swig of wine, the vinegary tang coating my tongue.

He moved back, crossing the floor in a panic. Josephine pushed past him, and he just turned away, as if she was no longer his concern. The front door slammed. She was gone. Tom shifted uncomfortably from one foot to the other, as if he was ten, doing a dance at a school disco. He looked ridiculous. 'Julia, I'm sorry. I'm so sorry. What can I do to make it up to you? Think of the kids.'

'The kids? You should have thought of that before. Now, for the last time, get out!'

I hurled my wine glass at him, he ducked, and it smashed on the door. It shocked him, and he stared at me for a few seconds. 'I am so sorry,' he said. Then he hung his head and went into the hallway to collect his bags.

He closed the front door quietly behind him.

Adrenaline pumped through me as I fetched the dustpan. After picking up the large pieces of glass, I swept up the small shards; alcohol coating the bristles of the brush. When I was sure it was done, I knelt and wiped up the rest of the wine. It left black marks on the parquet flooring; the stain would probably be there forever. My self-control slipped away; I was empty. Worthless. My life a dustpan full of detritus. I took off my glasses and rubbed my tired eyes with trembling fingers. Nauseated from the acidic wine sloshing about in my stomach, I swallowed and pulled out my phone to ring the police.

Chapter Fifty-Eight

It didn't occur to me that the police would arrive with their blue lights flashing, but they obviously thought it was necessary. I explained everything to the detective, while his team went up into the attic to retrieve the bones. He asked me for Josephine's address, and I wrote it down for him, folding the paper in half as if it was an important document.

'Will you be OK, Mrs Harker?' He glanced at my shaking hand as I picked up a mug of sweet tea a junior officer had made me.

'I'll be fine,' I said. He thought I shivered because of the bones – but it wasn't that. I was used to them. I shook because of Josephine and Tom – because I threw a glass at him. Because I knew that was the end of our marriage. 'My friend will be here soon, with my children.'

'I don't think your kids should be around while we're here,' he said. 'Can they go and stay with your friend?'

Disappointment stabbed through me. I wanted my kids where I could see them, but I knew he was right. 'OK.' I picked up my phone and wandered out to the back garden, so I could call Thalia in private. I didn't want him knowing I'd found the bones a few days before.

After I'd finished the call, I stepped back into the kitchen. He'd been watching me from the window. 'Can you go to your friend's house too? Or call anyone else to come and sit with you tonight?' he said. 'Or is there somewhere you can go? I don't think you should be here on your own, you're too shocked. I'd feel happier if you were somewhere around people.'

I didn't want to go to Thalia's – there wouldn't be room, she only had a one-bedroom flat, and the kids would be on the sofa bed in the living room. But I know exactly where I would go, back home to Mum and Dad's. The comfort of clean sheets and blankets, one of my Dad's hot toddies, and the knowledge that I would be safe. It was just what I needed.

*

A few days later, the kids and I were back in the house, and I explained the new living arrangements with them. I told them the truth, I didn't believe in sugar coating things, and I was sure they were happier knowing what really happened, rather than second guessing.

Obviously, I didn't tell them the details – I wasn't a total idiot. They were upset, especially Alex, but he brightened up when I told him that Tom was still working in Bristol. 'He's going to live with Mack for the time being,' I said. 'So, you can go over there and have a boy's night now and again. Watch football and play games.'

He seemed to like that idea, and Isla was pleased Tom would still take her swimming. But I was prepared for a rocky road; no divorce is easy for kids, no matter how much effort the parents put into making things seem normal. Tom wanted to give it another try with me, but I could never trust him again. He'd have to live with the consequences of his actions. As far as I knew, he wasn't seeing Josephine anymore, even though she'd been put on bail after being charged. So now, he didn't have anyone. Not me, not Josephine. What a fool.

I was surprised at how brilliant Lizzie had been. As soon as she heard about our breakup, she'd brought around a lasagne for me and the kids. 'If you need anything,' she said. 'I'm here.'

She'd even said she'd understood why I accused her. 'You knew he was having an affair, but you couldn't work out who. And you were bound to think it was someone young and attractive, rather than someone old like Josephine – no wonder you got it wrong.'

I tried to smile when she said this – I knew what she meant, despite it coming over as incredibly vain. But that was Lizzie all over, and to be fair, if it wasn't for her and Thalia over the days following the disintegration of my marriage, I'd have gone mad. I didn't tell Lizzie about the bones though; I didn't want rumours spreading around, mainly because of Olivia. It was bad enough for her knowing her mother was having an affair with a man young enough to be her son, let alone finding out she'd been involved with a killing. That was something Josephine needed to tell her. I shuddered at the thought of Josephine's court case – it would be in all the papers. Poor Olivia.

Mum and Dad had been amazing. Mum had said it was their chance to pay me back for all the help I'd given them when Dad had been ill. In fact, having me to fuss over seemed to give Dad a new lease of life. Mum drove him over to the house to help with the decorating now Tom had gone, and he seemed to enjoy every second of it. I never had thought a paintbrush, and a roll of wallpaper could be so good for mental health. Perhaps they should put it on the NHS?

The best thing about the house, was the heavy feeling of sorrow had disappeared, and so had the stench of sweet perfume. I no longer felt uncomfortable in the living room, and Isla had said 'the dark thing' had gone. Something had definitely been happening in Catcher House, and it was clear to me that the change of atmosphere was due to the bones being removed. It was no coincidence. Sue's remains had been laid to rest, and her spirit (if that's what it was) was now at peace.

Despite all this though, I knew I couldn't stay for much longer. There were too many memories. That was the thing about Catcher House it was like a web. It catches you and weaves your life intricately with the past, until the thread becomes too tight, and you can't escape.

*

One Friday morning, Olivia and I found ourselves together, staring at a coffin. After the coroner confirmed Roger North had committed suicide, and his body was released, Olivia had arranged a short service for her uncle, and it was held at the local crematorium. Poor Roger. I felt sorry for him, despite what he'd done, he'd obviously suffered from some mental health disorder. Sue's death had been an accident, and although he should have gone to the police, he must have felt terrible guilt. And to lose his daughter too – no wonder he went a little bit mad. I wondered too if Josephine had taken advantage of Roger for her own gains? I'd never know for sure.

Apart from myself and Olivia, no one else was there. Josephine hadn't come, which surprised me. I thought she'd cared for Roger in her own way. But once we got out into the fresh air, Olivia thanked me for coming and gave me a hug. 'You know I'm not speaking to Mum, don't you? That's why she's not here. I sent her a letter telling her she wasn't welcome. She shouldn't have sold the house when she knew Sue's bones were there.'

I squeezed her arm. 'You've been through so much, it's been a nightmare,' I said. 'I don't blame you.'

'I'm so sorry for what she did with Tom,' she said, as we walked slowly towards our cars. 'It's so awful. I still can't get my head around it. And then to find out on the same day that she covered up Sue's death for so long – I can't bear to see her ever again.' She pressed her key fob and the lights on a Ford Fiesta flashed. 'This is me,' she said, coming to a stop by the car. 'Keep in touch, won't you?'

'I will,' I said. Then a thought occurred to me. 'Do you like singing?'

She looked confused. 'Er, yes.'

'Come along to my choir with me then. I think you'll find it'll help. Take your mind off things. Something joyful.'

She tilted her head to the side, as if thinking about it. 'Yes,' she said. 'Yes, I think I'd like that.'

Chapter Fifty-Nine

Josh, the estate agent from Braithwaite's, let out a long sigh as he stood in front of Catcher House. He wasn't surprised the property was on the market again. He'd read about the hidden bones in the paper, and Julia Harker had told him she'd split up with her husband. He couldn't blame her in the slightest for wanting to move on. A few weeks ago, he'd come over to value the house, and although he could tell they'd done some decorating, the place hadn't really gone up in value. The skeleton would put viewers off too. But of course, there were bound to be ghouls who wanted to see 'the house of bones'. Funny how some people were fascinated with death. Luckily, Mrs Harker was only accepting viewings from people who had already sold their house. That way, only serious buyers would come.

He met Mr and Mrs Gulliano outside the house. They already had a prospectus, and when Josh shook their hands, they smiled; eager to get inside. 'We drove past last night, to see what the parking was like. It's not too bad, is it?' said Mr Gulliano. 'With it being permit holders only, and all.'

'It makes a difference, definitely,' said Josh. 'One of the perks of this street, it's a real bonus.' He didn't mention that most streets in the area had permit parking now. 'Ready to go inside?'

The couple nodded and followed him up the steps. Although it wasn't quite dark, the evening was gloomy, and a tingle went down Josh's spine as he remembered the first time he'd gone into the house. As soon as he stepped into the hallway, he reached for the light switch, exhaling in relief when the warm tone flooded the downstairs space. The Gullianos followed him in and glanced around. 'So, this is the hallway. On the left we have the dining room, and in here, we have the lounge.' He pushed open the living room door and stepped aside, allowing the couple to walk in first.

'Oh.' Mr Gulliano stopped. His back straightened.

Mrs Gulliano touched her husband's elbow and peered over his shoulder. 'What's wrong?'

Josh's heart sunk. What now? He slid past the couple and into the room. Sitting in a chair, facing the door, was Julia Harker. She was asleep with her head lulled to the side, her mouth open.

'Ah,' said Josh.

The Gullianos jostled out of the room in embarrassment. Josh cleared his throat. 'Mrs Harker?'

Julia's eyelids fluttered, and she raised her head. Her face flared with confusion before she realised what was happening, and when she did, she leapt to her feet. 'Oh my God, I'm sorry Josh. I fell asleep. I was going to go out. I'm so sorry; so mortifying.'

'No worries,' said Josh. 'Sorry to disturb you. Is it OK to carry on with the viewing?'

'Yes, yes, of course. Please carry on.' She hurried towards the door, immediately seeing the couple standing patiently in the hallway.

'This is Mr and Mrs Gulliano,' said Josh.

'I'm so sorry,' she said again. 'I didn't mean to startle you.'

'Please don't worry,' said Mrs Gulliano, smiling.

'I'll leave,' said Julia. 'You carry on.' She kicked off her slippers and pushed them under the hallway table, then put on a pair of trainers. 'Sorry, again.' She pulled open the door and shot out.

Josh turned to the couple, smiling. 'Well, I wasn't expecting that,' he said. 'Now, where were we?'

*

Mr and Mrs Gulliano didn't put an offer on the house. As the weeks passed by, it stayed on the market, even reducing in price. Julia couldn't bear living there any longer, and she went to her parents with the kids until they got a place of their own. Despite the estate agent telling them the house wouldn't sell unless it looked more homely, boxes had been packed up and were labelled either 'Tom' or 'Jules'. Julia couldn't be bothered to play at houses anymore. Tom begged her for forgiveness, but there was no chance of that. She could barely look at him.

One rainy Sunday afternoon, when the kids were out with Tom, Julia decided to go back to the house and tackle the attic. It had to be done. Hoping it would be the last time, she climbed the ladder and twisted herself around to sit on the floorboards. Dead flies lay under the window, and a lump of rat poison was still in position against the wall. It had a few bites taken from it. Thank God the rats had gone. The rain hit the windowpane, and ran dolefully down in fat, miserable droplets. It was dark as ever, the dull light from the window barely stretching more than a few feet across the floorboards.

She dragged the nearest box over and pulled it open. Inside was an old dinner set which had a few plates missing. She'd take that to the charity shop; she didn't know why they'd bothered to keep it. She pushed the box aside and crept further along. The blankets Roger had slept on were still there at the end of the attic, except now they were folded into a pile. The police must have done that after taking their samples. As she picked them up and hooked them over her arm, a rush of cold air hit her full on. The blast of ice was so bitter it felt as if her face was being slashed. With a gasp, she raised a hand to protect herself. She fell back, blinking violently.

A harsh voice whispered. 'Get Out!'

She steadied herself. Blood pulsated violently in her veins. Did she really hear that, or had it been her imagination? She gripped the blankets tight against her body like a protective shield. 'Who's there?' she said.

This time, there was a vicious scream right by her head. 'Get Out!'

With a gasp, she dropped the blankets and covered her ears – the voice was piercing. Her ear drums stung as if they would burst. She staggered towards the exit, but before descending, she twisted around and peered into the darkness, the chill air biting her skin.

She wanted to yell; a bellowing roar of defiance, but the words stuck in her throat and came out as a rough whisper. 'It's all yours, Roger.'

Her feet slipped as she hurried down the ladder, almost falling as she stepped off the last rung. She reached for the pole, and slammed the hatch shut, fastening the latch as tight as possible.

With her hand against the wall for support, she stumbled down the stairs. A bitter breath left her lips, fast and shallow. Pulling open the front door, she ignored her shoes, needing to feel the ground beneath her. She stepped out onto the wet doorstep. Her socks absorbing the rainwater which had pooled on the terracotta tiles. With her face to the sky, she let the rain-soaked air drench her skin. Never would she enter Catcher House again.

A couple sharing an umbrella walked by and glanced at the For Sale sign. They had their arms around each other and didn't seem to care about the black, wet sludge muddying their shoes.

As Julia watched them, the front door of Catcher House clicked shut behind her.

ACKNOWLEDGEMENTS

Thank you to all my wonderful friends and family who have helped and supported me in my writing and for being part of my life, I am lucky to have you all.

But there are a few people who deserve a special mention.

Thanks to Kathryn Clark: You did such an amazing job editing my story. I really appreciated your comments, expertise and kindness.

Thank you to Lesley Parr, my long-time writing buddy who I met on the Bath Spa MA Writing for Young People: I'm sad that none of my children's books managed to get published so I could join you on the bookshelves, but thank you for all your encouragement, support and understanding – not only with writing, but also with life in general!

Thank you to my sister-in-law, Linzi, and niece, Dotty: You gave me some marvellous feedback on the first three chapters and some top tips on book covers! You're both lush.

To my Mum and Dad, Diana and Brian Nason: You instilled a love of stories in me – both stories from books, and verbal stories that have been told to me over the years – I will never tire of the haunted hotel tale, despite hearing it countless times!

Thanks to my fabulous daughters, Ellen and Anna: for all your encouragement and putting up with my questions when I've been stuck on a bit of dialogue or plot. Thanks, Ellen, for your accurate proof-reading and Anna, for your excellent illustration of Catcher House. Also, a mention to Rachel 'Raccoon' Williams for giving her valued opinion on the book cover, and for putting up with all the nonsense we spout on our family's joint snapchat group.

Lastly to Jim: Thank you for supporting me through those two years of the MA, and through all the effort. false hopes and countless disappointments I faced trying (and failing) to get 4 children's books published traditionally. Thank you for reading my work, helping me with the formatting and for encouraging me to self-publish. I know I'm 'the limit' and a 'pain in the arse' but your love shines through and it is returned in equal measure, if not more.

Printed in Great Britain
by Amazon